The Le
John

Also by James Christie:
Dear Miss Landau

The Legend Of
𝔍𝔬𝔥𝔫 𝔐𝔞𝔠𝔫𝔞𝔟

James Christie

CHAPLIN BOOKS
www.chaplinbooks.co.uk

First published in 2015 by Chaplin Books

Copyright © James Christie

ISBN: 978-1-909183-96-4

A CIP catalogue record for this book is available from The British
Library

Design by Michael Walsh at The Better Book Company

Printed by Imprint Digital

Chaplin Books
1 Eliza Place
Gosport PO12 4UN
Tel: 023 9252 9020
www.chaplinbooks.co.uk

If, in the first century, Calgacus the Red came out of the hills to set the long brawl of Scots history on its course, it was only fitting that, two thousand years later, another red-haired Scot would look to other hills, thinking of a lost love, a forgotten book and a small Highland town named after Finnan's glen, wondering what it had all been for.

And not knowing he already had the answer...

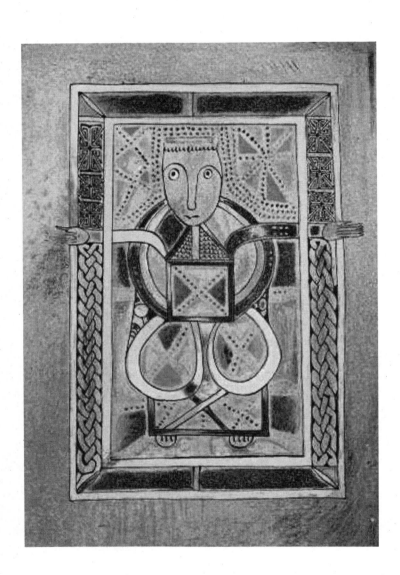

1

Glasgow: 1996

"I am Connor MacLeod of the Clan MacLeod. I was born in 1518, in the village of Glenfinnan on the shores of Loch Shiel. And I am immortal."

It was a good line, John Sandiman thought, and it struck a chord. Mind you, Christopher Lambert's 'Scottish' accent had as much to do with the Highlands as fromage frais did with Fort William, and *Highlander* as a whole felt like a flaky tribute video to Freddie Mercury and Queen.

He rewound the videotape to listen to that line again and see Lambert, playing MacLeod, stab himself in the heart with a silver dirk. *How*, he asked himself, *did such a film ever become a cult classic*?

For the umpteenth time, Sandiman also asked himself why he was still working as a librarian at a clapped-out college and staying in a small flat on the far side of Partick. He did not want to ask himself why he often ended up watching videos late at night on his own.

Perhaps it was because he had been a run-of-the-mill pupil at a run-down grammar school, and an apathetic student of Scottish History at a second-rate university.

He and his parents had been incomers from the Highlands. The kind of people whose fathers and forefathers had been described by John Buchan in *John Macnab* as *"a peculiar kind of tinker."* Scots travellers and storytellers who had known *"how to snare a dozen things, from hares to roebuck, how to sniggle salmon in the clear pools, and how to poach a hind when the deer came down in hard weather to the meadows."* His parents had died a few years before, succumbing to rare cancers of throat and tongue, but their way of life had disappeared many years earlier. Sandiman had gone to Glasgow and lived there a long time, but never called it home. He was a Roman Catholic Highlander who preferred shinty to football, whisky to beer and the Celtic cross to sectarianism, adrift in a Lowland, partly Protestant city.

Still, at least he had a nice flat. Framed reproductions of Patons and Vettrianos hanging on walls of Jacobite scarlet. A bay-windowed lounge. Shelves from Habitat filled with history books. A deluxe Gaggia espresso machine, and the address of a good pizza delivery place on the noticeboard in his L-shaped hall.

It didn't make everything all right, though. Sandiman stared at his scarlet walls sometimes, thinking of Jacobite rebels raising their glasses to the 'king across the water'.

Then he'd switch his gaze to his history books, trying to remember why he loved that subject so much. Perhaps because of its immediacy. Most people considered history to be a dry list of kings, queens, battles and dates to be memorised for exams. Few Scots realised their beliefs and prejudices had their roots in John Knox's dogmatic Protestant Reformation and Scotia's self-inflicted ruin via the Darien Scheme, the failed colony in Panama which bankrupted Scotland and made the subsequent Acts of Union with England more like a bailout than a bullying merger. Or perhaps because of his father. A small dark man who, on quiet days in the 60s, took his son north in the family's old Ford Anglia, determined that the young Sandiman would know a Scotland beyond the Central Belt. The land of the Gael and the kelpie.

He remembered fragments of the memories his father had handed on to him. Of standing stones at sunset on the Argyllshire coast. Of cool cloisters in Highland kirks illuminated by a faint spectrum of light from stained-glass windows. And of his father's voice, half-heard, like a radio just out of tune:

"Columba and Drostán came from Iona to Aberdour; and Bede the Pict was mormaer of Buchan on their arrival ..."

There had been other stories. Tales of Cuchulainn and Merlin and Tir Nan Og. Stories of his grandfather and great-grandfather, who had worked as ghillies on estates in the West Highlands. But like tales whispered to sleepy children at night, he could not quite remember them.

An oral history had been passed down to him, Sandiman realised later, but by then he had known other men truly had lived long before him. Men who had prayed beneath the same stained-glass windows, had fought, died, and been buried beneath Celtic crosses, and been forgotten.

But his past had been their present, and they deserved remembrance.

With remembrance came analysis, learned in lecture halls and honed in the Mitchell Library, and the present looked to be in a pretty poor state. A bit like the Mitchell Library, in fact. It was the largest public reference library in Europe and it was falling apart. He knew it well, for he'd mourned his parents in his own way, looking for his father's words in the Mitchell and in other libraries scattered like speckled jewels round that great old library's old green dome. He'd picked up quite a bit of library history as well. Islam had passed its reverence for the book onto Christendom, and history had shown that a society which neglected the sources of its knowledge was a society in decline.

Soon, Scotland would have a new Parliament, but that wouldn't stop things falling apart. It wouldn't magically cure all ills. Whigs, Tories, Labour and Lib Dems – he was against them all. Government just created more government.

The 'good old days' were a myth but, Sandiman sometimes thought, a man must have felt *alive* then, following his king into battle against the infidel, knowing he was on the side of the angels.

A lie, of course. Both sides usually believed the angels were with them, the infidels were often more enlightened than

3

the crusaders and were only defending their territory in the name of Allah, tribal prejudices were barbaric and death from gangrenous wounds was a slow, ugly process. Yet the lies had been beliefs devoutly held and the beliefs, evoked in scripture by holy men, had bound societies together.

What did society have now? Spin doctors shielding politicians who charged cash for questions. Diana Spencer, the divorced Princess of Wales with her conflicted desire for celebrity, taking army lovers and passing royal stories to journalists *sotto voce*.

That was all there was to the modern state and all there was to him, really. A maudlin man in his mid-thirties, wearing an old blue seaman's jersey and a pair of jeans. Hair, reddish blond. A small beard, neatly trimmed. Muscle tone not quite what it was, blue eyes clear and sharp. Someone had once told him he had an unsettling gaze, so he didn't look people in the eye much.

It was a maudlin end to a mediocre day. First the heating in the college library had failed again, then he'd found some junkie shooting up heroin in the toilets and had had to call the police.

Nil illegitimi carborundum, he had chanted to himself. Do not, as Plato should have said, let the bastards grind you down. Latin swear words did have a certain poetic eloquence.

The day had started out all wrong, even before he'd arrived at the library to find the heating failing and Mike (his psychotic part-time library assistant) blowing hot and cold about starting work. In fact, it had started going wrong the moment he woke that morning with a gnawing feeling in the pit of his stomach that told him there was something seriously rotten in the state of Denmark.

Or in this case, the state of Scotland.

It was 29 November 1996. Tomorrow was supposed to be a big day, but it didn't feel like it. After seven centuries the Stone of Destiny was returning to Scotland. In a couple of years, if Labour won the next election, the Scottish

Parliament would also be making a comeback, ruling a partly independent, *devolved*, state. The extent of devolution would depend on a referendum to be held the next year which would ask Scots if they really wanted their Parliament back and if it should have tax-varying powers.

The Stone, handed over two weeks earlier at Coldstream Bridge, was already in Scotland. Tomorrow it would be installed at Edinburgh Castle amid much pomp and circumstance.

Or at least pomp. Despite everything, he couldn't seem to raise a feeling of circumstance and neither could most people he knew. The great symbol of sovereignty had returned, and it was a *rock*. It could not walk the streets of Glasgow or Edinburgh and raise passions. It could not talk of the first king of Picts and Scots, Kenneth Mac Alpin, or William Wallace and the wars of Scottish independence. At the end of the day, it was a 336 lb lump of sandstone and that was all there was to it. It might not even be the right one. Some claimed the real Stone was made of black basalt and inscribed with hieroglyphs. Others said it had never left Scotland and was being guarded by the Knights Templar. A few believed it was the actual pillow stone upon which Jacob, grandson of Abraham, had dreamt of God while travelling from Beersheba to Haran. That same stone, they said, was taken to Tara in Ireland by Israelite refugees in the sixth century BC and became *Lia Fail*, the oracle stone.

In 1950, a bunch of Scots undergraduates led by a law student called Ian Hamilton had stolen the Stone from the Palace of Westminster. It had supposedly been returned to Westminster, but no one was quite sure about that. Some said the real Stone was buried underneath an ironmongers in Arbroath, but nobody really knew.

That morning, Sandiman had got off the train at Queen Street station and walked across George Square to his place of work. Usually he glanced up at Sir Walter Scott's statue. To his right was Glasgow City Council chambers. On the whole he liked doing this, but that day the mix of literary heritage and local government had pleased him not. Scott had been no more than a dead writer with pigeon shite on his head and the chambers empty shells of marble crammed with smoke-filled rooms where corrupt councillors created ever more layers of bureaucracy in which to employ their relatives and fly off on junkets to Jamaica.

The last he'd heard, Glasgow's debt was pushing £1 billion. *And men like these think they will rule Scotland come devolution.* He had shuddered at the thought. What was even worse was that everyone in Scotland would vote them in again, because they always had voted Labour and always would. End of story.

From a line of 113 kings of the blood royal to *this*, he had suddenly thought. What a comedown...

The library was right where he'd left it the day before – on the fifth floor of a gunmetal-grey office block abandoned by developers and swamped by the hordes of students that government was determined to stuff through the system like sausage meat through grinders.

At the rate they were going, people would soon need PhDs to be postmen.

Ruling the asylum was a finance manager who rode roughshod over the lecturers and pimped for the principal, a perma-tanned prat who had all the connections and catchphrases ('close that gap!') but simply could *not* make a decision unless it had been costed, debated, reviewed and referred to a steering committee or three.

As a result, no clear decisions were ever made and the college lurched onwards in a haze of fudged policy and unworkable ideas, a ship driven by a captain who could not decide whether to follow the moon or the stars, ably backed up by a first officer who truly believed that the ship would sail more cost-effectively if the thickness of its hull was reduced by half.

He nodded to George the security guard who sat asleep

by the door of the lobby, and walked up to his domain. Already drained of enthusiasm, he looked at the neat rows of grey bookshelves with beech endpanels, the black carousels displaying journals, the computer workstations, study desks and CD-Rom stacks. All the furnishings flanked the circular issue desk in the room's centre, the library trolley left askew the only sign of asymmetry.

The floor-to-ceiling windows let in plenty of grey, watery light but the very texture of the carpet breathed apathy. At least the first ned (non-educated delinquent) of the day – bent on accessing porn over the internet – had not yet loped in. Students at this further education college generally came in three sorts, he'd learnt: there were the bright ones who knew where they were going and were prepared to work to get there; the not-so-bright ones who worked hard but were a bit clueless; and then there were the neds foisted on them because the European Social Fund paid the college £50 per sad git.

The Royal Navy used to scour taverns and brothels in seaports, press-ganging the scum of the earth into naval service. The British Army did much the same, impressing men for a term of three years and a bounty of four pounds, paying them sixpence a day, treating them with contempt and regularly flogging them to death. Now Scottish Further Education was resurrecting the tradition.

Once, education had been all about quality. Now it was all about money, and nobody gave a damn about staff or students as long as the cash came in.

Then he realised it was about 10 degrees too cold, just as Mike walked in swearing it would be warmer in Murmansk.

Sandiman sighed, very deeply, and got on the phone to Maintenance.

Mike went home at lunchtime after threatening to crucify the next reader who breathed too heavily, which should have been a relief. But as he prepared to deal with the last query of the day, Sandiman felt his depression deepen. He just knew it wouldn't be one of the bright kids.

If I see one more pair of blank eyes beneath a baseball cap, he thought, *I'll...*

Do what? Cancel his library card?

As he feared, one of the neds was standing before him. Living proof that Neanderthal DNA did still exist. Neds marked themselves out by putting baseball caps on backwards, trying to shag female neds in corridors, and wearing T-shirts saying they'd been assimilated by the Borg and resistance was futile.

"Got any books?" the ned asked.

About 20,000. All neatly arranged on the shelves around you.

No, don't say that. Try and put it another way.

"Are you looking for any book in particular?"

"One on concrete."

How to headbutt the stuff or how to deal with the subject?

"Have you tried the OPACs?" he said, pointing to the terminals in the corner.

"The what?"

"The OPAC. Online Public Access Catalogue. Just over there."

"No."

Sandiman keyed his own OPAC and turned up a few possibilities.

"You can try *Richardson's Precast Concrete Production* at 624.173414, *Hurst's Prestressed Concrete Design* at 624.183412, or *Livesey's Concrete and You: In the Mix* at 623.7. Failing that, just try anywhere in the 620s. That shelf over there. Right there."

The student nodded vaguely and was about to turn away in the wrong direction when a thought occurred to Sandiman.

"By the way, what do you think about the Stone of Destiny coming back?"

"The what?"

"The Stone of Destiny."

Please God, at least let him have heard *of the bloody thing.*

"Oh. The Stone. Yeah. It's a good thing. Yeah. Good thing."

"Why do you think that?"

Sandiman watched the ned's eyes perform slow circles, then he saw a spark of inspiration stir within them.

"Better they send the Stone or we'll steal it again."

Sandiman almost smiled, mentally promoting the student from straightforward sad git to simply somewhat clueless.

"Best just consider it an overdue item ripe for return."

The student shambled away amiably enough and Sandiman was left alone with his thoughts. Perhaps he was becoming a bit too much of a cynical bastard. His colleagues occasionally said he'd picked the wrong career and might be better off being a mercenary in Croatia. Maybe they were right. Taking care of the overdues hardly seemed like the road to his personal Nirvana. Those university students who'd originally stolen the Stone back in the 1950s had gone a far better route, latter-day poachers or tinkers laughing at authority and taking real risks for their cause.

Still, at least he had a job.

"What're you saying today, then?"

That was Natalie, his other library assistant and his muse. Natalie who walked in beauty like the night. Except it was late afternoon and she was slouching over the issue desk. But she really was beautiful, and graceful as a wood-nymph. What a pity she'd wound up in this place. Why wasn't she away drinking Bollinger on a yacht off Cannes or gliding through marbled halls in Vienna with a Brad Pitt lookalike by her side?

No, that wasn't fair. She was a nice girl with a good mind. It wasn't her fault she'd turned up here early in 1995. Quiet girls from Inveraray with green eyes, red hair and slim hips often ended up doing a lot worse in the Big City.

He remembered interviewing her. He had asked her about Inveraray, what she'd done there and the like. She had looked straight at him, her gorgeous eyes wide and guileless, and said:

"I was born in a council house on Sinclair Avenue, and I worked as a dispensing assistant at the apothecary on Main Street West."

"Why did you leave Inverary?"

She had shrugged slightly. A smile had lit up her face.

"I didn't like oysters."

Sandiman had remembered the town's oyster industry, and found himself smiling back at her. She *had* been the best candidate, and it *would* be nice to have another Highlander around the place.

She'd got the job. They had got on well together ever since.

"Fancy a moan?" he said.

She rolled her eyes theatrically. He gestured around the library just as theatrically, letting his eyes wander over the scenery.

"Here we have the latest cutting-edge technology, computers with 200 Mhz Pentium processors, Internet access, an email server with 3.2 Gigabytes of memory, the best graphic design software packages. You name it, we've got it. We're wired up to everywhere except NORAD. And who's it all for? For people just passing the time between school and the DSS. For people who support Greenock Morton Football Club. For neds who can't even spell their own *names* properly."

"What's so bad about Greenock Morton?"

"They have this little problem. They don't know how to play football, but they really truly believe they're world-beaters. They're my metaphor for Scotland. They go on the field with high hopes and get the crap beaten out of them with monotonous regularity."

"You don't support them, then?"

"No, I don't support them. I don't even like football. I am tired of football, and I am weary of life."

"You're really having a bad day, aren't you?"

"Bad is not the word. Disastrous is the word."

Natalie looked at him intently and opened her mouth.

> *"What a life without a wife,*
> *And me without a lover,*
> *And the woman next door's got two..."*

Sandiman smiled despite himself. The next line seemed obvious.

> *"Her husband and her brother!"*

"That's sick!"

"It just occurred to me. Anyway it rhymes. What's the real last line?"

"Don't know. Don't even know where I heard it."

"Dear Natalie ..."

"Don't call me dear!"

"What would you rather I called you? *Babe?*"

"No," she said, picking up a pencil and fiddling with it angrily.

"Want to come out for a drink? It's late, I'm tired and right now suicide seems a pretty good career option."

"Don't say that. Don't *ever* say that."

Suddenly she had gone all Calvinist on him. He didn't know why, but all trace of the bantering Natalie he knew had vanished.

"I thought you were Protestant, not Calvinist?"

"What are you saying?"

"You're so serious all of a sudden – Little Miss Morals from Merchiston."

She gave him a look which somehow combined froideur with affection, and almost smiled.

"I don't know what I am. Anyway, no one goes to church any more."

"Go for a drink instead?"

She nodded and fetched her coat. As long as Natalie was all right, he reflected, not too much was wrong with the world. For a moment he wondered what sex with her would be like, then immediately dismissed it. She was his friend. And a good friend. So whatever lay unspoken behind that was damned well going to stay unspoken.

Resolving to think no more of it, he started the shutdown routines. As was par for the course in this dot.com age of instant gratification, it took fifteen minutes, several passwords which the bloody machine refused to recognise half the time, and monastic devotion to a page-long set of instructions.

Finally it was over, and they could lose themselves amid the throng of workers heading home.

The trains no longer ran from St Enoch Station, the *Glasgow Herald* had moved its offices away from the centre of town and the M8 snaked over and above the heart of Glasgow in a forest of pillars and flyovers. It was a bit of a comedown for the former second city of the United Kingdom.

Football was the city's new religion and Protestant and Catholic still fought each other, especially at Bridgeton Cross on Saturdays after Rangers played Celtic. Both sides were also quite happy to fight the Muslims on the Southside.

But stretching from Bridgegate to Rottenrow, the city's eight original streets still endured. Sandiman and Natalie walked around the old thoroughfares that evening, from the Merchant City to Argyle Street, slowly getting more and more bevvied as closing time got nearer and the nightclubs opened for business.

They ended up at an all-night pancake restaurant with private alcoves. Being fairly blootered, they simply sat staring at the streams of buxom bottle blondes and long tall brunettes heading out for the night.

"Best and worst night of my life," Sandiman said to Natalie, "sitting here pished one Sunday morning after seeing *Trainspotting*. Seeing Spud, Sick Boy and Renton saying it was shite being Scottish and shooting up on smack. Scottish miserablism summed up in one short sharp sequence by the station at Corrour."

Natalie dropped her eyes, not exactly enthralled by the fine example of miserablism sitting slopped over in front of her.

"I saw something interesting on *Reporting Scotland* the other day," she said after a short pause. "I'd been meaning to tell you."

"What?"

"Something about a book."

"Any book in particular?"

"A book in Cambridge. It's just as important as the Stone but nobody's ever heard of it. They walked all over Aberdeen asking people about it but nobody had ever heard of it."

"So what is it?"

"A really old book. The *first* book. First book in Gaelic."

"Does it have a title?"

"Can't remember."

"Helpful, helpful. Very, very helpful."

"The Book of Deer!"

"What?"

"That's the name of the book."

"Doesn't mean much to me."

"You used to be really into old books. Like when you and Gavin catalogued that old library near Arrochar & Tarbert," she said.

"I used to be. I'm not any more," he said vaguely. He hadn't seen Gavin Beatty for a while, but his old friend had recently been made Deputy Keeper of Special Collections at Glasgow City University.

She stared at him, looking even less enthralled than she had been before.

"I used to be a lot of things," he snapped, suddenly sober and angry. "That was before. Nobody cares any more. Not about history or anything else. Most people think the Scots fought the English at Culloden with Robert the Bruce, William Wallace and Rob Roy in the front line."

Sandiman saw Natalie's eyes narrow in contempt. He thought of apologising, but knew the mood had been broken.

Feeling wretched, he walked her to the taxi-rank in front of Central Station. She touched his arm before they parted, and he felt a little better. He watched as the taxi drew away, wishing he was with her.

After that, all there was to do was go home to his tidy flat. His tidy, *empty* flat.

Well, he was a loner so he could put up with it. Loners always got a bad press. If you were a loner you were probably a paedophile, and if you kept the flat tidy, you were most likely gay.

There was some truth to this, but he was just a bloke who lived on his own, and he was used to it.

Pretty much.

When he got back, he found he couldn't sleep. So he grabbed his emergency bottle of Glenmorangie and watched *Highlander*. He'd been drinking more recently, but he didn't think he was becoming an alcoholic. And he had a bottle of Irn Bru on ice, just in case.

He still felt wretched.

I was born in 1518, in the village of Glenfinnan on the shores of Loch Shiel...

The bloody quote was echoing in his head like a piece of oral history.

Sandiman slept late the following morning, and missed hearing about the ceremony celebrating the Stone's return to Edinburgh Castle. It was a muted affair, held on a windy street in front of a small crowd who, apart from a few William Wallace clones and some tweedy old SNP stalwarts, provided no characters or memorable images.

He lay in bed staring at the ceiling. He couldn't even look back nostalgically on his past. He was a librarian, after all.

There'd been a few bright spots. The girls he'd known at university. Like Susan from Strathaven who'd left him in a state of bliss for the better part of a week. Backpacking around Europe hadn't been too bad, either. He'd got as far as Istanbul, waking up on the deck of an early morning ferry from Izmir to see the dome of the Church of St Sophia rising above the Bosphorus.

Last stop for Christendom, he'd thought blearily, *all change for Islam*! As the mist had lingered around the dome, it seemed to float clear of the city without support. A palace set like a jewel above Byzantium by Constantine, a church to which Turks still turned their eyes in reverence.

A new Scottish parliament with its MSPs set on shagging their researchers didn't sound quite sae grand in comparison.

Of course, once there had been Jessica. He didn't want to think about her, but regret still gnawed at him. He'd loved her like his ancestors had loved the church and the land. No, more than that. She'd been warm but quiet, passionate but spiritual. She had completed him, he had fallen for her. And then she'd...

No. Try not to think about that today. It still hurt too much.

He walked over to the window and stared out at nothing. It had felt different in 1977, before the hurt. Back in the days of the Bay City Rollers and Ally's Tartan Army.

John Sandiman had not been born in Glenfinnan, but he had been there many times.

He'd been a spotty teenager youth-hostelling his way around the West Highlands for the first time. He had taken the postbus to Shiel Bridge and on the spur of the moment decided to walk the length of Loch Shiel, catch the train at Glenfinnan station and spend the night at the hostel near Morar.

Being young, stupid and full of testosterone, he had misjudged the distance, his stamina, and the weather. He spent that night shivering in a ruined bothy somewhere on the lochside wondering whether he'd die of hypothermia, his frozen dead flesh picked clean by swarms of voracious midges and his bones found by a shepherd several months later. Alternatively, he might survive to look back on this day with fondness and nostalgia.

Survive he did, and the next morning he'd staggered out of the bothy into warm July sunshine. Disorientated and grungy, he had looked around, trying to get his bearings. To his left were the calm blue waters of the loch, but to his right an early morning mist obscured the view.

Then, as he watched, the sun had broken through the mist.

He had seen the viaduct first, that long sweeping curve of suspended track which arced between the mountains of Fraoch-bheinn and Beinn nan Tom. As the mist cleared with infinite slowness, he had felt he was looking at a canvas upon which God must have woven a three-dimensional painting, for the viaduct centred the eye on the picture as if it had been created only for that purpose. With the eye drawn, the surrounding detail had been thrown into perspective. From the greens and browns of fir and pine by the lochside to the hard-edged flanks of the ancient mountains, home only to the eagle and the deer.

Like a stage curtain spun from spider's webs the mist had slowly vanished, letting the tableau take on a crystal clarity. He'd noticed a building in the foreground which he'd taken to be the visitor centre, and as he'd glanced to the left he had just been able to make out a church.

Last of all, he had looked at the figure on the monument standing as it had stood for so many years, whether in sorrow for Culloden's dead or assumption of the divine rights of kings.

Bonnie Prince Charlie, the Young Pretender.

Later, Sandiman could never quite remember just how long he'd stood there. The deep sound of a diesel engine hauling the blue carriages of the first train from Mallaig had brought motion and life to the tableau, like an artist adding the final touch to a masterpiece.

He'd stepped forward, as if to become part of the picture, and a stag had erupted from the heather before him.

Sandiman had jumped back, expecting the creature would head for the hills. But for a moment it had simply stood at bay, gazing at him with sorrowful eyes.

Then it had done as he'd first expected, taking flight so quickly he'd been left feeling he'd met, not a flesh-and-blood animal, but some creature of myth.

When Sandiman had first walked into Glenfinnan, he had not known much about the history of the township, but he *had* known he would not forget the tableau he'd seen.

Over the years he had returned to the village time and time again, getting acquainted with the scattered houses, old and new, which blended into the wooded slopes between ancient loch and Victorian station. He got to know the fish farm at the pier, the visitor centre by the monument and the big house at Slatach on the north shore.

He'd also picked up stories about local characters past and present. Like John Monahan, last station-master at Glenfinnan, who kept greyhounds in the signal-box and raced them in Glasgow. Or John Macdonald of Kinlocheil who propped up the bar in Glenfinnan's pubs and was known to all and sundry as Johnny Red Hair.

Now and then, he lunched at one or other of the hotels. One was by the lochside, the other at the top of the village on the road to the Isles.

Once, just once, he had gone up to the village with Susan from Strathaven. They had made love under the monument at sunset but she'd felt a bit inhibited, and sand got in the wrong places. They'd broken up soon afterwards.

So mostly he tramped about on his own. He discovered that the church, a Gothic design by Pugin & Pugin with a large bell in its grounds, was dedicated to Saint Finnan of Moville, teacher of the legendary Saint Columba, abbot of Iona. Accurately but unimaginatively, the bell was also named after Finnan.

The last time he'd visited Glenfinnan he had wandered down to the visitor centre, a black-wood building with a pine interior host to postcards, bottled jellies and bookshelves devoted to Wallace, Charlie, and the '45. Young women in blue National Trust jerseys buzzed about, and deep windows looked out onto the monument. It had been a slow day, one of the young women had been a bit talkative, and she'd ended up telling him how the church had been desecrated after the annual Highland Games. Sandiman remembered turning from the bookshelves to listen to her, a book he'd been browsing still in his hand.

There'd been a dance at the big house, she had said, and a late-night bar had been set up in a tent near the monument. Hearing about the bar, some little shits from Fort William had come up on the last train and drunk their fill. Then they had staggered up to the church, pissed on the pews, damaged the sacristy and smashed a couple of windows.

"They even mooned at me when I drove home!" she finished indignantly. She had been angry. He didn't blame her. He knew her slightly, had seen her occasionally over the years. A dark-haired, bright-eyed young woman who loved her church.

He and Jessica had spent time there as well, soaking up the quiet and the calm. It had been a sacrament of sorts. He'd heard the Church of St Sophia was the most sacred in Christendom. The absolute epitome of hush. He couldn't quite agree.

With the memories it held, Finnan's church was more sacred to him.

Now another little piece of his past had been pissed on.

It felt like a sad and final piece of proof positive that there was no respect left for church or state, that the past was forgotten, that the tales his father had taught him and the cool cloisters of Highland kirks stood for nothing.

He should have let his misgivings fade away, let himself be carried along on the tide of apathy which passed for his life, but he couldn't quite manage it. It would have been so easy just to see himself right but he couldn't do it. Some small voice from his id, as faint and out of tune as the memories of his father's tales had become, would not shut up and let him sleep.

Not much a librarian could do to change the world, though. Or was there?

A memory came to him, unfocused but vivid. The book he'd browsed through at the visitor centre. What was its title? Oh, yes. *The Return of John Macnab*. Based on *John Macnab* by John Buchan. He knew the original book, but had not read it for some time.

The douce young lady at the visitor centre had gone on talking. It had been quiet, a fine mist of rain falling on the loch, a lull before the next storm of tourist coaches. Some of the scenes in *Highlander* had been shot on the south shores, he remembered. Sean Connery had tipped Christopher Lambert into the loch to convince him he was immortal.

"John Macnab came from here," he heard her say.

"Who?"

"John Macnab. Like in the book in your hand."

"What do you mean?"

"There was a real wager. For a salmon, a brace of grouse and a stag. It happened by the Fort. Out at Inverlochy estates."

Inverlochy estates. His great-grandfather had worked there at one time.

Sandiman had glanced at the book. Had seen a reproduction of the updated wager.

A phrase had caught his eye.

For any further information, consult John Macnab *by John Buchan.*

He blinked his way back to the present. A fine mist of rain was also falling on Partick. He thought about the phrase. Perhaps he would consult *John Macnab* again. It would do no harm. It might even cure his boredom.

2

"Be a man, for God's sake, Mr Denver.
And if you can't be a man, at least
pull up your pants and be a principal."

(Stephen King)

It was Monday morning and Mike had an idea. Mike, the mad library assistant with the body-piercing fetish. Mike, who no one would ever own up to actually employing. Mike, who had a sociopathic hatred of students and occasionally drooled. Mike, who never told anyone, *ever*, where he lived. Sandiman suspected he curled up by the furnace in the basement at night, or skulked around some troglodytic realm deep beneath the streets of Glasgow that Alasdair Gray would have called Unthank or Provan.

Mike would probably end up taking a couple of delectable young students hostage, barricade himself into the library with an AK 47 and get himself blown away by the SAS. Shot to pieces in front of the social welfare section as he was shouting "Made it, Ma! Top of the world!" He was letting his imagination run away with him. So what if Mike had spots, smoked roll-ups and said 'arse' a lot? He wasn't basically evil, just a bit warped. Not surprising after ten long years in this particular library.

But all the same, it wasn't a very good idea.

"Where did you get this thing from, Mike? The local white witch?"

He reread the quotation:

"For him that stealeth a Book from the Library,
let it change into a serpent into his hand and rend him.
Let him be struck with Palsy,
and all his Members blasted.
Let him languish in Pain crying aloud for Mercy
and let there be no surcease to his Agony
till he sink in Dissolution.
Let Bookworms gnaw his Entrails
in token of the Worm that dieth not,
and when at last he goeth to his final Punishment,
let the flames of Hell consume him for ever and aye."

(Monastery of San Pedro, Barcelona)

"Bit drastic just for an overdue book, isn't it?"

"It'd bloody work! I got a cousin runs a second-hand bookshop in Camden who faxed it to me. He had trouble – this stopped it. Comes from a real monastery. Sixteenth century, he said."

"We're only meant to fine them if they bring a book back late, Mike. Just *fine* them, not consign them screaming to the fires of hell for all eternity."

Mike looked sulky and scratched his balls.

"So you don't want it put on the noticeboard then?"

"Let me put it this way. No."

"Arse."

Mike skulked out of Sandiman's small office with all the grace of the Hunchback of Notre Dame, leaving him to massage his temples. He felt pretty seedy, which was no surprise considering he still had the remnants of a bottle of Glenmorangie and several packets of Doritos in his system. The weekend had turned into a long morose hell of self-examination and the Irn Bru on ice had not, in the end, been of much help.

Natalie entered and said nothing, merely looked at him patiently.

"Yes, I know," he said.

She nodded and left.

He wondered why he kept on defending Mike. More and more, the college was becoming a pseudo-political bearpit of a place. Rivalry between departments was enormous and when a naïve personnel assistant had suggested a staff 'bonding' weekend at a posh hotel, one joker had said a 'square go' on Glasgow Green complete with razors and paramedics to mop up the blood afterwards might be a better idea. So it wasn't a good idea to rock the boat, and by keeping Mike on, Sandiman was doing just that. He had fielded subtle hints from the principal (and not so subtle hints from the finance manager) that Mike might be better employed somewhere else. Or unemployed somewhere else. Or basically just somewhere else, full stop. Perhaps Mike was still working because part of Sandiman's own personality occasionally yearned to tell society to go and get stuffed. Just like John Macnab.

Sandiman reached into his briefcase and pulled out a worn paperback. He had owned a copy of *John Macnab* for so long he'd almost forgotten where he'd shelved it, but late on the Sunday night he'd been staring sadly at his bookcase and noticed the title, right next to a book by T H White.

Consult *John Macnab*, he had thought.

Why not, indeed?

Sandiman turned the book over and over in his hands. He actually felt afraid to open it. There were ideas in there, and ideas had power. If he opened the book, he might be influenced by them. He might have to change his safe little routine. Maybe even do something different, exciting ...

The phone rang. It was the finance manager. The kind of guy who wasn't even good enough to play for Greenock Morton.

"Hello, Guy! How was your weekend, then? All quiet on the Western Front? ... Yeah. I've got a window this afternoon at two ... At one then. Well, if you insist ...You do insist. Right."

And that was the usual conversation with Guy Mannering, the finance manager from hell and quite possibly Mad Mike's secret brother. Everyone knew he lived in a posh part of Bearsden. Everyone knew he had a cousin in the Free Church who preached on the Isle of Lewis, and everyone suspected he sometimes engaged in unnatural sexual practices with his pet corgi. But nobody ever said it to his face.

He headed for the lift. The finance manager's office was on the top floor. Sandiman suspected Mannering looked out at the skyline every morning from his position of power and had a self-satisfied wank.

The lift bumbled upwards through the building, finally depositing him in Mannering's lair. The secretary, an old lady called Miss Partridge, waved him through with a mixture of disinterest (three parts) and contempt (one part).

In person, Mannering looked, not unsurprisingly, like an accountant. Apart, that was, from the way his eyes looked straight through you, clearly conveying the message that he had already made up his mind and simply did not care what anyone else had to say.

He greeted Sandiman with polite disinterest (the full measure) and proceeded to try and halve the library budget. It was an impossible conversation from the start.

"Guy, I appreciate that the college faces a deficit this financial year, but slashing the library's bookfund will only exacerbate the problem, not solve it."

"I'm afraid I don't quite follow you, John. Surely the increased Internet access, which has already been budgeted for, will compensate for fewer books on the actual shelves."

"I'm afraid, *Guy*, that the most user-friendly interactive medium on the market is still the book. We keep multiple copies of our core texts on the shelves for that very reason. Thirty students can read a text like *Building Technology* and leave the twenty-five PCs clear for other research purposes."

"But that is precisely my point, *John*. Information can be directly downloaded from the Internet, eliminating the need for so many books."

"Not all the information will be available via the Net, *Guy*.

In a pretty high number of cases it will only be able to provide nuggets of information or direct the student to the place where the rest of the information can be found. All knowledge residing in books *in depth* hasn't just been automatically transferred to computer."

"What exactly do you mean, John? I'm afraid I don't quite follow you."

"I mean," Sandiman paused and tried to stop grinding his teeth, "that books, computers, email and the Internet, all the buzz words which everybody gets so excited about these days, are just a means to an end. That end, in this case, is to give students access to information they need so they can pass their courses and we can stay in business. To that end, every one of the range of services we deliver is just as important as every other one. Our books aren't a luxury, they're essential for the long-term viability of this college!"

"I appreciate your point, John, but I'm afraid the principal and I are in complete agreement on this matter, and it is equally essential for the short-term viability of this college for cuts to be made. I'll need a breakdown of your projected economies by next Friday."

Or in other words, I've got the principal over a barrel and he'll let me do exactly what I want to do anyway.

Sandiman pursed his lips. He was not quick to anger, but once he became angry he tended to stay that way. And this man was making him angry. This man who simply did not seem to care that people's careers could be wrecked by his short-term economics.

He got up to leave, and as he was walking toward the exit Mannering sent a parting shot after him.

"Of course, John, cutting staff will always help us make economies. I believe it's time for Mike to be leaving us now."

Sandiman looked at the finance manager for a long moment, turned on his heel and left.

He sank gloomily down through the bowels of the building to the library, picked up *John Macnab* and headed for the canteen, a long grey room without windows or edible food. Natalie was sitting at a table in the corner. She looked steadily at him as he griped on about Guy Mannering.

"So I told him to take his planned economies," he finished up, "I told him to give them to his pet corgi and eat the resulting by-product."

"No you didn't."

"No I didn't. But I sure felt like it."

"What happens now?"

"I don't know. We've got a finance manager who thinks the college will be a more efficient place without any books in it, and a principal who backs this opinion up totally. This is the face of further education."

"What'd he suggest you do?"

"Fire Mike."

"You can't do that!"

"If I don't, Mannering will probably fire *me*."

"Would that be such a bad thing?"

"Sorry?"

"You're always saying how much you hate this place."

"It pays the rent."

"You can't fire Mike."

"Someone will one day," he said tiredly, unable to meet her eyes and instead trying to concentrate on the congealed macaroni cheese in front of him. At another college, he'd heard, the catering staff had accidentally added cleaning fluid to the bolognese sauce and killed a couple of lecturers.

"Mike has insulted too many people too many times in too many interesting and creative ways," he said. "Allah weaves the threads of men's destinies into many strange tapestries. This is Mike's destiny. They were always going to get him in the end."

"You've got a quote for everything, haven't you? And stop looking at the macaroni cheese like that – it won't bite you."

"Yeah, and I like that quote. I found it in the library Gavin and I catalogued up in Arrochar & Tarbet. And are you sure the macaroni is all right?"

"No."

Like the stiffening macaroni cheese, silence solidified around them.

"What's that?" Natalie asked eventually, pointing at the copy of *John Macnab*.

"It's a book about the kind of bloke who wouldn't take any shit from Guy Mannering."

"I'd like to meet him," she said, raising her eyebrows.

"You can't. He's a fiction within a fiction."

"A what?"

"Come on, I'll show you."

They went back to the library's reference section, where Sandiman picked out *Larousse's dictionary of literary characters*.

"There!"

Natalie looked at the entry.

'John MacNab'
John MacNab, 1925
John Buchan

A fictional character within a fiction, he is the invention of a group of bored gentlemen who create him to enliven the Highlands with the sort of mythic outlawry the present age lacks. More seriously, he fulfils Buchan's romantic attachment to the figure of the archetypal Lost Leader.

"So, he's a character in a book, based on a real person?" asked Natalie.

Sandiman opened the book itself, quickly found the relevant pages.

"Yeah. Basically, three members of the Establishment – Edward Leithen, John Palliser-Yeates and Charles Lamancha

– get tired of their gilded lives and decide to do something daring for a change. They make a wager with the lairds of three Highland estates based on a story they're told by a friend, Archie Roylance."

"What story?"

"This story. On page 17."

He began to read:

Archie was truly shocked. Then a light of reminiscence came into his eye. "You remind me of poor old Jim Tarras," he said thoughtfully.

There were no inquiries about Jim Tarras, so Archie volunteered further news.

"You remember Jim? He had a little place somewhere in Moray, and spent most of his time shootin' in East Africa. Poor chap, he went back there with Smuts in the war and perished of blackwater. Well, when his father died and he came home to settle down, he found it an uncommon dull job. So, to enliven it, he invented a new kind of sport. He knew all there was to be known about shikar, and from trampin' about the Highlands he had a pretty accurate knowledge of the country-side. So he used to write to the owner of a deer forest and present his compliments, and beg to inform him that between certain dates he proposed to kill one of his stags. When he had killed it he undertook to deliver it to the owner, for he wasn't a thief."

"So these three decide to get together," Sandiman went on, "and do the same thing themselves. They present their compliments to the lairds of three estates – here it is on page 22 – but they need a sort of group pseudonym as signatory so these fictional characters give themselves one name, also fictional. John Macnab. That's who John Macnab is, a fiction within a fiction."

"Fiction to you. Greek to me."

"My grandparents used to work on estates like these. It's no joke to me."

"Think you're John Macnab, then?" she teased.

"Of course not. I guess I'm just your average librarian." He avoided her eyes but she bored in again, probing for a response.

"You should go see Gavin. Ride into some other town like a couple of masked avengers and catalogue another old book collection that's gone to the dogs."

"Who do you take me for? Zorro?"

Damn it, she was leaning forward, staring right at him. He felt himself flushing.

"No, not at all. Perhaps you're right. Perhaps you *are* just an average librarian."

"Go take care of the issue desk, will you?" he snapped. He glared after her. He was more than just a librarian, damn it and damn her! Why did she keep pushing him?

Then his eyes turned back to the book, and he hesitated. He would sort things out with Natalie later; he'd just read a little while longer...

God, he hadn't felt so alive in *years*.

The afternoon dragged by. He neglected his duties with glee and carefully read through *John Macnab*. He found himself reading page 22 over and over again:

Sir, I have the honour to inform you that I propose to kill a stag – or a salmon as the case may be – on your ground between midnight on __ and midnight __ ... The animal, of course, remains your property and will be duly delivered to you. It is a condition that it must be removed wholly outside your bounds. In the event of the undersigned failing to achieve his purpose he will pay as forfeit one hundred pounds, and if successful fifty pounds to any charity you may appoint. I have the honour to be, your obedient, humble servant."

A good way to tilt at windmills, Sandiman thought.

Before he knew it, however, it was a quarter-to-five and the computer system had to be turned off before the library itself closed at five. Still looking hurt, Natalie called him in and he started the shutdown routine.

Halfway through it, a youth he knew strutted up to him and dumped a book on the issue desk. Unlike the rather amiable sad-git-promoted-to-clueless from earlier in the day, this one was classic ned from head to toe. A rail-thin yob with plastered-down hair who thought a hard stare and attitude would solve any problem.

"I need this book out," said the youth.

Sandiman felt a twinge of annoyance. He was halfway through the routine and the system couldn't backtrack to do withdrawals now.

"I'm afraid the library's closing. We can keep it for you overnight. You can pick it up tomorrow morning, but you'll have to bring in some of your overdues first. Your card's full."

"What're you saying, man?"

"I'm saying your card's full. I know it's full, and all the books on it are overdue. I've sent several letters to you about it and about the fines you haven't paid. Come back tomorrow with your overdues, pay your fines, and then you can take this book out."

"I ain't paying no fucking fine!"

Sandiman felt his annoyance change to anger. It was quite pleasant, like the keen edge of a knife. He drew himself up to his full height and stared back at the youth.

"Bad language is not allowed in the library," he said in a low voice. "Your card's full. Come back in the morning."

"I ain't coming back in the morning!"

"I'm tired of repeating myself. The library's closing. I don't want you in it. If you'd rather a report didn't go to your tutor, the exit's that way."

"You're talking pure mince, man."

Sandiman felt the blood draining from his face. He went

on looking right into the youth's eyes, beginning to see uncertainty in them.

"You want to walk out on your own, or would you like the janitor to help you?"

The youth blinked, opened his mouth like a flounder a couple of times and then resorted to the Glaswegian answer to all adversity:

"Get tae fuck!"

"I think you can do that to yourself quite effectively."

Sandiman never quite knew where that retort came from, but all he felt next was a rush of air and light impact as the ned threw a clumsy punch which clipped him on the jaw.

The ned tried to scramble over the issue desk. In slow motion (or so it seemed to him), Sandiman saw him raising his right arm like the crudest of clubs, caught the violent fist and looked him right in the eye.

"On second thoughts, just don't come back in the morning."

The ned slid back onto the floor and made for the exit. Sandiman watched him go. He felt little pain in his jaw, just relief in the knowledge that even that prat of a principal would have to expel a student who'd assaulted a member of staff.

Even this lousy college couldn't have gone so rotten they'd cover *that* up.

3

"Darlin', is that you?"

"Well, John. As you've just called my home phone number at half-past-two in the morning, I think you can be pretty sure it's me. And don't call me darling."

"Natalie. I'm really, really sorry about calling you now."

"You know, you really are a right old pervert," she said. "I'm twenty-two, you're at least thirty-five and you're my manager. I could get you thrown out of the library for sexual harassment and sodomy. All I'll have to do is turn up in front of Mr Mannering tomorrow, look vulnerable and flash my poor bruised tits at him."

"Natalie. I swear to God I haven't phoned about your tits."

"You'll be the first man alive to do that then. That's all you lot ever think about."

"I'm sorry, Natalie."

"You're not sorry, you're drunk. But John…"

"What?"

"I'm drunk, too. It's the Scots disease. We all drink."

"Why're you drunk, too?"

There was silence on the line for about ten seconds.

"Hello?"

"I'm still here, you big, self-pitying jerk. You're damned lucky I'm still even talking to you."

Despite himself, Sandiman suddenly burped. It was one right old eructation of a belch, the room seemed to shake and the walls somehow cringed. He'd have to quit that damned Glenmorangie, and soon.

"I'm empty inside, Nat."

"You certainly are after that performance."

"It was good today, though. Felt like a man. Stood up for myself."

Silence again.

"Natalie. You still there?"

"Yes. I'm here," she said softly. Even pissed at half two in the morning, she thought, he was a better man than Murdo had ever been.

"I'm sorry, Natalie. I've been thinking too much."

"Don't be sorry about that. What have you been thinking about anyway?"

"About being on the side of the angels, about whether I'm Christian, Catholic or Celt. Which foot do you kick with yourself, Calvin?"

"I don't know," she said. "I got dragged to the Free Church a few times, nearly died of the cold, said I wouldn't go again because the fires of hell would at least be warmer. Quite like the idea of praying, though. Kind of wish there was someone good out there who'd keep me warm. I just think they've wrapped so much ornament and ritual and rubbish around it that it's all rotting to pieces and turning to nonsense. They've taken all the meaning away from it. I can't remember what the words are supposed to say."

He was quiet for a long time.

"Natalie?"

"John?"

"I'd like to die in battle with my king. Really."

"There aren't any more kings, John. Not real ones. Neither here nor across the water. They're all wrapped in ornament and ritual and rubbish, too. But I know what you mean."

"Could you tell me, then?"

"You're looking for a life with passion and honour and valour. The world your mythic outlaw Mac-what's-his-name would have lived in. But that world's gone. If it ever even existed."

"Macnab. John Macnab."

"Whatever. It's either that or you're having an absolutely massive midlife crisis."

"You're the wisest girl I ever met."

"Wiser than Jessica?"

Sandiman went stock still save for a sharp indrawn breath he didn't even know he'd taken. Why did she have to mention *that* name of all names? Then he found it within himself to laugh a little.

"See you tomorrow, Nat. At least there'll be one less ned to worry about on the day."

"See you. Try and get to bed if you can remember where it is."

"Night, Nat."

"Night, John."

4

It was the morning after the day before, and Sandiman knew the wheels were turning in the offices above. He'd made an official complaint, the CCTV footage was sharp, clear and indisputable, and now the ned's fate was being decided by Mannering and a committee of grey men upstairs. He wasn't too bothered. However rubber-spined they were, there was no getting round the fact that a student had assaulted a member of staff, and the little lug would get his comeuppance. So while he should have been thinking about his job, about Mike and about the whole silly little stushie, he wasn't. He was actually glued to a biography of John Buchan. What that biography told him stirred up a burning sense of excitement in his chest. Either that or he was getting angina.

John Macnab had indeed been based on reality. In 1897 one Captain James Brander Dunbar of Pitgaveny had successfully bagged a salmon, a brace of grouse and a deer on Lord Abinger's estate at Inverlochy, less than twenty miles from Glenfinnan. Years later, Buchan had even autographed Dunbar's copy of *John Macnab*.

A thought struck him. Some of his own ancestors might have been working on Abinger's estates when John Macnab was hunting the deer.

The strange quote he'd found when he and Gavin Beatty had been cataloguing the library in Arrochar & Tarbert came once more to mind: *Allah the Compassionate, the Merciful, weaves the threads of men's destinies into many strange tapestries.*

Allah had done a good job this time. Sandiman didn't have a clue what it all meant.

He did know that Natalie had been right, though. She always was, damn her. He probably was having a midlife crisis, Mannering would certainly not be pleased that one of his students would have to be expelled from the college and Sandiman would also have to decide what to do about Mike soon. That knowledge had dogged his footsteps as he had dragged himself to work that day.

I hate you, Mannering, he thought. *I hate you so much it surprises me. I think I hate you enough to destroy myself if I could bring you down with me. Or at least just tell you to fuck off.*

He sat at his desk for a full fifteen minutes, scarcely moving. He looked at the computer in front of him, at the Bic biros in their blue tidy tubes and the old picture of Jessica, taken a long time ago at the pier in Kyleakin. He could see the Sound of Sleat behind her. There'd been no Skye Bridge then, just the old Caledonian MacBrayne car ferry. It had been windy. He remembered the breeze catching her hair. Remembered her smile as she tried to pat it back into place.

The phone interrupted him. They'd made a decision and they wanted him upstairs for the verdict. Mannering, it seemed, would deliver it.

Once again he took the long walk from the lift to the office as Miss Partridge looked on dispassionately. For a moment he thought of vampires and their familiars.

Mannering was much as he had been before. God-Emperor of Finance and walking cliché. Guy I Mannering he should have been, and the 'I' would stand for insincerity.

Later, Sandiman would be surprised at how little he reacted. He sat in a waking dream. Everyone likes to believe that what they do has some meaning. When they learn that it does not, there is a period of disbelief. There is a numbness before perception finally kicks in and confirms that, no, there isn't going to be a happy ending.

"Come in, John. Sit down."

Right where I tell you to.

"Thanks, Guy."

"I appreciate the fact that the aforementioned student assaulted you in the heat of the moment... But I have discussed the matter with the department heads, discussed it at some length as a matter of fact..."

Surprise me. Tell me about a committee meeting that was short, sweet, democratic and logical.

"And we're not going to do anything."

Sandiman just sat there. He would never forget that last sentence. Not ever. At first it made no great impact on him. Only later would it slowly come back to him. At odd moments: at night, alone. Or in the cafeteria, or (another cliché!) when he was just walking down the street, thinking about nothing at all.

"We're not going to do anything."

The words repeated themselves in his head. The message painfully clear. The students could do what they like and get away with it, because they made money for the college. £50 a head from the European Social Fund. And the college, personified by its finance manager, did not care about anything else. It did not care about libraries, lecturers, knowledge or wisdom. It did not give a damn about Plato's Republic or the Groves of Academe, and once it had sucked their bones dry of income the college didn't even care about its students. All it cared about was the £50.

Mannering's short sentence summed up the whole problem so perfectly, without fanfare or drum roll, that there really was nothing more to be said.

No words came out of Sandiman's mouth. He realised he was staring at Mannering. There was nothing behind Mr Mannering's eyes either, he thought. Nothing at all.

He got up to leave, and he was halfway out of the door when Mannering mentioned Mike again. Sandiman went on walking. He went back to his office and stared at the wall, feeling chills pass through his body.

He did nothing else for the rest of the day. Then he went back home and stared at the scarlet walls of his flat, feeling nothing but the chill. That was all there was for him. A life of fits and starts, of dead-ends and cold regrets. He had little to look back on and less to look forward to. He wasn't even much of a man any more, and that was the worst of it.

The Irn Bru stayed on ice. He drank some Glenmorangie and thought of Gavin. Of the time they really *had* gone off cataloguing books. Hardly the stuff of masked avengers: a small adventure, but one which had given them back some self-respect, made them feel a bit like men.

Before becoming Deputy Keeper at the University, Gavin Beatty had been in charge of Reference Services at the Mitchell Library but had been getting disillusioned with librarianship for some time and for a while he'd been drinking too much. He turned up at Sandiman's flat one evening with a bottle. They spent a long night of the soul talking things through and the next day Gavin took the pledge.

Sandiman could still remember the conversation word for word. Gavin was a short swarthy man with thick dark eyebrows and big ears. All in all, a fairly typical West of Scotland type. Good post-war nutrition had saved him from bow legs and a good brain had rescued him from becoming one of the men so often seen being thrown out of pubs at closing time and getting into fights at Bridgeton Cross after an Old Firm match.

Gavin had been a Bridgeton boy all right, but instead of propping up the bar at one of its many pubs he'd found himself a job in Bridgeton Library and educated himself by reading the books he returned to the shelves each day.

His diligence was its own reward. He was promoted to a post at the Mitchell Library where he met others like himself. Librarians who had made their way out of the poverty trap with the help of books. Librarians who believed that that was what made their jobs worthwhile. Every so often, he walked through Bridgeton and the Barras on a Friday night, reminding himself of the harsh truth about hard liquor and hard men who lived in rooms called single ends, took home carry-outs and beat their wives. Men who had always done their thinking with their fists and always would.

That was the fairytale. Local boy makes good and goes on to a glittering career helping others help themselves. Lah-di-dah.

The truth, even for a Glaswegian who'd escaped the lure of strong drink, was a sobering experience. One best experienced with the help of a friend and a large glass of whisky.

"They took the greatest public reference library in Europe," Gavin had said to him that night, "and they cut it up. And while they were cutting it up they sank three million quid into turning the Stirling Library into a Gallery of Modern Art. Go into that gallery and what's the first thing you see? A devil with balls and tits.

"And you know what happened then? That parcel of rogues at Strathclyde Region decided they wanted our spare space for their archives. Ten years worth of our growing-room! Everything we had. Filled up with *statistics*. I knew a manager at the Region. He told me they sent him so many requests for stupid numbers that he started making them up. He did it properly of course. Used a slide rule and tables. Even added a 10% distortion factor so they couldn't prove anything. But they never guessed. Said they were some of the best statistics they'd ever had. That's the truth. The damned honest truth. That's what they filled us with."

Sandiman nodded. Strathclyde Region had been full of it, all right.

"Still, we had books. Okay, half the time we couldn't find them on the shelves ourselves, but at least they were there. I thought we were still getting through to people. I thought people were still at least *reading*, but I was wrong.

"There was a lad hanging about in the reading room with his mates one day. The usual arseholes you see mucking around on street corners. They were making a bit of noise so I went over to quiet them. They didn't like that much, and just for once I said what I felt. 'Why don't you read a book and learn something?' was what I said. And it went quiet, just for a moment. Then one of them got up and looked at me. Just looked at me. And he said, 'nobody reads anything any more.'

"Getting lip is one thing. I'm used to getting lip. But I looked at him and I saw he wasn't trying it on. He was just telling the truth. Nobody was reading anything any more. That's when I knew it had all been for nothing. I went home and had a drink that night. The next day I heard they were going to have a reorganisation. I knew what that meant. I know a quote about it. Want to hear it?"

Sandiman nodded again. He knew the quote.

"We trained hard," said Gavin slowly and clearly, "but it seemed that every time we were trying to form up into teams, we'd be reorganised. I was to learn later in life that we tend to meet any new situation by reorganisation and a wonderful method it can be for creating an illusion of progress while producing confusion, inefficiency and demoralisation. Petronius said that in AD 66. *Fuck*."

The last word was said with great weariness. Sandiman had never heard Gavin swear before, not once in twelve years. He'd seen the man angry, once nearly hysterical; but obscenities were part of his past, never again to be uttered. Until now.

He let Gavin sleep in the spare bedroom that night. The following day they walked into a pub on the stroke of eleven. Gavin had bought a pint of Tennents and stared at it. Sandiman had seen his friend's hand shake very slightly. Seen the disinterested look on the barman's face. Gavin had gazed at the pint for a long tense minute before he turned and looked at Sandiman.

"I don't think I'll drink today," he said. "You have it."

With that, they once again become part of the world around them. Sandiman had a pie with the pint. They watched a bit of football on the pub's telly. Talked a little shop. That had been the start of his friend's cure, but fate and luck had helped complete it.

An old man in an old house forty miles north of Glasgow had an old collection of books. The books needed cataloguing so, late in 1994, he'd advertised for volunteers in *Scottish Libraries*. When Sandiman saw the advert he had realised it was just what Gavin needed. A chance to get back to what it was all really about. To handle books which had shaped history.

Every Saturday of 1995, the two men took the West Highland Railway up to Arrochar & Tarbert. The old man was always there, waiting on the platform. He would offer them a nip of whisky from his battered hip flask then drive them, badly and bouncily in a battered Land Rover, down a potholed private road.

The house itself was a cold and grungy neo-Gothic monstrosity, the library shuttered up for the best part of a century and the plumbing unspeakable. It was said a servant's body had been left to rot in the water tank in 1897. But the books had endured and they provided better testimony to the learning of its past owners than the present occupant, who obviously changed his underpants no more than once a week and regularly took a crap in the compost bin.

Poking and prodding their way through books unopened and undusted for decades, Gavin and Sandiman began to remember what had attracted them to their profession in the first place. There had been plenty of rubbish. Every era has its share of potboilers and bad writing. Amid mouldy old books by the likes of John Oxenham, Rafael Sabatini and Baroness Orczy were many dated melodramas set in Chelsea salons. A blonde by the name of Betty always wanted to marry a dim hero called Desmond. Once she nailed the witless dope they'd depart the London scene for his stately pile in Devon. There they would sponge off his senile parents, run down the estate and produce fat children called Jeremy.

Then there were works from the First World War with titles like *The Glory of the Trenches* which saluted soldiers for 'cheerfully' laying down their lives; and volumes on agriculture with specialist sections delving into the latest advances in manure spreading.

But here and there they found pearls. Books written by the greatest thinkers of times past. Works with leaves of typed wisdom, knowledge stored like dried flowers on pages kept too long from the light. Books like *Apologia Pro Vita Sua* by John Henry Newman, the Oxford Cardinal who shocked England's church to its very core by defecting to Rome in the eighteen-forties. Or Walter Bower's *Scotichronicon*, a history of ancient Scotland covering a thousand years. A copy of John Evelyn's diaries also turned up late one afternoon, and so did an early edition of Adomnán's *Life of St Columba*.

There was even an old Qur'an, picked up in Persia perhaps by a son of the house commissioned into the Army and sent out East in the days of the Raj. Sandiman had glanced at some lines jotted on the flyleaf, and the words had stayed with him:

"Allah the Compassionate, the Merciful, weaves the threads of men's destinies into many strange tapestries."

And above the lines was the owner's name: Dunbar.

Sandiman had also browsed through Adomnán's *Life of St Columba*. He had read it once before and it was good getting to know it again. One quote near the end of book three about some place small and mean but revered by saints sounded familiar. Perhaps his father had taught it to him.

Columba and Muhammad, he had thought. They were like two sides of the same coin. They had lived at much the same time. What if they could have talked to each other?

He had tried to find the quote about Allah in the Qur'an itself, but there was no sign of it. He'd finally gone to a mosque in Glasgow and asked a Muslim scholar about it. The scholar had invited Sandiman to his home, a top floor tenement stacked from floor to ceiling with golden-brown books. A great and splendid book, robed like royalty in a binding of tooled goatskin leather, was resting upon a carved reading stand of dark wood in the middle of the room. Sandiman realised it was an ancient Qur'an. Its edges were defined by silver borders strung taut between sharp metal cornerpieces and the binding was studded with scarlet gemstones and embossed with flowers. The flowing patterns contrasted with the clear lines of the arabesque star at its centre. A golden circle lay at the heart of the star, etched with Muhammad's words by a calligrapher from Persia or the Ottoman Empire.

Here in this room, with a Muslim scholar who truly believed that the Qur'an held the Words of Allah as recited by Muhammad, Sandiman felt a little awed. Before him was a true and holy copy of the icon which had risen from the sand seas of Arabia, whose dynasties of followers had taken Jerusalem and gone from there into Asia, Africa and Europe.

The scholar himself, clad in a long black gown and a neat little cap, had bright blue eyes and shining white teeth. The perfect teeth contrasted with his dark beard when he smiled, which was often.

"The book speaks of itself as radiant with light," he said, and Sandiman believed him. The bound volume from the Middle East with its luminous text reminded him of the cool cloisters of Highland kirks he had seen as a boy, bathed in light from stained-glass windows. The same calm, spiritual atmosphere he had known as a child in the kirk seemed to come from the pages of a book crafted half the world away.

The Qur'an, he remembered, was both glorious book and illuminated work of art. Words for the scholar. A glimpse of paradise for the faithful.

The scholar nodded, as if hearing the librarian's thoughts.

"Purity of writing is purity of soul," he said, seeking agreement, but Sandiman had not been able to meet his eye. Like the gospel books of the West, its purity had too often been used to defend days of infamy. The original Qur'an might actually have been written in the eighth century to justify the Muslim occupation of Jerusalem in the seventh, but Sandiman knew it wasn't a good idea to suggest that to an Islamic scholar.

They talked on though, and the scholar explained that Muhammad had said many things that had not been included in the Qur'an. There were many papers with his words which were, even now, uncatalogued and unclassified. The phrase could even have predated Muhammad. In the end, nobody really knew.

A thought had occurred to Sandiman.

"The Muslim community on the Southside isn't very well integrated, is it?"

A shadow had crossed the scholar's face.

"No. Both Islam and Christendom worship the one true God. English editions of the Qur'an even translate his name as God, not Allah, because there is no difference. And Jesus and Muhammad, peace and blessings be upon him, were two of His prophets."

It had seemed too simple. "So what are we fighting about?"

"You believe Jesus was the actual Son of God and literally spoke the Word of God. We do not agree. We believe Jesus was a great prophet, but only a man. The only record of God's Words is the Qur'an. So the Qur'an is as holy to us as Jesus is to you."

"People don't often debate theology on street corners, I'm afraid."

"True. Perhaps it is also because we raise mosques to God instead of churches, although a mosque is a church. Perhaps because we have dark skin and do not drink alcohol. Perhaps because we support neither Celtic nor Rangers."

"I don't like football, either," said Sandiman. "In fact, I hate it."

The scholar smiled broadly.

"You are a librarian, yes?"

"Yes."

"Here in the West, librarians were once venerated as prophets, magicians and keepers of books. To be a *librarius* was a mark of high station."

"Not any more."

"No." The scholar gestured at his books. "You have lost touch with your history but we carry ours with us. Via the angel Gabriel, Muhammad recited to us the Words of Allah in verses or *suras*. To submit to them, we had to preserve them. We learnt papermaking and calligraphy from the Chinese, borrowed the craft of fine bindings from Amharic scribes in Ethiopia. With this knowledge we recorded Muhammad's verses in the Qur'an, illuminating the Words and founding great libraries in Damascus and Jerusalem to honour the glorious books we had created.

"We are people of the Book. To be a custodian of the Book – to be a *librarius* – is truly to be held in high esteem."

"I hadn't thought about it that way before. Most people just call us the pearls-and-twinset brigade. I don't wear pearls any more and there's always someone else wearing the trousers."

The scholar smiled and nodded, the blue eyes alive with memory.

"Yes, many Westerners are unaware of the past they share with us. We held Jerusalem for a thousand years and more, pioneered algebra and astronomy in Baghdad, and built a library of half-a-million books in Cordoba when the greatest collections in Christendom numbered no more than seven hundred volumes. We recognised the Torah and the Bible as other Qur'ans, recognised Jews and Christians as fellow peoples of the Book, recognised Jesus and Muhammad as sons of Abraham and Adam, but you would not recognise *us*. And at the same time as you fought us, you learnt the arts of illumination from us, combined them with your Words and created manuscripts of your gospel.

"This is a tragedy. A pope once said to a caliph that they both believed in and confessed one God, admittedly in a different way. But you and I, we fought over Jerusalem and we fight still, though the illuminated gospels prove that your culture is part of ours and our culture part of yours."

There wasn't much answer to that, and the tolerance of true Islam was a refreshing change from the slow drip of sectarian poison Sandiman sometimes felt in Scotland. The original quote about destiny and tapestry had stayed with him, together with an image of the bright-eyed scholar and the beautiful Qur'an. *That* was how to respect a book, he thought, but it wouldn't mean a damn thing to the likes of Mannering and his ilk.

However, the collection in Arrochar & Tarbert still had to be catalogued. Late one afternoon Gavin had uncovered a volume printed by one of the Scottish historical societies which had flourished in the nineteenth century. They'd glanced through it quickly as the light was getting low, noting it was a product of the Spalding Club of Aberdeen, but its title had meant little to them.

It was only later that Gavin had said to him:

"Sure you never heard of a Book of Deer?"

Sandiman had shaken his head and picked up a copy of the *Herald*. It had an extract from a new book by Andrew Greig called *The Return of John Macnab*.

"Can't say I have, no."

The long days working on the collection with their bare hands began to pay off. In an era where librarians' thinking was dominated by computers and information technology, it was a relief to handle books without apology and stick two fingers up at political correctness. To see a collection put back in order by dint of sweat and muscle, the order being a hierarchy of knowledge composed by thousands of minds, now dust, the collection as a whole far greater than the sum of its parts.

Sandiman had even found himself thinking about Jessica less often.

Slowly, Gavin had come back to himself. Then had come the chance to work with rare books in the University's Special Collections department. They had kept in touch. Scotland not being America, they had not swapped heartfelt pledges about helping each other out; but Sandiman knew that if there was one person in the world to whom he could turn, it was Gavin.

Once they'd finished cataloguing the library near Arrochar & Tarbert he had taken the train up to Glenfinnan. He'd heard about the vandalism of Finnan's church and on the way back down south, a thought had shot through his mind.

Fellow people of the Book, are we? What kind of people would tear up their own past?

The thought hadn't faded away like retinal flash. It had settled in Sandiman's mind like a festering boil. He didn't sleep that night and dragged himself back to work the next day. Natalie smiled when she saw him coming, but the smile dropped dead on her lips when she saw his eyes. He walked back into his office and toyed with the picture of Jessica.

For a moment he thought of his lost love at the Church of St Finnan, and of the blue waters of Loch Shiel so easily seen through the half-open door.

What if he had done something differently then? Could he have changed things?

Probably not. What if he did something different now? He knew the answer to that. Three P45s would be handed out instead of one.

Finally, he steeled himself.

"Mike, have you got a minute?"

"No."

"Mike, just come in here a minute, will you?"

"Why?"

"Look, it's just..."

He came to a halt. His face said it all and their eyes locked in mutual understanding. Natalie turned away.

"It's just..."

And then it happened. Sandiman felt that flicker of anger again, but this time he didn't try to control it. This time he poured some petrol on it and let it ignite. It felt good.

"It's just that ... that Mannering would like to make some cuts. Any idea how we could reduce costs?"

Mike looked at him for a long moment and they really saw each other. The college kid and the dropout. Both library workers on the surface. Both anarchists at heart. Both coming to the end of their respective tethers.

"There's no way we can reduce anything, boss. And that's all there is to it."

"That's your final word?"

"My final word. No. Fucking. Way."

"You know something, Mike?"

"What?"

"I think that's my final word, too."

Mike actually looked surprised.

"What do we do now then, boss?" he said.

"I think," Sandiman replied with a delicious sense of anticipation, "I'll send Mannering a memo."

"Thanks, John."

Sandiman glanced up. Mike had never called him by his Christian name before. He smiled without mirth.

That afternoon Miss Partridge was roused from her desk by a choking sound from the office. She entered to find a choleric finance manager clutching a crumpled sheet of paper which had arrived shortly before via internal mail.

He waved it at her like a drowning man, and despite her surprise at seeing her dapper superior reduced to the level of sweaty human frailty, she grasped the memo and read it.

To: Guy Mannering, Finance Manager

From: John Macnab
         Mike McCorquodale

Dear Mr Mannering,
Re: Proposed budget cuts (library)

Nuts.

Yours sincerely,
John & Mike

PS: Enclosed is a suggestion from Mr McCorquodale aimed at improving the rate of overdue book returns. May we circulate it via noticeboard and email?

"For him that stealeth a Book from the Library,
let it change into a serpent into his hand and rend him.
Let him be struck with Palsy,
and all his Members blasted.
Let him languish in Pain crying aloud for Mercy
and let there be no surcease to his Agony
till he sink in Dissolution.
Let Bookworms gnaw his Entrails
in token of the Worm that dieth not,
and when at last he goeth to his final Punishment,
let the flames of Hell consume him for ever and aye."

(Monastery of San Pedro, Barcelona)

Miss Partridge had never seen anything quite like it. The sputtering spectacle before her bore no resemblance to the Mr Mannering she thought she knew. Miss Partridge – who'd last stumbled through sex when Callaghan was Prime Minister – was a genuine example of that enduring breed, the dried-up old spinster. She spent her days grappling with crosswords, reading the *Scots Magazine* and watching *Countdown* on Channel 4. In another age, she would have been a denizen of Miss Cranston's tea rooms.

Her job was her only other reason for living. As a result, although able to master Windows 95 and control multiple spreadsheet applications with much the same agility she had displayed as a comptometer operator in her faraway youth, her relationship with the world was governed by a cast-iron set of rules which tolerated only certain types of behaviour.

Mr Mannering, who impressed even Miss Partridge as a singularly cold fish, obeyed much the same rules. Even if he did seem a trifle too fond of the picture of a pet corgi discreetly displayed on his desk. But now the axes of her existence had been upended, nay, utterly polarised!

This kind of thing just *was not done*.

So she stood there and did nothing. Mannering slowly regained control of himself. Gradually the sputters wound down and some semblance of normal service was resumed.

"Miss Partridge?" His voice was high and squeaky, and for a moment she feared his appendix had burst.

"Miss Partridge, please telephone the library and ask the ... the *gentlemen* concerned to come to my office immediately."

"Yes, sir."

"Gross insubordination, Miss Partridge. Gross. Absolutely gross."

"Yes sir. Gross."

"Nuts, Miss Partridge!"

"Sir!"

"I mean the word in the memo! What does he mean ... *nuts*?"

At last, a query for information. Something into which Miss Partridge could sink her perfectly preserved teeth.

"I think it's based on the answer given to a German general who demanded the surrender of the Allied forces occupying Bastogne during World War II, sir. The Americans were basically telling him he was up the creek without a paddle."

Mr Mannering's face darkened. It was a very ugly expression and Miss Partridge realised, very clearly, what he intended to do to the unfortunates from the fifth floor.

She turned to go, so his next question caught her by surprise.

"And who the hell is John Macnab?"

"I really *don't* know, sir."

When the call came, Sandiman and Mike were sitting at the issue desk with their feet up while Natalie hovered nervously. Sandiman picked up the phone slowly and deliberately.

"Yes, Miss Partridge. I think that would be possible. We'll be along in about half-an-hour ... Sooner than that? Oh, you mean *now*. Well, I'm afraid that won't be possible ... Oh so he's a bit upset, is he? Well – and this is just between us – frankly, my dear, I don't give a damn. Anyway, we've got a window at two. We'll see the old bastard then."

Sandiman put the phone down gently, thinking of his mortgage and personal pension plan. Not much chance of financing either of those without a salary. Then he looked up and saw Natalie watching him. Saw a warm glow in her eyes. That made it all worthwhile.

With the advent of information technology, gossip travelled round the building even faster than before. So when Sandiman and Mike took the long walk up to the finance office, it just happened to be the time everyone decided to take their tea break. There were a few smiles and nods, the occasional disapproving frown, but on the whole they felt a cheering wave of tacit support buoying them up. Nobody actually walked with them, but that was life.

They walked past the passive Miss Partridge like latter-day desperados as she cowered behind her desk, perhaps fearing she'd be infected by some virus of rebellion. They went slowly into Mannering's office and came to a stop in front of his desk, looking straight at him.

Mannering had intended to let loose a tirade of carefully cultivated abuse on the petrified underlings he was expecting, but when he saw their eyes, he hesitated. He hadn't expected to find two men standing in front of him who ... who ... Damn it! Who didn't look *afraid* of him.

Nevertheless, he was still the finance manager and these two fools had committed a sackable offence.

"What was the meaning of this memo I received this afternoon?"

"Mr Mannering," Sandiman spoke slowly and deliberately, "did you know that the Mitchell Library is the largest public reference library in Europe?"

"What?"

"I said..."

"I heard what you said! No, I was not aware of that fact and it has nothing to do with the present situation. It is, I must also say, the last thing I would expect someone in your position to allow to take place. Where's Macnab, anyway? Haven't you brought him with you?"

"I'm afraid I don't quite follow you, Guy. I didn't *allow* this to take place."

"I'm sorry?"

"No you're not, but that's beside the point. I did not allow this to take place. I did it."

"You did it! What the hell for?"

"Like I said, did you know the Mitchell is the biggest public reference library in Europe?"

Mannering took a deep breath. "No, I can't say I was aware of that."

"That's a pity, Guy. Because nowadays it's a wreck. Because of cuts. Because of people like you making cuts and, up 'til now, because of people like me letting you make cuts."

Mannering looked completely flummoxed. For a moment Sandiman almost pitied him, but the moment swiftly passed.

I'm supposed to have an unsettling gaze, thought Sandiman. *Let's put it to work.*

He skewered Mannering with his eyes. Then he spoke:

"Let me put it this way. If there were no books, no libraries, there would be no civilisation. When the first clay tablets were shelved in Sumeria five thousand years ago, Man for the first time – *the very first time, goddamn it* – could pass his hard-earned knowledge on to his son. Because of books. *Books*. Not CD-Roms, not the internet – books. We're people of the Book and before books, each generation learnt the facts of life the hard way. Made the same mistakes over and over again. So now, thanks to books, what do we have? Civilisation, culture and science. So how do we say thank you? We elect morons and Morton supporters to high office. They then bequeath the Gallery of Modern Art £3 million and cut the staff at the Mitchell by a third. Brilliant."

"I don't quite..."

"Yeah I know, Guy. You don't quite follow me. You don't quite get it. And you know what? Neither do I. Five thousand years after struggling out of the slime from which we evolved, what have we got in the way of culture? I'll tell you what we have got. The closest we get to culture is neds pissing in a fountain in Florence – or wherever the World Cup is being held – in the Scottish national dress of football jersey, kilt, black socks and Reebok trainers. A can of lager in one hand and their willies in the other!"

In the adjoining office, Miss Partridge uttered a faint cry of distress and prayed for a swift coronary to take her away from it all. But it was not to be.

"John, I don't think…"

"I don't give a damn *what* you think," Sandiman continued, cutting him off with relish. "What I really object to is that you just don't get *anything*. All the progress from Babylon and Byzantium, built on the words of scholars who died for their beliefs, and you don't know a damn thing about any of it. The Crusades. The Holy Roman Empire. Augustine and the City of God. Adam Smith and the Wealth of Nations. You think it's just boring old history. You don't think it has anything to do with the present situation. You think some shiny plastic frisbees networked to a few smart desktops make it all obsolete. Five thousand years of work to put you behind that desk and you'd tear it up tomorrow if you could. You're a man of the Book just like me, but all the great houses of knowledge – from Alexandria to the Mitchell – they're all wasted on you. Because you – and all those like you – are blind to anything except buzz words, spreadsheets and memos. You're here *despite* books and history, not because of them. In a nutshell, *Guy*, you're just fucking ignorant."

Mike watched, wide-eyed, wondering if that library curse of his had worked and his boss been possessed by some demon from hell.

"If you don't stop this tirade I'll..."

"You'll do what?" said Sandiman. "Take us outside, have us executed and stick our severed heads on the city gates? You know something? You won't do that. Oh for God's sake, Mannering, be a man. If you can't be a man at least be a good manager. And if you can't even do *that*, go roger your pet corgi some more and stop pissing us about.

"And one more thing. I'll make no more cuts. Not now, not ever. I've had enough of mean old men like you, deaf to tunes of glory."

Sandiman came to a stop. Mannering just stared at them as they walked back out of his office, past a cringing Miss Partridge and down the corridor. Neither man said anything for a few moments. Then Mike spoke up:

"Guess that's our Christmas bonus fucked then."

5

The 1996 Christmas season found the new John Macnab (as he was beginning to think of himself) at a backpackers hostel on the far north western tip of Skye; fresh from a long evening's boozing in the local hotel bar and now in bed with the beginnings of a hangover.

The spirit of John Macnab persisted despite such diversions. Weeks earlier it had seemed like a good idea, but a few cold and sober dawns had despatched it to the nether regions of his mind. The harsh reality of unemployment and the slim chance of finding another job in another library had also had quite a lot to do with it.

He had about thirty years of working life left. All of which looked to be well on the way to being wasted because of one beautifully delivered speech, one pure and simple moment when he'd said what he actually thought about things.

Still, Natalie had looked more than a little impressed when he and Mike, feeling like a couple of Bosnian war veterans, had walked heavily back into the library. Word of their exploits had already began to circulate around the college as the modern equivalent of jungle drums – faxes and email – started beating out the news. Even the students had noticed and with a precision worthy of the Hitler Youth at their best, every baseball cap in the place had swivelled to look at him when he walked in.

She watched as he cleared out his desk. It hadn't taken long. He'd always refused to be buried under paperwork and the few remaining files were binned in seconds. Throwing out the official library journal, the *Library Association Record*, was actually quite cathartic. It really was the most boring magazine he'd ever read. Last of all, he was left with Jessica's photograph. He looked at it briefly – had she been the real reason he'd done it all? – then gently put it in his wallet.

It occurred to him he would never see the interior of the library again, the place where he'd worked for six years. Then he realised he didn't care. The walls had no memory.

Once, librarians had been prophets, magicians and keepers of books. Now they were just glorified clerks. Why the hell hadn't he admitted that to himself sooner? Six years of enduring slow humiliation by stupid people in senior positions, all to pay the mortgage...

Mike had rolled a cigarette while John finished packing. Sandiman knew they were both out of a job. Maybe Natalie was too.

Guilt rose up in him. Mike saw the wavering look, nodded.

"My brother's got a second-hand bookshop in Camden. Always said he'd give me a job if I needed one."

"You don't like London," said Natalie tonelessly.

"Don't like it here much either," Mike replied ruefully. "Anyway, I live at the Red Road flats. They're full of asbestos."

"That's where you live?" stammered Sandiman. Walking tall in front of Mannering had been a walk in the park compared to this revelation.

"Yeah, so what?"

"You never told us where you lived, Mike!" Natalie said as Sandiman collapsed speechless into his chair. Telling Mannering where to go was as nothing compared to finding out Mike's address. Up to now, that had been a secret more closely guarded than the lost Ark of the Covenant.

"Aye, well. If some of our student pals from Easterhouse had found out where I stayed I'd probably have had an unfortunate accident involving a broken window and a twenty-storey fall. They fucked up my bike a few years ago. I'd found two neds – or was it three? – having sex in a store cupboard and threw them out. That was their revenge. Thing is, it was a 750cc Norton Commando. Twin-cylinder, 1968 vintage. It was an absolute fucking classic and I'd spent two years restoring it. Once, just once, I came into college on it and they took a hammer to it. Then they took a shit on top of it."

"What happened to them?" asked Sandiman. He'd heard of Norton Commandos. They were the kind of bikes Hell's Angels took to rock festivals on the Isle of Wight after the Summer of Love.

"Fucking principal let them off. Told me I'd be out of a job if I pressed charges, too. So I didn't press charges. But I knew a guy in Castlemilk who broke legs."

There was a short silence

"I think we all need a drink," said Natalie.

"Good idea," said Sandiman. "We might as well shut up shop for the day."

"Nothing you want to come back for?"

"Nothing."

The pub, a Victorian establishment with gilded handrails, Rennie Mackintosh mirrors and Tennents on tap, lay just off the Drygate in the shadow of the Necropolis. With the library and their jobs behind them, they found an alcove and reminisced. Dignity and decorum had that day been blown away by the metaphorical equivalent of a pump-action shotgun; civilised intercourse had now to close the breach.

Later, much later, John Sandiman would remember that night as one of the happiest of his life. Poised between past and future, he had sat in a smoky Glasgow pub with his friends, laughing.

At least it was better than sitting around waiting for the DSS, the local council or the Parliament to decide his fate. Because none of them would. Hell, if there was going to be a Parliament, why not just shut the councils? It sure would lessen the paperwork.

Why not indeed?

He drew on his pint, looked at the amber fluid intently. Why not close half the pubs in Scotland? Tough on the publicans but if the money otherwise poured down throats and pissed on pavements was used for the good of the country instead, they'd probably have a land of milk and honey inside three years.

Why not outlaw sectarianism? Better still, why not outlaw Celtic and Rangers, or at least make them play English clubs regularly? They'd never find out how good they really were otherwise. Seeing Rangers play St Johnstone, St Mirren or even (God help them) Greenock Morton, was like seeing a German Panzer division scything down a bunch of French peasants.

Worse still, the French peasants sometimes won. Berwick Rangers had knocked Glasgow Rangers clean out of the Scottish Cup in 1967.

And wouldn't it be *wonderful* if, the next time Celtic and Rangers played each other, Celtic wore blue and Rangers wore green! Why wouldn't it happen? Because people were scared of change. Because people liked the status quo. Because people wouldn't do anything. That was 'just the way things were', and that was all there was to it.

Still, he *had* done something. They all had. And it felt good.

But the following evening Mike had taken the Scottish Citylink bus down to the Big Smoke. Sandiman had walked with him up to Buchanan Bus Station on Killermont Street and watched as the blue and yellow coach headed off on the low road south. Mike had had a last surprise for him, though.

"You know the principal has an email facility he never uses?"

"Yeah. So what?"

"I spend a lot of time on the Internet. Found a pretty interesting web site with an email list facility. Specialises in bondage, sadomasochism and lesbian schoolgirls. It's easy to add another address to their list."

"Mike, you didn't..."

"Aye, I did," said Mike, and in the stark neon light of the bus station his face looked cold, hard and Celtic. "Aye, I did."

"Can he trace it back to you?"

"No he can't. He'll suspect, but he won't *know*."

Then Mike shook his hand firmly, once, and boarded the bus.

After the bus left, Sandiman hung around for a while, not sure what to do with himself. He had forgotten just how lonely a city could be when the money dried up and friends were notable by their absence. Now he was forcibly reminded of it. Scotland's library community was small. His little contretemps with Mannering would not soon be forgotten.

Eventually he started walking. He had no idea where he wanted to go, but guided by habit he ghosted past the grey pillars of the M8 bypass and headed for the West End. He walked for a while along the cold streets. He walked and walked, sometimes in circles, and finally in the wee small hours he walked through a doorway with the words WE NEVER CLOSE printed above it and found himself in a café called Insomnia. Arty paintings hung from the mauve and pale-yellow walls, circular fans suspended from the sky-blue ceiling turned slowly and tropical fish swam round in a bath by the window.

He looked at the menu, ordered a caffè latté and sipped it. The café itself was virtually empty save for a small man with a goatee beard sitting muttering in a corner and a Chinese student reading a small red book. He could faintly hear jazz on the radio and the staff, bless their hearts, didn't trouble him. On the whole, he reflected, he felt all right. Quite all right, really. He just couldn't face going back to his flat yet.

He'd probably have stayed and watched the fish weave

their patterns in the water until dawn, but a bunch of drunken clubbers fresh from the Garage nightclub straggled in at twenty past two in the morning. As he watched them struggling to enunciate their orders and generally behaving, well, like kids, he felt himself shrivelling into middle age. This was no longer his place.

Maybe he would go back to Glenfinnan and chill out for a while. That was still his place. He thought of the quiet church and the clean air, and wondered why he'd stayed in the city so long.

Perhaps because he knew damn well he could be just as lonely in the country.

He tramped up Woodlands Road and onto University Avenue. Once past Byres Road it wasn't far to Partick and he soon found himself at the unwelcoming stairwell leading to his flat. There was a small bottle of Buckfast standing on the bottom step.

He fumbled for his keys as he doggedly climbed the stairs and so did not see Natalie huddled by his door. Clad in black leather and blue with cold, she stared at him.

"What are you doing here?" he said, gobsmacked.

"Freezing. Waiting for you. What do you think?"

"How long for?"

"Do you want to keep asking questions, or do you want to ask me in?"

Sandiman opened the door, conceiving unmentionable notions as he looked at the dull gleam of the leather she wore. At the pub, she had sat next to him the entire night, flicking her hair back and looking at him intently. He hadn't been sure what to make of it at the time, although several possibilities had occurred to him. All the usual barriers were breaking down, all the carefully constructed zones of personal space arcing into different orbits.

Natalie got stiffly to her feet, walked into the lounge and crouched in front of the electric fire. Sandiman felt better. With two people in it, the flat came quietly to life.

"You need a cup of coffee," he said. "Colombian Supremo?"

He thought he saw her roll her eyes.

"Still buying it from that Edinburgh emporium?"

"I guess so. Up until the other day, that was the most exciting part of my life."

"Java would do. Got any Java?"

"Yeah. Somewhere."

"You're a poor sad man," she said kindly. "You know that, don't you?"

He nodded, made her coffee, then made a cup for himself. They sat in silence on the sofa in front of the fire for several minutes, dunking biscuits and avoiding each other's eyes. Finally, he looked across at her and saw a tear drying on her cheek. Just one. His mouth dropped open. He'd never seen her cry before. He'd always thought of her as the feisty sidekick. Robin to his Batman. He'd classified her all too readily, but he'd been wrong. She had feelings and now they were showing.

He hugged her. She put her head on his shoulder.

"I was in my flat," she said. "And I started thinking about you. Thought I wouldn't see you again, and... it's all so different. We won't go to the library again. See each other again. I don't know. I just wanted to see you."

He looked at her intently and opened his mouth.

> *"What a life without a wife,*
> *And me without a lover..."*

She smiled slightly. "We're just poor sad people, aren't we?"

"Seem to be. Seem to be."

She took his hand and went into the bedroom with him, curling up under the duvet like a cat seeking warmth and cleaving to him with a simple uncomplicated need. For a moment, some remote, rational part of his mind informed him that the Dewey Decimal classification number for sexual love was 306.7. He pushed the thought away but as they began to make love, he realised he was reaching the end of a story. The library, Mike, most definitely Mannering, were all becoming part of the past. Part of another country.

And now he and Natalie were together. Her hands slid over his back and her breathing came faster and faster. After a while, she stiffened and cried out softly. He felt her legs grip him sharply for a long moment, then relax completely. As they lay still, he heard her sniffling.

He turned over and looked at her. Their eyes met, and he felt as if he was looking into a dark empty room.

"My boyfriend committed suicide," she said huskily. "Ever since, I've had a bit of a problem about losing people. I know it's going to happen, but I can't quite handle it when it does."

Sandiman waited, knowing she would talk when she wanted to.

She did not meet his eyes. "His name was Murdo. He was always saying he couldn't live without me but he didn't want to leave Inverary, and I did. He liked selling tourists tickets to Inverary Jail, liked getting drunk every Friday at the George Hotel, liked going to Oban to play pool every so often. I wanted a career.

"He had a car he loved, though. An old Ford Zodiac he'd found in a garage in Taynuilt and rebuilt. Usual thing, he wasn't much for the schooling but marvellous with his hands. Most weekends he took me for a drive. Once he took me all the way to Kyle of Lochalsh. That was the day I told him I was going to Glasgow.

"Perhaps I shouldn't have told him then, but I did. Wrong time. Wrong place. Wrong everything. Anyway, he turned round and took us back to Inverary, foot on the floor the whole way. How we got back in one piece I'll never know. But we did. Then he threw me out of the car and tore off towards Tarbet."

"And that's where he crashed?"

"No. He got stopped by my uncle – a sergeant in the police – and Murdo got banned for six months. But my uncle also had a second home – a flat on Hyndland Road. He needed a tenant, I wanted out of Inverary, and we both knew Murdo needed time to cool off. At first it seemed to work out all right. Murdo got a job fixing cars in Dunoon and did okay. But he kept saying he'd come to Glasgow to find me. After the six months were up, he came steaming down the Rest And Be Thankful at about a hundred miles per hour and lost it. He crashed and burned, and I think it took him a wee while to die."

Her voice faltered.

"I know he wouldn't have been going so fast if he hadn't been thinking about me. I know it. I thought about it as I watched them put him in the ground."

"Jesus."

"I don't go back much now. It's a small town. People talk."

She curled up closer to him and they stayed together until dawn and a new day arrived.

They shared a quiet breakfast. There were the usual awkward silences, but he found he liked having her around in the morning. At least he didn't have to try making conversation. This was Natalie, after all. She already knew what a grouch he was before ten o'clock.

Trouble was, where did they go from here?

"I'm probably heading up north for a while," Sandiman said. She nodded, looking totally unsurprised.

"I would, if I'd done what you did. I probably wouldn't come back."

"You won't be losing me. I've just got to decide what to do next."

"So do I," she said simply. "I don't want to work in that place any more."

They were both in the same mess, he thought. Stuck between past and future, and not welcome in either country.

"I'm going to do something," he said suddenly. "I just don't know what."

"Become an MSP. Think of all those researchers you could shag."

"Natalie..."

"Only kidding."

"You still stay in Hyndland Road?"

She nodded.

"I'll look you up when I get back."

He walked her home down streets of sandstone tenements. At her door she impulsively caressed his cheek. He squeezed her hand, then took his leave.

Christmas was coming, the goose was getting fat and both his parents were dead. That left him with no ties and free to take some time off. There was Glenfinnan, and then there was a hostel on the north western tip of Skye where he could get away from it all and decide what to do next.

That was why, a few days later, he found himself waiting for the 12.42 to depart from Queen Street Station to Mallaig. He should have taken the 08.12, but he'd been too lazy to get up in time. So now he was stuck with staying the night in Mallaig and getting the first ferry to Armadale in the morning.

Well, what the hell! He was in no hurry, and the West Highland Railway held a lot of good memories for him. However, hanging around George Square in the freezing wind interested him not at all, so he decided to kill some time in John Smith & Son's bookshop on St Vincent Street.

He was browsing through the Scottish History section on the ground floor when his eye fell upon an unusual title:

The Book of Deer
Roy Ellsworth and Peter Berresford Ellis

At first the name meant nothing to him. Then a memory surfaced. Natalie had said something about a Book of Deer that night at the pancake restaurant. Gavin had also referred to it once. An old book of some sort.

The *first* book. That was what she had said. The first book in Gaelic. And now here it was, right in front of him. He took the book from the shelf, scanned the notes on the back cover.

'One of the principal antiquities of Celtic Scotland' *was how this ninth-century Gospel book was described in the nineteenth century. Written and illustrated by at least two monks of Deer, near Aberdeen, its art is not as sophisticated as some of its better known brethren like Kells, Durrow or Lindisfarne. Nevertheless, it has a fascinating visual vibrancy showing strong pagan Celtic motifs. One is reminded that this was the last Celtic area to become Christianized in the sixth and seventh centuries. It is no coincidence that Deer takes its name from* doire, *the place of oaks associated with Druidic worship. Now in Cambridge University Library,* The Book of Deer *is priceless, not only for being the oldest indisputably Scottish Gospel manuscript, but for its marginal notes written in Gaelic, showing the transition into the Scottish form as opposed to Old Irish, made in the eleventh and twelfth centuries.*

Sandiman stared at the words for a long moment, then opened the book and read further:

*Colum Cille, sometimes known as St Columba, AD 521-597, made a journey to see Bruide Mac Maelchon (c. AD 556-584), king of the Tuatha Cruithne, more popularly known today by their Latin nickname, Picts (*picti, *painted people). The purpose of this visit was to Christianize them and after a conflict with the Druids of Bruide, Colum Cille set in motion the process. According to the story, in about AD 580 Colum Cille, together with one of his disciples, St Drostán Mac Cosgrach, came to a place named Aberdour. This is not to be confused with Aberdour in Fife but was a spot on the southern tributary of the River Ugie, just to the west of modern Peterhead in Aberdeenshire. The missionaries decided to establish a religious settlement at the spot which was later called Deer.*

Interesting, thought Sandiman. This book, The Book

of Deer, basically the first Scottish book, was created in a monastery founded by Columba, Scotland's greatest saint. And Finnan of Moville had been Columba's master in Ireland. Finnan, patron saint of that church by the shores of Loch Shiel. The church sacred to Sandiman, the church vandalised by those bloody Highland neds.

It felt as if a thread was being spun. A fragile, tensile connection between himself, Glenfinnan, Columba and the Book of Deer.

Well maybe, maybe not. One thing he did know, however, was that he badly wanted to buy this particular book.

It took but a moment for him to make the purchase then, book tucked safely under arm, he was back on the street, walking briskly to catch his train.

There was still a short time to kill, so he strolled out to the far end of platform two, his mind pleasantly occupied. The train would be leaving soon. Should he get a newspaper? No, he had enough reading matter to be going on with and the papers seemed to be full of nothing but stories about Princess Diana's problems. He was getting damn tired of hearing about them.

He boarded the train without a backward glance.

No rain fell as the train passed through Helensburgh and trundled up the gradient to Garelochhead. Sandiman looked down the mountainside at Loch Long, letting the scenery help clear his head, and as the train pulled into Arrochar & Tarbert it seemed he felt the threads coming more firmly together.

He had found that phrase about tapestries there, looked at a copy of the Book of Deer there. He flicked through Ellsworth and Ellis's book, noting that:

> *When the Celts converted to Christianity there was a need for manuscript books, copies of liturgical texts and of the Christian Gospels. The models for such books were manuscripts produced by the cultures of Eastern Christendom and particularly the Coptic Church ...*

As the Muslim scholar had said, Christendom learnt those skills from Islam. The arts of calligraphy and fine binding used to create that splendid Qur'an in the flat had passed into the hands of the Celts. They recorded gospel instead of suras, illuminating the Word made flesh and crafting books like Deer, Kells and Lindisfarne.

He browsed on through the book. Another phrase stuck in his mind:

The word 'Cathach' means 'battler' and the book was so called because it was carried into battle as an icon.

The train skirted Loch Lomond and climbed towards Crianlarich where the carriages would split between the Oban and Fort William/Mallaig lines. Smokers flocked onto the platform for a fag while the carriages were uncoupled and once this was complete his part of the train headed north. Past Tyndrum and Bridge of Orchy, through a winter landscape of white mountains and dead grass, where smooth boulders broke the flow of icy streams and plantations of skeletal trees supported the frozen earth.

An unforgiving land, indifferent to the fate of those who'd fought and died for it.

The train crept out onto Rannoch Moor. The flanks of the mountains fell away. Above, a blanket of cumulus cloud stretched across the firmament. Ruffled and patchy, it diffused the radiance from above. At the edge of the picture, faraway hills stood like sculptures in ice, tinted a deep blue-grey. Nearer, Sandiman saw small black bogs studded with rocky outcrops, outposts in a sea of scrub. He did not see anything move.

God's spare room, he thought, and smiled. What else could you call it?

Apart from a few electricity pylons there certainly was little sign of life, but his own ancestors had tramped across the moors on drovers' roads before asphalt and the iron horse had opened up the territory.

He had met Jessica near here.

The train climbed towards Rannoch station and laboured on from there to Corrour, highest point of the line. This was the loneliest place of all, with no roads and few houses. A tableland nearly fourteen hundred feet above sea level. To the east were Loch Ossian and Ben Alder. There was a youth hostel near the loch. Perhaps he would stay there one day.

He heard his father's voice again, telling him how Columba and Drostán came from Iona to Aberdour, from the west coast to the east. That was as dangerous as a journey into the heart of Africa in Victorian times, through forest and lochan in a country full of savage Picts.

From Corrour, the train ran down by Monessie Gorge towards Fort William. The Falls of Tulloch were in spate and the water foamed, surged and fell in torrents through the confines of the rocky canyon.

Just before the Fort itself were Lord Abinger's estates at Inverlochy. Where his grandparents had worked. Where Captain Dunbar had chased the deer a century ago, creating the legend of John Macnab.

North of Fort William and Loch Eil lay Glenfinnan, home to him since he'd first seen the tableau of mountain, train and deer in 1977. Then there was Finnan's church. For him, a sentimental shrine to his memory of Jessica. For others, a place to drink, piss and...

A hot flash of Celtic rage shot through him. What a pity Dunbar couldn't have stalked those bloody little vandals instead of a harmless deer!

Perhaps it was time to take a look at *John Macnab* again.

What if my destiny really is a tapestry? he mused. If so, then Finnan, Columba and the settlement at Deer are certainly on one thread, a thread running east from Ireland to Aberdour and Buchan. The Book of Deer itself? Well, it can only lie at the centre of any design. It's a work of art, an icon and a Cathach. John Macnab? He's like a loose thread, or a loose cannon. But I'm John Macnab now. Finnan's glen is home to me, my own ancestry is tangled up with the creation of John Macnab at Inverlochy, and perhaps my destiny is too.

But to fulfil that destiny, what do I – what does John Macnab – have to do?

Soon the harbour at Mallaig came into view. He stayed in a small backpackers' hostel that night, took a nostalgic look at Eigg and Rum from the seawall early the next morning, then boarded the ferry for Armadale on the Isle of Skye. From Armadale there was the Skye-Ways bus to Portree via Kyleakin, where Jessica had been born.

He didn't want to go through Kyleakin and be reminded of her, but there was no other road to take. Sure enough, he saw her everywhere he looked. On the pier, up at the viewpoint, standing silent in the street. Not quite looking at him, never meeting his eye. A gloomy spectre, like that other side of the Highlands seen only in winter. A place of out-of-season poverty, free of hope or prospects, haunted by suicides. He was glad to leave that place, relieved to reach Portree and impatient to catch the postbus to the hostel on Skye's northern coast. The hostel on the edge of the world.

Far enough.

Sandiman drifted into the hostel and crashed out on the bunk, weary as a man on his deathbed. Later that evening, though, he roused himself and went to the nearby hotel bar, where all the talk was of tolls on the Skye Bridge and all eyes were on the ample bosom of a buxom young lady from Paisley. A blonde wearing black leggings beneath a Pringle sweater. A Lowland outsider in the Highlands.

He drank too much and woke with a hangover. He headed for the toilet and noticed the lack of a loo roll, so he found a copy of the *Sunday Post* and wiped his arse with that instead.

A shower, a shave, and a shit! That was the best way to start the day, and it certainly was a fine morning. He needed a walk in the clean air and where better to walk to than the Quirang, a high plateau looking towards the Outer Hebrides.

Sandiman trudged along the one-track road, past whitewashed villages mired in torpor. Once he might have called them charming and rustic. Now they looked depressed and threadbare.

Near the township of Uigg he saw a ruined church. It stood alone and stark, broken gravestones in the cemetery, stained glass windows smashed. Slates were missing from the roof and he could imagine the smell of mildew he would find if he opened the door. He didn't want to open the door. He walked on.

It was a long way from the church to the top of the Quirang, but the view – a panorama encompassing Wester Ross and the Western Isles – was worth it. The summit was a vast flat plain, a bit like Tara. The Hebrides themselves looked bleak as the mountains of the Moon. There was no better place to go for clarity of thought. Raw calm desolation. A great emptiness with not a hint of green, softness or warmth to distract him.

Sandiman looked out over the waters of the west. Feeling as if he was at a turning point, remembering the words that had pushed him over the edge.

Better to stand and die with your king in battle...
From a line of 113 kings of the blood royal to this...
We're not going to do anything...
For any further information, consult John Macnab...

He *had* done something, but verbally abusing a finance manager wouldn't exactly set the world on fire. There *had* to be something more dramatic he could do.

Sandiman began to feel excited. He was free. Master of his fate, captain of his soul. With a life to live and his destiny to chase like a deer.

Excitement turned to exhilaration. There *was* more he could do, but how to make something happen? How to be heard? Dying with his king in battle wasn't really an option, and the Stone of Destiny had already been stolen once...

Lost in thought, he went on looking west.

In pristine silence, for there was no wind, he saw a

CalMac ferry going on its way to the Isle of Harris. It seemed to leave no wake on the ice-blue waters. For a moment he felt he was looking at a ghost ship taking an ancient tribe to their destiny, like the *curragh* (a leather-hulled longboat) which had carried Columba and his disciples to Iona. On the way across, probably on Colonsay, Columba had climbed a hill and looked back at Ireland for the last time. Then he'd founded the Abbey of Iona and later, the settlement at Deer.

According to legend, Columba had been exiled for copying a book without permission. He had been tried for this, the decision had gone against him and, piqued, he'd started the battle of Cul Dreimne.

Sandiman smiled. They had certainly taken breaches of copyright seriously back then! But books had been sacred...

His mind stopped dead. Something that nice, clueless ned had said in the library.

"Better they send the Stone or we'll steal it again."

Steal it *again*...

Quite suddenly, it all came together.

Of course.

Not the Stone of Destiny.

The Book.

Once as holy to Christians as the Qur'an still was to Muslims.

A Cathach. Taken by clans into battle.

There were still battles to be fought, still a need for clansmen to carry the Cathach.

Clansmen like John Macnab.

John Macnab, who would steal the Book of Deer.

6

"David king of Scots, to all his 'good men', greetings.
You are to know that the clergy
of Deer are to be quit and immune
from all lay service and improper exaction,
as is written in their book,
and as they proved by argument
at Banff and swore at Aberdeen.
Wherefore I strictly enjoin that
no one shall dare to do any harm
to them or to their goods."

(The Book of Deer)

I t all started quietly a few days after Hogmanay 1997, with a tall man getting off a train at Queen Street station and walking past crowds of shoppers, his mind on a different agenda to theirs as he made his way to his Partick flat where he opened a book he had read several times. He looked through it once more.

It started quietly, with a small article in *Scotland on Sunday* written by the president of the Adam Smith Institute:

The Stone of Destiny came home in 1996, but 1997 could become Scotland's year of destiny. It might well take its place with the other momentous dates which used to be taught to schoolchildren: 1603, 1707, 1746. Why should this year be compared to those in which Scotland's history was determined? How can it be ranged alongside those which saw the Union of Crowns, the Treaty of Union and the Battle of Culloden?

The reason is that 1997 may be seen by future historians as the year in which Scottish independence and the break-up of the United Kingdom became inevitable...

Thomas Rose had no reason to suspect the librarian who turned up at his bookbinding business late one afternoon in February of 1997. He'd met John Sandiman once or twice before. An intense individual who occasionally needed a book rebound or deacidified. This time, however, he hadn't asked Rose to restore a rare book, but to create a facsimile of one in order to display the duplicate and keep the real copy in a safe. Christie's, Sandiman had explained, had recently valued the original work and it had turned out to be too expensive to insure if kept on display. The copy, of course, only had to resemble the exterior binding. The pages could be left blank.

Sandiman gave Rose the measurements which he'd copied from a description in the Mitchell Library: six inches by three. He'd spent a lot of time in the Mitchell over the last month or so, piecing together the history of the Book of Deer.

As Rose copied the measurements down, Sandiman sat and sweated. Librarianship was a small world and Thomas Rose was an expert. What if he worked out what he was duplicating? There weren't that many ninth century manuscripts around, after all. Sandiman had had to mention the number of folios which made up the book – eighty-six bound in a small octavo. That was standard practice, but archive work, a colleague once told him, was like being a detective. An intuitive and forensic process of piecing together seemingly innocuous clues separated by thousands of miles and centuries of time in order to identify a manuscript. Clues obscure enough to tax the wits of a Philip Marlowe or a Sam Spade.

Sandiman looked at the second hand of an old clock on the wall slowly moving. Time seemed to stretch out. Surely Rose would realise something wasn't right. See something. Have a flash of insight.

But Rose simply finished copying down the specification and gave back the notepad.

"I can have it ready for you in about a fortnight."

Sandiman nodded, feeling his stomach start to unclench. But Rose's next question caught him off guard.

"Where's it being displayed, then?"

Sandiman paused just a moment too long.

"Probably abroad. The chap I'm working for right now also has a place in Massachusetts. He's a cautious man."

That was the best answer. A wealthy bibliophile, probably a Harvard man with property on both sides of the Atlantic, simply trying to keep his collection safe. Rose was discreet. Sandiman doubted the man would have much interest in a collection he'd never be able to see.

He thought back to the research he had done at the Mitchell Library. It had been a surprisingly easy job, because there wasn't that much written about the Book of Deer. It boiled down to two books: Ellsworth and Ellis's text and a book called *The Gaelic Notes in the Book of Deer*, written by Professor Kenneth Hurlstone Jackson in 1972.

Ellsworth and Ellis had outlined the basic facts:

This text was written by a uniform hand ... so that while one monk wrote the text, at least two were responsible for the illustrations ... The textual scribe of the ninth century has added the usual colophon asking for prayers for the work and its creator to his Latin text ... This gives the book value for the scribe writes in Gaelic and not in the usual Latin form found in Irish books: 'Forchubus caichduini imbia arrath inlenbrán collí aratardda bendacht foranmain intruagáin rodscríbai...' *A colloquial translation of this would be:* 'Let it be on the conscience of everyone who uses this splendid little book, that they say a blessing for the soul of the wretch who wrote it.'

Sandiman had found himself wondering who the wretch

had been. The colophon sounded a fair bit more heartfelt than the usual pieces of Celtic self-flagellation. The splendid book had indeed been written by a single scribe, so it looked like the wretch had been exceptionally well-motivated.

Unfortunately, there was no way of finding out what his motivation had been. Nevertheless, the completed Book had remained at Deer, although *"a Cistercian monastery replaced the Celtic Abbey in 1219."*

Then something strange had happened. The Book vanished from the monastery and was not heard of for four centuries.

All Ellsworth and Ellis could say was:

We know that it 'disappeared', probably taken as booty in the attempted conquests of Scotland by the English, for in 1697 it emerged as part of the library of John Moore, Bishop of Norwich. This library was bought for 6,000 guineas by King George I (1714-1727) on the advice of his secretary of state, Charles, Viscount Townshend (1674-1738), who later advised George to take harsh measures to repress the 1715 uprising in Scotland. George I gave the library as a gift to the library of Cambridge University.

Professor Jackson had been more precise, consulting John Evelyn's diaries and discovering that the Book of Deer had turned up again in London on 10 March 1695. In his entry for that day, Evelyn had described dining at the Earl of Sunderland's with Lord Spencer. Evelyn had been shown *"a MS. of some parts of the New Testament in vulgar Latin,"* by a colleague, Doctor Gale. There was little doubt that this manuscript was the Book of Deer and Lord Spencer, it turned out, had been Robert Spencer, ancestor of Lady Diana Spencer and a hypocritical bastard if ever there was one. A man who had allied himself to both Catholic and Protestant faiths simply to increase the power and influence of the House of Spencer. He was without doubt the kind of man who would pay any price to be king, or failing that, for one of his descendants to take the throne.

Not the kind of man who should have the Book of Deer in his hands, but that was what had happened. Sandiman had been getting very tired of hearing about Princess Diana and her problems. Now he felt a bit more sympathetic. She was just the latest pawn in a long and ruthless historical game.

The Book was then sold to Bishop John Moore by Spencer, becoming part of the collection given to Cambridge University Library in 1715 by George I. Rather ridiculously, the library then lost track of it for about 140 years until a library assistant called Henry Bradshaw found it in 1857 and showed it to the Celtic scholar Whitley Stokes.

Stokes translated the Gaelic annotations but, apart from an article in *The Saturday Review* of December 1860 and a facsimile of the book printed by the Spalding Club of Aberdeen in 1869, there'd been no great crusade to reclaim the iconic manuscript. So the Book of Deer had remained a lost fragment of Scottish history until 1972 when Professor Jackson published *The Gaelic Notes in the Book of Deer*. Careful study of Ellsworth and Jackson's texts had then made it possible for Sandiman to deceive an expert.

Time to get moving. Rose might start asking more questions.

On the way out, Sandiman also reminded himself of a simple fact. He had proved that there was relatively little record of the Book of Deer in history. Ask for a 336 lb lump of sandstone and everyone would immediately think of the Stone of Destiny. Ask for a binding and nobody had much reason to be suspicious.

It was a pity so few knew the story of the Book of Deer, though. Columba's journey into enemy territory, his confrontation with the High King of the Picts and the founding of the Abbey of Deer was all pretty exciting stuff. A thread woven with the bravery of a frontiersman.

But was there also a story behind the founding of the Church of St Finnan? Why had a church far from Finnan's ecclesiastical school in Ulster come to bear the name of Columba's teacher? True, the word *finnan* or *finan* was part of many place names in the Highlands, but perhaps Finnan had had a greater influence on his pupil than history knew. Perhaps the first step east along the road leading to the creation of the Book of Deer had been taken, not by Columba, but by his master.

Perhaps, perhaps, perhaps! All my talk is of maybes and all I can say is perhaps!

Sandiman felt the fury of the frustrated academic. There was a truth out there. He could feel it. But there were neither books, records nor storytellers' tales to prove it.

Finnan of Moville, what led you to the glen that bears your name? I'd sell my soul to find out.

Perhaps God, the Devil or another deity heard him; for that night he dreamt a deadly dream and by morning all memory of it was gone.

The Tale of The Book of Deer

Part One

"Ex oriente lux!"
[From the East, light!]

Once, some fourteen hundred years ago, the province of Argyll dominated the west of Scotland, and on its coast lay the stronghold of Dunadd. A great stone wall encircled the rocky mound like the crown upon a high king's brow. Hardened and ancient, dwarfing the curraghs berthed at its base and flanked by circles of sharp-edged standing stones dotted across the flood plain, Dunadd stood guard against assault by land or sea. It is true to say that the tapestry which would one day lead to a brainwave for a man on Skye began first to be woven, not in Glenfinnan, but here.

Within its walls, Dunadd's terraces swarmed with life. Fishermen selling their catch, the haggle of barter and trade by the well, merchants in brightly-coloured cloaks displaying Greek pottery and Gaulish wine jars, their chatter underscored by the hiss of molten metal being poured by goldsmiths, soon to be spun into delicate confections of jewellery or hardened into axeheads.

And at the summit, where the kings of Dalriada were crowned, stood a holy man. Long-haired, grey-bearded and green-eyed, he was neatly tonsured from ear to ear. He wore a splendid white habit but stood so quiet he seemed carved from stone. Like the fortress, he looked stern on the outside. Inside, his thoughts were flying frantically around.

The citadel on the river Add was virtually impregnable. Once it had served as shelter for barbarians fleeing the Roman legions; now it was capital of the Royal House of Dalriada. Forged by the Irish Celtic tribe of Scots, Dalriada stretched from Ulster in Erin to the hills of Morvern on the west coast of northern Alba, wild territory yet to be united under one king as the Nation of Scotland. Dunadd was the most northerly outpost of Christendom, the union of Church and Empire ordered by the Rule of St Benedict and radiating outwards from Rome, Constantinople and the Byzantine Empire.

The old man's foot nestled securely in the footprint carved into the flat rock, weathered into smoothness over generations. Many kings had been inaugurated here: Fergus Mor, Domangart, Comgall, Gabran; and now Conall, reigning king of Dalriada.

Surrounded by the buzz of industry, at one with tradition, he should have felt secure. He did not. The encircling ridges oppressed him and the thought of the endless forest beyond weighed heavily on him. The kingdom did not stand alone and its territory was always under siege. In Erin, from the south by the tribe of the Cruithin, and from the west by the northern tribes of the Uí Néill. In Alba, a pact made by Fergus Mor with the powerful Britons of Strathclyde held sway. Without that pact the House of Dalriada would not have been able either to gain or keep its settlements in northern Alba, but it was still humiliating. They had not conquered this land by the sword. They had been *allowed* to settle it. Not exactly the stuff of which legends could be woven by bards.

The Scots of Dalriada were surrounded by their enemies as surely as Dunadd was encircled by the hills. Dunadd itself was no more than an uncertain foothold at the edge of a land peopled by barbarians; a foothold which would *remain* uncertain because of the blasted mountains! Druim Alban, the Ridge of Alba. A spine of hills bisecting Alba from north to south. The Ridge had defeated the legions of Rome and its forests of alder, oak, rowan and pine sheltered the Picts, pagans who had ruled the north and east for centuries.

The hard ridges seemed to mock him. They'd probably also mocked Conall during his inauguration but, subject as he was to the overlordship of Brude Mac Maelchon, High

King of the Picts, Conall wasn't even a true king. Gabran had bravely led an expedition into Pictish territory a few years earlier, but had been defeated and thrown right out again. The overlordship under which Conall now laboured had been the result. The king of the Orkneys, or so he had heard, was also subject to Brude.

A Pictish kingdom stretching from the Tay to the Orkneys. There was certainly no way to outflank them. And it was no use looking further south. Beyond the border kingdoms of Strathclyde, Manau, Rheged and Gododdin, southern Alba was dominated by Angles and Saxons.

Slowly but surely, the Scots of Dalriada were being squeezed out of existence. They could not defeat the relentless tribesmen of Erin. They could not unseat the Britons of Strathclyde. Could they conquer the Picts?

The omens did *not* look good. Perhaps that was part of the reason he'd crossed the North Channel. He'd made for Dalriada's frontiers when he could easily have stayed at Moville, the ecclesiastical school he'd founded twenty years before on Ulster's east coast. The school itself was no more than a bunch of huts standing sentinel over Strangford Lough's harbour, but it was perfectly sited. No one knew what lay to the west – probably nothing but endless ocean – but the light of civilisation had come from the east. A past lost in legend, a history he craved to learn. A natural teacher, he'd transmitted this craving for knowledge to his pupils and earned himself the title of abbot.

Abbot Finnan of Moville, a fine title...

But something had happened at the school, something which had shaken him free of his cloistered life of matins, vespers and meditation. Forget the Cruithin, forget the Uí Néill, forget the possible fall of the House of Dalriada. Those were large, impersonal matters, like cloud over moorland.

One of his own deacons had dared to steal from him, and in a house of God! One of his first pupils! Crimmthan – a man with piercing grey eyes, a fiery temper, and a great deal of promise. Finnan had caught him copying from a book of psalms in Finnan's own church. A book carried from Ninian's church at Whithorn on northern Alba's south west coast. Worse than the discovery of the theft was the man's defence. He had stoutly insisted he had not defaced or damaged the book in any way. He'd merely made a copy of it. Granted, he hadn't actually thought to ask Finnan's *permission...*

But such books were sacred. Called Cathachs or, more commonly, 'Battlers', their vellum pages, cut and sewn from the skin of unborn calves, held the Word of God and placed it within the grasp of Man. Their bindings and scripture were illuminated in gold and silver by artists whose skills had been handed down to them by holy men of the Eastern church. Carried onto the field of battle in bronze reliquaries by custodians called dewars, their gospel inspired armies.

Words alone could not always touch a layman's soul. Few could read, and it was for the missionary to speak the Latin words, not always well. The art, sometimes crude (even semi-pagan, he admitted to himself), raised the message to another level. It was one thing simply to hear a sentence spoken. It was something else, much more, to let the eye be drawn to the spirituality evoked by the union of gilded words, designs and colours on the vellum pages. A spectrum of shades running from ultramarine, indigo and bright red to deep brown and verdant green. Pigments ground locally or brought to Erin's ports by merchants from Byzantium, Egypt and the Far East. Any man who looked upon such a book and opened his heart would be brought before Christ, bathed in his love, held in grace.

Such books acted as a sacrament, as windows opening onto the kingdom of Heaven, as doors to Paradise. They were venerated as icons, for they held the image of God in word and art.

This iconic imagery united the faithful with the one true God, converted the faithless and defined that faith. Copied by scribes, elaborated by illustrators, preached to the laity by martyrs and missionaries, that grace and love had been passed from monastery to monastery across Europe, overwhelming the babble of pagan beliefs with the clear light of liturgy. Cathachs had broken through ridges far worse than Druim Alban.

To copy such an icon without permission and produce a crude replica which literally distorted the Word of God was blasphemy, but the deacon refused to see it that way.

The difference of opinion, if such an abomination could so simply be described, had eventually been referred to a king of the southern tribe of the Uí Néill, Diarmait Mac Cerbaill. The deacon was descended from kings of the northern Uí Néill so to avoid warfare and placate tempers, a kindred member of that dynasty had to judge him. Diarmait, a pagan who gave lip service to the idea of Christianity when it suited him, was the only logical choice. An assembly was convened at the seat of the high kings, a hill fort on a plateau in Meath called Tara, dominated by an icon from the Holy Land – *Lia Fail*, the oracle stone.

Unfortunately, although the choice of Diarmait and location of Tara eased tribal tensions, the deacon and the king hated each other's guts. Diarmait's judgement was quickly reached, and summed up in a single sentence:

"To every cow belongeth her calf, to every book its little book."

Or in other words, no man had the right to separate a copy from the original.

Crimmthan had gone white with sheer fury. Finnan, standing nearby, felt the heat of that pent-up anger pass through the assembly. If magic had been involved, the look with which the deacon had then favoured Diarmait would, Finnan had no doubt, have struck the king dead on the spot. Had the two men been alone, he was also perfectly sure Crimmthan would have achieved the same end by liberal and bloody use of a sword, an axe and a mace.

But despite everything, the deacon was a good man. Finnan

saw him master an anger so intense it was like a sheet of raw flame, hone and refine it so although it curled deep within his belly, he stood motionless and outwardly respectful.

That should have been that, but with a sneer Diarmait had then ordered Crimmthan to return the copy to Finnan in front of the assembled monks. A calculated humiliation. He had done so, but his control had finally faltered. When the book had been placed in Finnan's hands, Crimmthan had turned and in a low, rasping voice said to the king:

"This is an unjust decision, O Diarmait, and I will be avenged!"

No one ever found out if the deacon was the cause of the battle which then took place between the northern and southern tribes of the Uí Néill, but he *did* have the ear of a king and he *had* sworn vengeance in public. Not only that, when the two armies clashed in 561 at Cul Dreimne in the west of Erin, Crimmthan was seen fighting on the northern side, not half-a-mile from a small church at the foot of Ben Bulben which he himself had founded.

At dawn the tableau of church and Ben had been defiled. As druids allied to Diarmait had cursed the northerners from the overlooking crags, the two tribes of horsemen had flung themselves upon each other with a prodigious roar of war-horns. Swords had been loosed from bronze scabbards and finely wrought shields glinted in the sunlight as the armies met. The bloody clamour and consequent slaughter lasted until dusk as the Celtic fighting spirit exhausted itself. As usual, everyone forgot what they were fighting about after the first half-hour or so.

What Finnan would never forget, though, was crossing the battlefield at dusk and finding Crimmthan, a man he'd thought of as a son, standing near the church. A sword was in the deacon's hand and his side was drenched in blood.

Behind him Finnan had heard men moaning and screaming, dying slowly from ugly wounds. The northern tribe of the Uí Néill had won, but the victory had cost nearly three thousand lives.

Finnan had looked into Crimmthan's grey eyes and the message which passed between them was clear.

You would sacrifice men's lives for a book?

For the words of Martin, bishop of Tours, passed to Ninian of Whithorn from Rome, Constantinople and the east, I would indeed sacrifice much.

The only thing greater than the book and the words within, are the soldiers of Christ who fight to bring such words to the pagan. You have thrown these soldiers' lives away with your petty arguments and your petty arrogance.

Crimmthan had been humbled. He had also been excommunicated and now, a year later, a synod was gathering to decide his fate. That was partly what was troubling Finnan, and as he looked out the kingdom and its islands he found himself wondering whether, for good or ill, Dalriada could afford to lose such a man at this time.

The way ahead was in shadow. Finnan would have to travel a good bit further before it became clear to him; until he gained some insight into a broader tapestry he could only vaguely sense.

He had to meditate upon the answer, and realised he couldn't find it from the comfort of his cell at Moville. He would have to travel to the borders of the kingdom. Only there could he face his fear, master it and (hopefully) look clearly at the truth behind it.

Only there would his demons be unafraid to approach.

When Finnan asked for twelve oarsmen to row him north and west to the frontier in a curragh, the commander of the fortress nearly refused. It was unheard of (not to mention highly dangerous) for so high-ranking a personage to go so close to the Pictish territories! To say nothing of the dark magic of the forest, home to the raven, wolf and deer.

But he was an abbot, and few in the kingdom would refuse an abbot's wishes. So he was soon able to set sail in the curragh, the sturdy craft leaving its berth at Dunadd with the tide. South of Islay was Erin, and Finnan imagined he could see his school on the coast, but they had to turn north via the Firth of Lorne to hug the coast, looking for an inlet to a sea loch deep enough to take the curragh's shallow draft.

It would be the Feast Day of Beltane soon. The mid-point of the year was usually a time of optimism as nature renewed itself, but it was also a time when demons walked the earth and communed with men.

His oarsmen were not happy. They would rather have been with their families at Beltane, but Finnan had blessed the boat before they sailed so they bent to their oars with few grumbles. It was a calm day, and for a time there was little sound save for the quiet slap of oars slicing through the water.

They reached Dunollie, kindred fortress of Dunadd, that evening. Sitting at the northern edge of a harbour overlooking Mull and Lorne, it protected Dalriadic trading ships from Picts. It was also the last outpost before the frontier. Knowing this, Finnan's men tried to lose their senses with ale and women. Finnan himself walked along the ramparts and looked out over the anchorage towards the green and golden hills and valleys of Mull. He'd always believed the vault of sea and sky was the true church of his faith, had always felt uplifted by their presence, but now that comfort was gone.

They set out the following morning, small signs of dissent more noticeable as the curragh neared Pictish territory. With the unwelcoming mainland looming to starboard and the friendly hills of Mull disappearing to port, they felt isolated and vulnerable. The wind picked up and a light rain began to fall.

Late in the day, Finnan saw an inlet. He could feel the silent force of the men's entreaties to enter it, to do what he'd set out to do and quickly return to Dunadd. But still he shook his head. They weren't close enough yet.

They beached the curragh at the mouth of the locah and ate some rations. Finnan, understanding their fears as well as his own, sat with them and told them legends of Cuchulainn, the ancient Irish hero; and tales of the cavalry general who had united the border kingdoms of Strathclyde, Rheged and Gododdin. With a likeness of the Virgin Mary on his shield, he and his horse warriors had defeated the Picts, Angles and Saxons after the Roman legions had finally departed over a century before. His victories had helped to preserve Christianity and Celtic civilisation in northern and southern Alba from the barbarians after the fall of Rome.

His name?

The general had been called *Artorius miles* – Arthur the soldier – and he'd simply used military tactics and discipline learnt from the Romans to outfight the barbarians. Yet already the bards were rewriting history, saying Arthur had been helped by a druid known either as Lailoken or Merlin.

Supposedly, Arthur and his horse warriors would return to unite the tribes of northern and southern Alba if need be. But other tales said that Merlin was a *librarius* – a magician, prophet and keeper of books who would reappear every seven centuries, and whose reappearance would herald a spiritual renaissance.

Arthur had helped to preserve Christendom in the early sixth century, so if the tale was true, Finnan mused, Merlin would return in the thirteenth century. And again in the twentieth century.

Last of all, he told them of Tir Nan Og, the place of heaven found beyond the sunset. Telling that last tale was, Finnan admitted to himself, an act of pragmatism. Men who felt they were at least partly on a quest for Tir Nan Og would be less likely to grumble about sailing even further away from their home port the next day.

The sun came up and the ship went north. To the west, Finnan could see Coll and Tiree. Beyond were the island fortresses of the Fir Bolg – an ancient race driven out of Erin centuries before.

By sunset, the abbot and his oarsmen could see the point of Ardnamurchan far ahead. They were perilously close to

Pictish territory but only now did Finnan feel it was time to seek safe harbour.

Following the shoreline as the evening mist closed in, they came upon an inlet which could shelter them from the tide. By now, however, the men didn't even want to go ashore. The forest was home to the raven, the wolf and the deer. It was well known that Cernunnos, father of the gods, and Donn, god of death, could take the form of deer. Finnan's men were Christian, but their faith was not strong enough to free them from their pagan past. Especially at Beltane.

They made it through the night, although one man refused to leave the curragh and spent a chill evening on the deck. Finnan was not surprised. The crewmember was little more than a boy and scared out of his wits, but when all the oarsmen were assembled, Finnan stood before them at the bow.

"I swear we shall travel no further," he said. "I have come here so I can best decide what must be done to safeguard the future of the House of Dalriada. I could not do this at Moville. It is a decision I could only make here, facing the bloody heathen.

"I will pray for guidance tonight. I ask you to leave me on an island further down this river, and return in the morning."

There was a murmur of surprise. It was one thing for holy men to seclude themselves in cells within the precincts of their abbeys. It was quite another for them to be left unarmed and defenceless on the frontier.

Finnan could virtually hear their thoughts. He even agreed with most of them. Up to now, he had not even been quite sure what had driven him this far. Dissatisfaction with his privileged life? Perhaps. A need to confront the absolute reality of the threats the House of Dalriada was facing? Maybe. A wish to truly understand what had driven the deacon to act as he had?

Definitely.

Finnan's self-doubt disappeared. The men saw it happen

and drew strength from it. Even the youngster looked a bit more confident.

They soon found a suitable island. Rising from the centre of the flat blue waters of the loch like a keystone, it sat poised between hard-edged mountains and the heavens' vault. A kernel, balancing the trinity of land, sea and sky.

Except for a scattering of oak trees, loosely grouped into a circle, the island was quite deserted.

That, Finnan knew, was the place to which he had been drawn. A place of oaks, where druids carried out their rituals on the Feast days of Samhain, Imbolc, Beltane and Lughnasa. A place where spiritual forces converged. Where demons might speak with their subjects.

They oarsmen left the abbot there. They vowed to return for him in the morning but doubted they'd ever see him again.

Finnan was no longer worried. This was the place where his beliefs would be put to the test. Either they'd be vindicated, or he'd disappear from the pages of history. Simple.

The wind, it seemed, did not breathe. The loch was still as glass. Looking around, Finnan could clearly see every last detail of the rocks, shoreline, ridges and gullies. He found he was holding his breath.

He let the air out of his lungs and bent to the task of building a fire. His furs were thick but the night would be freezing. In defiance of the pagan gods, he even made the fire in the middle of the place of oaks. The druids would not like a Christian treading on their patch, but he was going to do it anyway. He smiled at the thought.

Slowly, the abbot began to fall into a meditative state. Staring at the flickering tendrils of flame, Finnan's calm became absolute. An eyeblink, and an hour had passed. Another blink, and the sun had set.

I am beyond the sunset, he thought. *I am come to Tir Nan Og*.

Even then, he did not stir. Not 'til the faint tolling of a bell, very far away, roused him.

Once again he smiled. The bell's chimes were comforting, a summons to prayer for the penitent. Except there was no bell within earshot, and he was the only penitent around.

He stretched out tiredly and only then did he see the deer, standing motionless at the edge of the glade.

It was a stag standing there, staring at him unblinkingly. Now, Finnan began to feel true fear. Animals ran from Man because they feared Man. Animals had no souls. Deer were respected for their speed, alertness and strength, but they were not Man's equals. They ran. Always.

This one, presumably, had other ideas.

Its eyes, hard and melancholy, bored into him.

Cernunnos? he thought. *Donn?*

Still the creature stared him down. Filled with vigour yet as finely sculpted as an oak tree, it defined the dark and loveless country surrounding them.

A thought occurred to him.

What if you are not Cernunnos? What if you are not Donn?

After all, if those two pagan gods could change their shape was it not possible that his own god, the one true god, could do the same?

Of course it was possible! Maybe he wasn't going to get killed after all.

Finnan felt a sudden sense of contentment. If this was his god, he had nothing to fear. If not, a swift charge would bring a quick end.

Finnan stood up. He crossed the glade with measured steps until he faced the creature. He could see its glossy brown hide, smell its scent, see the flaring of its nostrils. He reached out and patted its muzzle.

This could not be Cernunnos. Nor could it be Donn. But did it have the answer he sought?

He knelt before it, in the shadow of its antlers.

Afterwards, he could never recall quite what happened next. A shaft of sunlight broke through cloud, and it seemed he was raised up suddenly, far beyond the ground. He found himself looking east, much as he often did from Moville, but this time his vision was far more clear and sharp. He felt as if he was flying above hills and glens. Across choppy seas. Over jagged mountains wreathed in snow. On to a city on seven hills, dominated by cathedrals and surrounded by olive groves.

Rome, he thought. *Rome in Constantine's day.*

Would the vision draw to a close here? No. The land was becoming brown and sunbaked. He was travelling further and faster. Passing over a colourful city laced with a filigree of gold and silver spun, in supplication, around the dome of a great church.

Byzantium. Constantinople and St Sophia.

He saw Greek isles basking like white droplets in the blue Mediterranean. He reached the shores of the Holy Land, came upon Jerusalem and still the vision went on. Still he flew further east. Now he saw a land between two rivers, his vision finally slowing and settling upon bronze temples. Focusing on marbled halls where scholars read from tablets written in a strange wedge-shaped script.

This was a time far in the past, Finnan realised. The history he'd longed to embrace. The east where the light of civilisation had first shone, where knowledge had first been recorded. Echoes of Gilgamesh could be heard. Images of the empires of Sumer, Akkad and Babylon could be seen. The scholars were long dead, the names of their royal houses so old they'd become legend, but their words had survived.

He thought of Martin. Once a Roman legionnaire, later bishop of Tours. Martin whose Gospel had been given to Ninian of Whithorn. His own deacon, copying that word. Of the House of Dalriada, armed with words from the Holy Land to be spoken to the heathen.

How could this be done? The Ridge of Alba was still in the way, and it was too cruel a test for a priest. A soldier could endure, a statesman backed by soldiers could negotiate, but a priest alone could not break the Ridge.

Yet both soldier and statesman needed the priest's simple faith.

It was another trinity, but how could it be achieved? The House of Dalriada had no one who could...

Wait.

The encounter with the deacon at Cul Dreimne came back to him. A man willing to fight. Able to negotiate. Of unquestioned faith.

Soldier. Statesman. Priest.

Miles Christi. A soldier of Christ.

Cathach. A battler.

Only such a man could carry the word over the Ridge. He could also carry a Cathach.

The stag moved back, and once again it seemed the abbot could see further than any mortal man was able. Beyond the flat blue waters of the loch.

That was the challenge, Finnan realised:

To carry the word over the Ridge and beyond. Into the east. To take the sceptre of the kingdom. For Church and Empire to carry that sceptre and, with it, to unite a world.

Finnan stood, facing the stag. The challenge was accepted and a price would have to be paid. He wondered how it would be exacted. No deity would give up a kingdom lightly and Royal Houses, now and forever, would fight like bloody savages to claim the sceptre.

An uncertain future, but one which now had some shape. There would be a place for the Scots of Dalriada if they were willing to fight for it. Better the chance to fight, anyway, than slow humiliation by pact and overlordship.

But, he thought again, *at what price?* Images of Cul Dreimne tormented the abbot. The memory of crossing the battlefield at dusk to find the deacon standing near the church, sword in hand and side drenched in blood. The sound of men screaming and cursing as they slowly died from ugly wounds.

He didn't have all the answers. Perhaps the best he could do was have faith and believe.

They oarsmen found their abbot in the morning, sitting safe by the remnants of a small fire. Some of the men crossed themselves when they saw him and, on the return journey, they all treated him with veneration. It would have been pleasant to bask in their hero worship but Finnan did not let it deflect him from his purpose. That would take months to arrange, but he would manage it somehow.

Late in 562, a synod was convened at Teltown in Meath. Its purpose, ostensibly, was to excommunicate and exile the unrepentant deacon. Finnan, however, had had time to go to work behind the scenes, carefully pulling strings until the outcome had become less a sentence and more an opportunity.

Rather than simply being cast out, never to return, Crimmthan was ordered to convert as many pagan souls as the soldiers who had been slain in battle at Cul Dreimne. To do this he would be exiled to northern Alba, but with him he could take twelve disciples. Not only that, an island had been provided for him. This was Finnan's greatest achievement. Armed with the notoriety his voyage had given him, he had sought an audience with the king and made Conall negotiate with his overlord, Brude Mac Maelchon, to grant the deacon and his disciples possession of a small island west of Mull.

The soldier of Christ was already armed with faith. Now he'd been granted a foothold on enemy territory. It was up to him whether he disappeared from the pages of history or wrote some of them. Carefully observing the man's tightly leashed anger as the synod's clerics droned on, Finnan doubted Crimmthan would squander his chances.

Still, Finnan had taken care to visit him in his cell the night before sentence would be passed. The abbot had found him staring out of the small window and into the east. Yet when the deacon turned to greet his master, Finnan had seen tears in his eyes. He had understood immediately. It was a great thing to be given the chance to go into the east and convert the pagan, but a terrible loss never to see home again.

That, however, was the price that had to be paid.

Aloud, Finnan said a single word:

"Arthur."

The tears did not cease streaming silently down Crimmthan's face, but Finnan saw a light begin to sparkle in the grey eyes.

"They will speak of you as they speak of *Artorius miles*, Arthur the soldier. They will speak of the man who broke the Ridge and carried the Word to the pagan. They will call you *miles Christi*, the soldier of Christ. *Cathach*, the battler..."

"Then the House of Dalriada will survive?"

Finnan almost smiled. "Yes."

"To safeguard a kingdom is a king's task. I am a priest."

"A priest can place the sceptre of a kingdom in the hand of a king. The king, once consecrated by the Church, can rule a world."

"A Christian Empire? You have a rich tapestry laid out for me."

"I did not lay it out. I merely looked at it. All I have done is negotiate with Conall to give you a place to live."

"What place?"

"Iona."

Crimmthan, later to be known as Columba, set sail from Derry for Iona in 563 with twelve disciples. He knew he would not see Erin again, but as the hills of Antrim vanished over the horizon he felt threads tear in his soul. At his command, the disciples landed on the nearby island of Colonsay. Columba climbed the highest hill, from where he could just about see the outline of Erin's coast. He thought of Tara. He always seemed to end up facing his destiny from the tops of hills. First Tara, then Colonsay. Iona would be next. It wasn't necessarily a bad thing, though.

And then he looked towards the east.

There's a grey eye that looks back at Erin, he thought as he turned. *It will never hereafter see the men of Erin nor their women...*

Forging the future would always demand a forfeit.

Crimmthan clasped the leather satchel Finnan had pressed into his hands just before he set sail. He had not opened it, because if it contained the Gospel of Saint Martin he would know Finnan had forgiven him, a weight would lift from his heart and the Gospel would become his Cathach, an icon to unite him with the land and people awaiting him.

But if it did not, then he would have to live with the knowledge that, despite all the talk of Arthur's deeds, his teacher was basically just pleased to be rid of the arrogant deacon who'd sacrificed men's lives for the words of a book.

He dreaded the latter possibility, but the truth would have to be faced.

He would open the satchel soon, and if Finnan had forgiven him, go gladly into exile.

He looked away from the west, toward the light of the east, and began the long walk down the hill.

7

*F*ebruary 1997 gave way to March, and 1 May was set as the date for a general election. The move towards Scottish devolution quickened its pace as Labour promised to ratify the 1997 Scotland Bill if it was elected and, amidst the hue and cry for independence, hardly anyone noticed that Alex Salmond, leader of the Scottish National Party and MP for Banff & Buchan, had begun to lobby for the return of an ancient manuscript belonging to a village in his constituency. A village called Old Deer.

About then, a sharp-eyed local might have seen a tall man walking up the hill above the ruins of the Cistercian Abbey of Deer. Few people bothered to come and see the fallen stones. They had not been restored and, compared to Scone Palace or Edinburgh Castle, were of little interest to anyone except Historic Scotland.

John Sandiman stayed awhile on the hilltop before walking back down to the village, a tidy grey granite settlement with a wide main street. At one end of the street stood two churches, Deer Parish Church and St Drostan's Episcopal Church. At the other was the Aden Arms Hotel. Sandiman stopped for a moment at the first church and noticed a plaque on the bell tower. He smiled as he read the inscription:

In the Celtic Monastery in this vicinity
was Written
"THE BOOK OF DEIR"
Which includes the oldest known examples of
Scottish Gaelic

The original monastery, as far as anyone knew, had been built on this site inside a loop of the South Ugie Water. It was good to see it remembered. He walked past St Drostan's, stopping at the Aden Arms for a pint of beer and a toastie. After that, he took the bus to Inverness where he spent a night in the youth hostel on the Old Edinburgh Road. The next day, he spent reading about Loch Lochy and the Great Glen, and the day after that travelled to the hostel in that area.

As he got off the bus it occurred to him that the general election was being held on an historic day – the Feast Day of Beltane. An ancient date, reaching back to the time of the druids. It was said that on the Feast days of Samhain, Imbolc, Beltane, and Lughnasa, spirits were freed to walk the earth and do whatever they pleased.

Back then, druids would probably have been making human sacrifices to the God of Death to try and keep the peace. Right now, spin doctors on all sides were probably invoking pagan deities to help their parties get the votes.

Sandiman stayed at the hostel for several days, walking in the hills, making notes and lunching in Invergarry. Then he boarded another bus for Fort William, intent on fading away into the hills of Moidart and working out what to do next.

Now that he'd seen the site of the Abbey of Deer, the tale of Columba's journey across the Ridge to face the High King of the Picts was becoming more and more real to him. Ancient history, once spectral as a ghost, was now clothing itself in flesh and blood, reminding him of the men of whom his father had talked, and who deserved remembrance.

The Tale of The Book of Deer

Part Two

> *"Sovereignty did not lie with the actual state
> (that is, the government of the day),
> but with a symbolic representation
> of the continuity of the state."*

(Lindsay Paterson)

Once he was a warrior, thought Columba. Now he is become a king.

The warrior in question, Áedán Mac Gabran, knelt before Columba and the assembled brothers in the main church of the Abbey of Iona. Although he could not see the sky as clearly as Finnan had, Columba felt the same sense of calm fulfilment which had possessed his teacher some twelve years earlier. He himself was now Abbot of Iona; the small island where his teacher had meditated was now known as *Eilean Fhionnan* or Islandfinnan and the tale of Finnan's encounter with the stag was being enthusiastically woven into heroic legend. The glen itself would probably end up being called Glenfinnan.

It had been a long road back from Columba's arrogance, disgrace and excommunication. That first winter on Iona had tested them to their limits, and if their crops had failed... He didn't even want to think what might have happened. Thankfully, the fort of Dunollie had been nearby and the local kindred had helped build the abbey. The wooden monastic enclosure, made up of the main church, domestic buildings and guest house, now lay safe within its circular boundary bank, the fields on the machair gave good produce, and the seal harvest was bountiful.

And there had always been the Cathach his teacher had bequeathed to him. Early on, he had built a wooden cell beneath a rocky knoll to which, on difficult days, he would retreat and read from St Martin's Gospel.

During the crossing to Iona, Columba had refused to open the satchel until the outline of the isle had begun to coalesce out of the mist. Only then had he withdrawn the book from its covering and learnt he'd been forgiven.

It had not been the original gospel, but his own illegal copy. In complete defiance of Diarmait's ruling, Finnan had separated the calf from the cow, the little book from the book!

To take such a risk was brave indeed. Finnan had placed his trust in Columba, and Columba vowed he would be worthy of that trust. It seemed a shaft of sunlight had broken through cloud at the same moment. Perhaps he was rewriting his own past, but Columba was sure he'd then taken the book in his hands and, reading from it, blessed the isle they would shortly reach.

Now, perhaps, Finnan's designs would reach their culmination. A culmination which knelt before him in the person of Áedán Mac Gabran, whom he would shortly consecrate as King of Dalriada. To the certain knowledge of Columba and his apostolic brothers, no consecration of a king by an abbot had ever before taken place on Alba's mainland. So this ceremony was unprecedented.

He wondered how many more kings would be crowned in this way.

Conall, the former king, had died in Kintyre and for a time it seemed sure the throne would pass to Conall's cousin, Eogan. Politically, Eogan was the correct choice but Columba had suspected that Eogan's brother Áedán had the stronger character and greater prowess on the battlefield.

When he made his misgivings public, though, the politicking had begun in earnest. Ignoring the clear and present problems of the Picts and the Ridge, the clerics argued endlessly among themselves and vied for position. Columba finally lost patience with the petty wrangling, sailed across the Firth of Lorne and parked himself on a small island south of Dunollie. He liked the place. It was warm and calm, and the ripples on the water seemed soft as silk. On a clear day he could see Ben More on Mull, and not far beyond the Ben was Iona.

He lazed about nibbling shellfish for a while but eventually made himself meditate. The time had drawn out slowly, and it had been the third day before he dreamt.

In his dream, he had seen an angel. In the angel's hand was a book for the ordination of kings, and when Columba awoke the first name on his lips was Áedán. He would have to consecrate Áedán, then, and damn the politics. He had been reluctant, for he both knew and liked Eogan better, but the next night and the night after that the dream had recurred.

Áedán would have to be king, and that was all there was to it.

After all, Columba thought, he himself had not been the best choice to become Abbot of Iona, but Finnan had realised only he could actually do the job. There would still be a real chance of civil war, but for the Scots of Dalriada to survive, that chance would have to be taken. Áedán had his faults but he could unite tribes and that, in the tradition of Arthur, was the crucial qualification for a king.

Still, Columba wasn't going to let him get cocky. That would cost lives.

Returning to the present, he reverently placed the sceptre he was holding upon the book, before turning back to the man kneeling before him.

"Make no mistake, Áedán," he intoned, "but believe that, until you commit some act of treachery against me or my successors, none of your enemies will have the power to oppose you. For this reason you must give this warning to your sons, as they must pass it on to their sons and grandsons and descendents, so that they do not follow evil counsels and so lose the sceptre of this kingdom from their hands.

For whenever it may happen that they do wrong to me or to my kindred in Ireland, the scourge that I have suffered for your sake from the angel will be turned by the hand of God to deliver a heavy punishment on them. Men's hearts will be taken from them, and their enemies will draw strength mightily against them."

And to avoid such evil counsel, he reflected, they would have the books. Icons uniting Church and Empire with their words which, copied by clerics and preserved in abbeys, would endure for centuries.

If they weren't hauled into battle as Cathachs too often, anyway.

Áedán looked chastened, then smiled as Columba placed the sceptre firmly in his hand and laid both hands on his head in blessing.

This was the moment of consecration. Channelled by the symbols of sceptre and gospel, evoked by liturgy, the Lord's sacrament made flesh the sovereignty being conferred upon Áedán.

Columba felt warm strength flood from his fingerprints as a radiance briefly bathed the congregation in light. A light which focused on the young warrior.

No, no more a warrior. Now and for all his days, he would be king.

It was done. There was a new king of Dalriada, by the grace of God, and history would take a different path.

Six years passed by. A political settlement was hammered out at the convention of Druim Ceatt in Derry which, despite control of Dalriada's navy going to Erin's kings, secured independence for the House of Dalriada in northern Alba.

The weekly round of worship on Iona, with fasting on Wednesdays and Fridays and the celebration of the Eucharist on Sundays, also began to establish itself. Raids by Picts were rare and a fragile peace seemed to be evolving.

Except every so often, worries wormed into Columba's gut and, turning from a manuscript he was writing, he would stride into the open and look to the east. What he saw reminded him starkly of how delicate the peace really was. The Ridge still held firm, Brude Mac Maelchon still thought himself overlord of Dalriada's king, and Dalriada's Scots were still besieged in Erin.

He was a soldier of Christ who carried the Cathach! If only he could do something.

But it wasn't the right time yet.

In the spring of 580, the right time arrived. The royal curragh sailed to Iona and as Columba and his brothers waited, the king, followed by his retinue, made his way to the abbot. Columba knelt before the king, who immediately bade him rise, and the abbot took the opportunity to have a good look at his sovereign. Áedán wore a king's circlet upon his brow and a long cloak fastened by a golden brooch, but little other ornamentation. His hair was longer, his beard now full and pointed, and his eyes were those of a seasoned sovereign who'd seen death and made hard decisions. There was little trace of the cocky young warrior Columba had consecrated. He had matured into a king.

Their eyes met and the abbot realised the king knew exactly what he was thinking. A smile played upon Áedán's lips for a moment.

Columba never forgot the words Áedán then uttered to him:

"I am a king, but to break the Ridge I need a prince of the Uí Néill."

The king and the abbot had talked late into the night. The pressures on the House of Dalriada in Erin were becoming unbearable, and the Picts were still too powerful to challenge directly. Nevertheless, the Ridge had to be broken. A monastic settlement deep within Pictish territory would have to be established. At the same time, other settlements in the Orkneys would have to be created, boxing the Picts in.

"I don't think Brude will just *let* us do this," said Columba sceptically.

"He certainly won't allow soldiers to create a fortress, but he might allow soldiers of Christ to live a peaceful monastic life, and once we have a foothold in the east we have a chance to survive."

"Finnan negotiated to send me here. I negotiated to make you king. Now you expect me to negotiate with Brude for you?"

"Brude will not come to me, and if I were to go to his stronghold he would doubtless consider it an act of war. I wouldn't even blame him for doing so. However, a man of God would pose no threat, and a prince of the Uí Néill would command respect in his court."

Columba looked at his king for a long time. However clearly it was explained – and the logic was irrefutable – whoever faced Brude was still risking torture and death. Druids often carried out rituals involving human sacrifice and impalement, usually in places of oaks. Captives might also suffer the tripartite death of burning, drowning and stabbing which supposedly satisfied the elemental forces of earth, fire and water. The victims' entrails were then spread on bloodsoaked altars and used to divine the future.

They were in the main church. Columba stood up and looked towards the lectern upon which the copy of St Martin's Gospel lay.

"I am over fifty," he said at length. "I am a little bit worn. A bit like the satchel in which I carried this book here; but it is still useful, and I am still useful. If it is the will of God that I face Brude as Arthur would have, then that is what I must do."

"You won't have to go alone. Your nephew Drostán Mac Cosgrach will accompany you, as your cousin will accompany me to the Orkneys."

"My king, you *yourself* are going to the Orkneys?"

"Creating a settlement that will last needs the authority of a king, but I can't be in two places at once. If you, the prince, can start an abbey in the east, I, the king, may be able to found a fortress on the Isles."

"And you expect Brude to allow you to set foot on the islands?"

"If you tell him only that some of our people have sailed off to find a place of retreat out at sea, and that their travels may bring them to the Orkneys, he just might."

"Must I lie for you, my king?"

"It is an omission, not a lie, but I will not order you to do so, my abbot. I will only ask you to. I can think of no other way to ensure our people's survival."

Columba began to shake his head. Once he had been young and arrogant enough to deceive his abbot and sacrifice men's lives for a book. Now the mere thought of lying horrified him. He didn't think he could do it.

Then a memory came to mind. A legion of soldiers standing to attention. The dead of Cul Dreimne. Headless men, bloody corpses, butchered boys, all gathered on a mound of shields in crimson twilight. Every one of them staring at him with eye or eye socket. Unlike Columba, none of them were alive and able to moralise about right and wrong in comfort.

I have moved beyond arrogance, I have humbled myself and I have repented, but I will always be a wretch because of what I did. Three thousand died at Cul Dreimne because of me. I have no right to hide behind morality, and the only way to redeem my wretched soul is by doing anything I can to stop more slaughter. I have already placed the sceptre of the kingdom in Áedán's hand. If I must lie in order to carry the Word beyond the Ridge then so be it.

Finnan had indeed chosen well. A priest would have refused, but a soldier of Christ could be a little more mercenary and a humbled wretch would do much to redeem himself.

His cheeks burning with the memory of his disgrace, Columba bowed his head to his king.

They could not travel overland; the forests cloaking the Ridge were even more dangerous than the Picts. They would have to voyage via inland waterways, hauling their boats between lochs, following the line of the Great Glen towards the Pictish fort of Craig Phádraig at the mouth of the River Ness. Even on water they would be vulnerable, but Áedán had told Columba that Brude wished to meet the Abbot of Iona in person. Therefore they'd probably get there alive. Most of them, anyway.

The thought did not cheer Columba up at all. He would have to choose the men to accompany him and any deaths would be on his conscience. Meditating on it, he decided to include Comgall and Canice. Both were Irish Picts and both able to talk to the barbarians in their own tongue.

In the end, he picked the others at random. He and Drostán looked at them with pride as they bent to their oars and Iona receded into the distance. Columba thought of Finnan heading out into the quiet emptiness years before, then turned to look at the waters of Loch Linnhe.

When they reached Loch Ness, they began to hear the drumbeats. A green mantle of leaves reached from the shoreline to the high ridges, the forest masked the hills, the trees masked the contours of the glens and the branches masked the movements of the Picts. The drumming went on and on, an unbroken beat which began to fray their nerves. Each man began to look at his kin with irritation as the constant beat wore their nerves ragged. It was made worse because, no matter how many times they scoured the water's edge with their eyes, not once did they see a living soul.

Like ants crawling across hot glass in bright light, they ground their way across the loch, each man becoming an automaton to try and block out the maddening beat. Columba himself stood before them and thundered challenges to the mountains, holding the book aloft in its satchel and daring the pagan gods to strike him down.

He noticed Drostán looking at him askance and realised he was smiling. Columba's eyes were alight with a fire Drostán had not seen in many a year. A light which, for good or ill, had not shone since Cul Dreimne.

They made landfall near the mouth of the River Ness that

night. The drumbeat had subsided, so the monks cooked a choice salmon in the fire and made wary conversation. No Pict had yet been seen, although the odd rustle told Columba they were close by. The party began to relax and at first nobody noticed that the firelight seemed to be growing brighter. Then a few stray cinders wafted past them and the truth became apparent.

A human sacrifice was taking place on the hillside less than a mile away. They could hear screams as the tripartite ritual of death unfolded. The poor devil was being burned half to death, then his head would be held under water until he was on the point of drowning. Lastly he would be hung from an oak tree and stabbed or decapitated.

There was a general rush to free the victim from the flames, but Columba looked at the faces of Comgall and Canice and saw the truth. To interfere with a human sacrifice was sacrilege to the Picts. If they did so, Columba and his monks would be cut down there and then.

They had no choice but to sit and listen.

The night passed very slowly. The screams faded and after a pause they were replaced by faint gasps as knives stabbed between the man's ribs. Columba's men sat stonily by their own fire.

"May God have mercy on that man's soul," said Drostán heavily.

Columba looked at him for a moment.

"May God have mercy on the soul of the man who put him there."

The sentence hung in the air between the cousins. Drostán could almost hear the unspoken end of Columba's sentence.

Because I won't.

The next day, when at last it came, found the abbot and his companions walking uphill to Craig Phádraig. Like Tara, the ancient stone fortress was built on a plateau. Unlike Tara, the path winding up to it was marked out by human skulls skewered to stakes. Picts in blue warpaint stood still as statues at regular intervals along the way, their silence exuding menace. It was all part of the softening-up process and Columba had to admit it was effective. The thought almost brought a smile to his lips but he kept his face blank. Any expression would be interpreted as weakness. He clutched the satchel more tightly.

The fortress loomed before them, layer upon layer of vitreous rock topped by timber ramparts, the gates firmly locked. Columba knew it was part of the game Brude was playing but unchristian anger still boiled up inside him. He fought it down. The Battle of Cul Dreimne had left him with a livid scar on his side. On the other hand, the sacrifice he'd witnessed the night before had left him feeling willing to risk more slaughter for a chance to strike Brude's head from his shoulders ...

Columba and his followers stopped at the gates, uncertain what to do next. Brude might well leave them out there until they starved or retreated.

Of course, there might be a way round the problem. Like any high king, Brude had an ego and if the reports were anything to go by, Brude's ego was bigger than most. That would be the weakest link in his defences.

Brude would not like being challenged.

An idea came to Columba. Simple and devilish. He grinned at the thought of it.

He filled his lungs and spoke, loud and clear, to his assembled brethren. He knew Brude would hear every word. The high king might not understand it all at first, but he would get the message sooner or later.

"Brothers, we can only assume that the high king does not wish to let us enter Craig Phádraig. He doubtless believes that, were we to do so, we might carry out acts of Christian worship and claim his fortress in the name of the Lord. We respect his beliefs, but now we're stuck out here we must pass the time somehow and vespers are as good a way as any to pass the day. Let us remember the words of the forty-sixth psalm and hope they'll carry to the ears of all the Picts in this fine and sturdy fortress."

A Christian service in the Pictish capital. Brude would not like that at all. It was a risk. They'd either be quietly invited in or not-so-quietly executed.

The monks grinned too. If this was their day to die, it would be a good way to go. Carrying the Word into the lair of the pagan. They grouped themselves together, crossed themselves and bowed their heads.

Columba began, filling his lungs with a certain relish.

"God is our hope and strength: a very present help in trouble.

Therefore will we not fear, though the earth be moved;

and though the hills be carried into the midst of the sea ..."

Columba preached for a very long time, turning from the forty-sixth psalm to other verses, taking the book from its satchel when his memory failed. Someone had once said that when Columba preached on Iona, they could hear him on Mull. It hadn't been a joke.

Later, Columba could never remember exactly which parts of the gospel he'd recited. The words seemed to echo beyond the farthest hills. Perhaps that was true power, far more enduring than false and fleeting victory in battles like Cul Dreimne.

Columba had been preaching for three hours when he and his brethren heard the sound of bolts being violently driven back. The gates slowly opened. *Someone*, Columba thought, *has become exasperated*. He made the sign of the cross and waited to see what would happen next.

Brude, wearing the double-linked silver chain of Pictish sovereignty, stood in the centre of the compound with the druid Broichán by his side. Behind him were his nobles and on the ramparts stood his warriors. The king and his court surrounded by a sea of square shields, the kingdom of the Picts made flesh. Heavy-bearded, black-eyed, as squat and aggressive as an evil little troll, the arrogant monarch would not consider a band of monks dangerous. But the supernatural was another matter entirely. Brude suspected Columba might be a match for Broichán.

Brude eventually spoke:

"You are Columba, Abbot of Iona?"

"I am he," replied the abbot, relieved they could communicate.

"What business do you have here?"

Columba paused before saying, a little hoarsely:

"Some of our people have sailed off to find a place of retreat somewhere on the trackless sea. Commend them to the care of the sub-king, whose hostages you hold, so that if their wanderings bring them to Orkney, they should meet with no hostility within his boundaries."

He didn't mention that King Áedán of Dalriada was one of those people, and once Áedán's fleet had secured a presence on Orkney, the Picts would be trapped between North and South, between the Scots of Dalriada and the Britons of Strathclyde. And finally, the Ridge would be breached.

Brude measured Columba carefully, looking for any weakness in the cold grey eyes. He found none. He had heard Columba was a battler as well as a holy man. He had doubted what he'd heard, but the truth now stood before him.

The abbot stroked the silver cross on his habit and saw a shadow cross Brude's eyes. The Pictish king moved closer to Broichán. He *is* afraid, thought Columba.

"The signs will have to be consulted over this," said Brude. Columba saw an evil gleam in Broichán's eyes and realised exactly what that would mean. There would be another sacrifice, and if Columba and his men did nothing but look on while it happened, they would become unwilling converts to paganism.

It was brilliant. Columba would be humbled, Christianity tarnished and, once the news got around, the Picts would stay in power and the Ridge remain unbroken.

Unless I do something.

Brude saw the realisation cross Columba's face, and then produced his masterstroke. Slowly, casually and sadistically, he said:

"There is a slave girl from Erin here. In honour of your visit, and as you are also a native of Erin, she will be the sacrifice."

To attend the disembowelling of one of my own people! That would be the final humiliation.

Columba heard a rustling amidst the ranks of nobles. Tittering? No. The slave girl was being brought forth.

She was dirty. She had certainly been beaten, had probably been used by several men. But still she was beautiful. A tall, firm-breasted girl with a rosebud mouth, green eyes and a mass of dark auburn hair, shoulder length. And her spirit seemed unbroken. Her eyes were still proud. She still held herself straight.

"What is your name, my girl?" asked the abbot.

"I am Eithne, Father, daughter of Feargal. I come from Antrim."

A flame of anger built up in Columba. Eithne had also been his mother's name. He might even have seen the girl herself in Antrim. He stared at Broichán.

"Know this, Broichán. Know that if you don't free this captive exile before I leave Pictland, you will have little time to live."

"I know no such thing, and it is not I who only has a little time to live."

As one, twelve swords leapt from twelve scabbards behind Columba. The abbot himself had come unarmed. His brothers had been a little more pragmatic. Quite literally, the situation was now balanced on a knife edge.

"If you cut me down," Columba said mildly, "my men will kill you, as many of your nobles as they can, and your king."

"I doubt that," said the druid.

"But you cannot be sure. It isn't wise to do battle with an enemy who has nothing to lose."

Columba saw Broichán's eyes cloud over slightly. The druid was used to political games. He was not used to foes who would freely embrace chaos and their own deaths.

But that was what being *miles Christi* was all about.

Columba saw Brude and Broichán realise that. Then the abbot turned to Drostán and a smile lit up his face.

"Pass me your sword, brother, that I might teach this barbarian a thing or two about faith."

With that, he tossed his satchel to Drostán, catching in return his kinsman's blade. He felt nothing save a fierce joy. Perhaps he had been waiting for this moment all his life. Past and future hung in the balance, but at last the waiting was over.

The sea of shields shaped themselves into a circular arena for Columba and the druid. The abbot easily took up his stance on the hard earth. He was sure he could smell the blood of previous contests underfoot, but the sword was in his hand and he felt his old mastery of its quicksilver motion return. With a studied move, he slit the druid's cloak, opening a shallow cut over the man's ribs. Enough to provoke, but not to kill. Enraged, Broichán grabbed a heavy war axe and slashed wildly at Columba.

That is your first mistake, thought the abbot. A thruster would always beat a slasher. And the war axe was twice as heavy as the slim blade. Broichán was nearly Columba's age and unless he had practised every day, his hands and wrists would soon become desperately tired. The training of a druid was gruelling, but it was not the training of a swordsman.

And Columba himself? In his youth he had been something of a swordsman, and he'd never let himself get entirely out of practice. Now he moved inside and outside the arc of that razor sharp weapon, making the druid miss while conserving his own energy, which would shorten the fight still further.

Of course, if he got careless, a blow from the axe would bring things to a sure and sudden halt. He could hear hoarse invocations from the ramparts above. The Pictish warriors were sure their druid's wizardry would be too much for the Christian. They were wrong. No one except the participants could really tell what was happening in a fight. They could only see Broichán as the victor but that, Columba assured himself, was not going to be the outcome.

Broichán continued to rage, the humiliation of being outclassed in front of his people making his blood boil. *That is your second mistake*, Columba observed. Keeping absolute cool was crucial in a fight. Anger soon exhausted itself and a worn out fighter was easy prey.

So the abbot carefully circled the slashing, tiring druid, occasionally inflicting a light flesh wound for show. Listening to Broichán's ever more laboured breathing. Noting the extra moments it took the druid to heft the axe and swing again, only to hit empty air. His own heart felt light in his chest, his tread soft and airy.

When it came, the end was anticlimactic. A slow motion slash with the axe was deflected, the axe parting from numbed fingers to fly into the crowd and accidentally sever a nobleman's hand. Broichán dropped to his knees before Columba, struggling so frantically for breath the abbot thought he was having a seizure.

Columba turned to Brude, saw fear in his eyes again. *Fear of God, I hope*, he thought. He levelled his sword at the king and for a moment felt tempted. He'd consecrated one king; he could kill another. He could behead Brude and take the spoils back in the satchel.

No. No, he could not. Iona was not the place to display such things. Nor was he the man to do so. He had learnt much since Cul Dreimne.

Aloud, Columba said, "If you are intransigent and refuse to release Eithne, you will die on the spot."

"On your way home," gasped the druid, "I hope you meet an adverse wind, a thick mist, sink and drown!"

"The power of God rules all things," retorted Columba,

"and our comings and goings are directed by his governance. Not by yours."

Gently, he tapped Broichán behind the ear with the hilt of the sword. The druid dropped without a word. Columba saw Eithne's face light up with a smile sweet as dawn breaking over the hills. The abbot noticed Drostán was looking at that beautiful smile even more intently than he was himself.

Now what to do? Perhaps gentler diplomacy was called for. He was getting tired of death threats, whether in God's name or anyone else's.

Columba strode up to Brude and softly told the nonplussed king:

"We can walk one of two ways today. You may execute us and try to cover up the fact. You will fail, of course. The truth always comes out. Or if our people reach Orkney, you can show your regal munificence and tolerance of the Christian faith and its emissaries by commending them to the care of your sub-king."

There was a short pause, but Brude had been High King for nearly thirty years and knew a good deal when he heard one.

Loudly, Brude said:

"You are brave men. I will spare your lives, and those of your kinsmen on the trackless sea, if you return home."

"We will gladly do so," said Columba equally loudly, "but," he added more quietly, "with your permission, my brethren and I would like to travel on into the east for a short time."

This was the most delicate moment. Brude knew a settlement would surely spring up if he allowed Columba's men to march further east. An abbey beyond the Ridge might further annex Pictish territory and convert Pictish tribesmen to Christianity. Brude, however, already had enough enemies and could do without making any more. And a *supernatural* enemy was surely to be feared.

On such delicate moments does the wheel of history turn. Though neither man could know it, Brude's answer to

Columba's request would shape the future of northern Alba for centuries to come.

Grudgingly, Brude agreed.

Columba gritted his teeth to avoid smiling. The day had gone well. Bloodshed had been avoided. He'd achieved his aims and Christianity was poised, slowly and surely, to spread a little further. Brude was certainly less than happy, but Pictish kings tended to have short bloodsoaked reigns. In ten years' time Brude's mutilated body would probably be lying in a field somewhere with several spears sticking out of it and these negotiations would be forgotten. The Ridge, however, had been broken, not with violence (well, not *much* violence) but with words.

Brude did indeed die bloodily in 584 during the battle of Asreth in Angus, but in 580 Columba and his monks reached the area of land Bede had granted them. They had faced death and been spared, so they marched joyously into the east, the land opening up around them, dank forest and crowding trees giving way to rolling hills of emerald green. The cries of seagulls came ever closer, the sea air invigorated heart and lung, promising light and life as Columba, his new disciples and Eithne, hand in hand with Drostán, marched towards the land between Garnait's stone and the rock of the spring. This was a sheltered valley twelve miles from the eastern coast of the territory which itself lay between the Grampians and the Dornoch Firth. They founded the Abbey of Deer there, on a knoll called Tap Tillery by the South Ugie Water.

The territory itself, ruled by sub-kings or *mormaers*, had been fought over by Calgacus and the Romans five centuries before. Centuries later it would be called Moray. Some would say that the abbey really had been named after Drostán's tears, but the English word *deer* and the Gaelic *doire* probably both derive from an ancient Pictish word meaning oak. This valley was home to great gatherings of oak trees, the kind of place where druids would choose to carry out their rituals on Feast days, but also the kind of place where Finnan had met with the spirits at Beltane. Perhaps Columba had wished to mollify Brude by naming a new abbey after an old ritual to bridge the gap between the Picts and the Scots, and to unite beliefs by founding a Christian church upon a place of oaks.

Or perhaps it was just a good site. Carrying the Word to the pagan was not going to be easy, but the future was beckoning and the sceptre of the kingdom was there to be taken.

Columba and Drostán parted at Tap Tillery. The oaks towered above them, enduring and magical. Eithne stayed by Drostán's side, fresh and happy to be free. Columba stood slightly apart from the others, listening to the stream flowing down to the sea, remembering why he had come to this place.

Soldier, statesman and priest was he, but also something of a mercenary and a bit of a wretch. Finnan and Áedán had had the measure of him, all right. And those characteristics had taken Columba a very long way, to the eastern coast of a new territory. There was still so much further to go, though. Further east. Beyond Rome and Byzantium. Past Jerusalem and the Holy Land.

He found himself thinking of another place of oaks, and of Finnan's vision. Of the land between two rivers, the bronze temples and marbled halls where scholars read from tablets written in a strange wedge-shaped script.

He yearned to talk with the scholars. He knew he never would.

"Perhaps you should consecrate the new abbey by burying this book in the foundations," he said to Drostán and Eithne, taking the satchel from his shoulder. "We wouldn't have reached this place without it."

"Better it be read by other fine men," said Drostán. He and Columba clasped hands, tears in their eyes.

"I am not a fine man," Columba said, "I am a wretch, and all I ask is that you say a blessing for my poor soul every now and then."

Drostán nodded, and in the years to come he prayed many times for Columba's soul, occasionally wondering why the great abbot had seemed so humble that day.

Neither Columba nor Drostán knew that, ten years before they parted at Tap Tillery and not far from the land between two rivers, another fine man had been born.

He was an Arab of the tribe of Quraysh, his birthplace would become known as Mecca and he would make the Word flesh in another way. His name was Muhammad and he would be remembered as the prophet chosen to give God's word to his people.

Muhammad's followers copied down the verses the prophet recited. They created a holy book called the Qur'an and founded a religion called Islam.

They were few at first but they quickly grew in number, for they had created their own Cathach and with it, they too would break many Ridges.

8

On 1 May 1997, the voters made their mark and changed history. The Conservative government was wiped out by the pro-devolution New Labour party. It was the Tories' worst defeat since 1832 and with a Commons majority of 179, Labour's greatest victory. The political map of Britain moved from Tory blue to Labour red and the island kingdom which had first begun to be united by Arthur and Columba fourteen hundred years before would never be the same again.

Once in power, New Labour ministers began to squabble about Scottish devolution, putting Secretary of State for Scotland Donald Dewar under intense pressure as he tried to sell devolution via referendum to Scotland *and* Westminster. At least the date of the referendum had already been decided. On September 11 1997, Scots voters would be asked if they agreed that:

Yes, there should be a Scottish Parliament and Yes, it should have tax-varying powers.

A No-No vote would mean no change, while a Yes-No vote would create a tartan talking shop with no power to do anything. Although New Labour was now firmly in power at Westminster, only a Yes-Yes vote in Scotland could empower a restored and devolved Scottish Parliament. The decision rested firmly with the Scots themselves.

The writer William McIlvanney once said *"Scots are forever chapping on doors for years begging to be let in and then when the door finally opens they back off saying:* 'No, no, I didn't want to come in after all'. "

Either way, the United Kingdom was coming to a turning point. Tied together by one political party on the surface, riven by old tribal hatreds beneath. Not certain where it was going, but heading for a referendum dependant on a people who might back off.

Who might not do anything at all.

Walking in Moidart, John Sandiman took little notice of the political storm. Compared to the way Kenneth Mac Alpin had united Scotland in 843, the present election and referendum was nothing more than a distracting bore. Now that he'd made the break from the daily grind and embarked on his crazy quest, he was pleased to find out he really was a bit of an unreconstructed macho idiot. He'd never thought much of politicians. Government just created more government and devolution was a joke which would only further divide a deteriorating country.

Kenneth Mac Alpin had achieved exactly the opposite with brutal efficiency. What would the wretches in modern-day Parliament have made of him?

Wretches.

The word stuck in his mind. Regarding the Book of Deer itself, it was very important. His research work at the Mitchell Library) had uncovered the fact that the whole manuscript had been written by a single scribe at the Abbey of Deer in the ninth century. Rather than glory in his achievement the man had added a downright downbeat colophon as his epitaph, asking only that everyone who used that splendid little book to say a blessing for his wretched soul.

There would never be any way of finding out what the scribe's motivation had been, or why he'd composed such a humble elegy.

Perhaps only a writer of fiction could bring that noble wretch back to life. Perhaps he could also weave a coherent story from the plot elements hovering about Kenneth Mac Alpin's consecration in 843, the wars between Pict and Scot along the Ridge of Alba and the Cathachs, but nobody would ever know what had *really* happened ...

The Tale of The Book of Deer

Part Three

*"There's but ae law for Jew an Greek
an ane alane for Scot an Saxon"*

(The Declaration of Arbroath)

*"We believe in and confess one God,
admittedly in a different way."*

(Pope Gregory VII to
Mussalman ruler
al-Nasir, 1076)

The Scots, it is said, had journeyed from Greater Scythia by the Tyrrhene Sea and the Pillars of Hercules, had dwelt in Spain among the barbarians and, twelve hundred years after the transit of Israel, had won that habitation in the west known as the Kingdom of Scotland.

The Byzantine Empire had succeeded Rome in the fourth century and reached from the Holy Land to the borders of Alba. Free from Roman rule, Western Europe was now a rough patchwork of kingdoms where holy men like Martin of Tours and Ninian of Whithorn brought the word to warring Lombards, Franks, Visigoths, Britons, Angles and Saxons. Monasteries were founded and icons venerated as a Christian unity was slowly forged.

For one empire, one church. A universal or, one might say, *catholic* Church. At and after the Synod of Whitby in 664, this Roman Catholic Church began to hone itself on the slow forge, Romanised Angles and Saxons fighting with Gaels and Irish Scots to decide what form the orthodox church of the British Isles would take. But elsewhere, another church was also evolving into an empire.

Muhammad's people had swept out of Arabia, pushing back the borders of Byzantium to conquer North Africa in the west and convert the Persian Empire in the east. They reached Jerusalem in 638 and invaded Crete, Sicily and Spain in the eighth and ninth centuries.

The followers of Muhammad believed in no god but God, but also, according to his words in the Qur'an, that all should submit to Islam and be known as Muslims – those who practised Islam.

They had not been to the Synod of Whitby, and nor would they have accepted an orthodox non-Islamic church if they had. This was a pity, for with knowledge of papermaking and bookbinding gleaned from Chinese prisoners and Ethiopian scribes, Islamic calligraphers and illustrators were copying and transforming Muhammad's verses into works of art to equal the iconic Cathachs of the Celtic world.

Christendom and Islam. Two empires united by one God and the books which held his word and image, but divided by theology and locked in struggle over possession of Jerusalem.

More the pity when the struggle was misguided. Muslims had learnt some tolerance for the Christians and Jews they conquered in Jerusalem but Western Christendom had learnt no such tolerance for Muslims. Confusing theological challenge with conquest by sword, Christians painted Muslims as monsters while Muslims accepted Christians as 'people of the Book.'

Forgetting Finnan's respect for the light of civilisation from the east, Christians waged war against barbarians who were making great strides in science and the arts, pagans who invaded other countries and treated the local populations well and savages like the caliph al-Aziz who built a great library in Cairo. At a time when the largest libraries of Western Christendom had only a few hundred manuscripts, the caliph's library held over half a million books.

Twenty-four hundred of them were illuminated Qur'ans, and as the empires chafed at each other's borders, Christian scribes learnt the art of illumination from Muslim calligraphers.

'Threatened' from without by so-called barbarians and threatened from within by power struggles for kingdoms and their sceptres, Alba warred with itself for the next three centuries. Arthur and Columba were but memories and without a king to unite the tribes, Picts battled against Irish Scots, Britons fought their way north of Strathclyde, Angles took part in border skirmishes and Norsemen pillaged the coast. Bloody conflicts spilt back and forth across the Ridge as the House of Dalriada moved east from Dunadd, the dewars carrying the Stone of Destiny to Fortriu, a kingdom in central Scotland sheltered to the north by the Grampians and to the west by the Ridge.

Picts and Scots found common ground at Fortriu and peace was made in 843 when Kenneth Mac Alpin, consecrated at the Palace of Scone on the Stone of Destiny, became King of both Picts and Scots. He inherited a country of kindred tribal lands growing up around abbeys like Iona and Deer which, like Constantine and Áedán before him, he began to unite.

By the mid-ninth century, the Pictish way of life in Moray was dying out. Some Picts were being raised as Christians at the Abbey of Deer. Others had fallen in battles with the Scots, Britons, Angles and Norsemen who continued to squeeze their territories in a vise from west and north, so when the son of Alpin was crowned it seemed that the day of the Picts was well and truly done.

On a cold grey morning in 848, a stubborn old monk walked away from the Abbey of Deer and towards the sea. Although nominally a Christian who fasted on Wednesdays and celebrated the Eucharist on Sundays, he lived more in fear of the pagan gods and the blood sacrifices they demanded of his Pictish ancestors than he respected the Divine Offices of a pacifist Lord. He was an able Latin scholar with an artist's hand, but he'd sidestepped the abbot's recent requests for him to copy a new book of gospel in the Vulgate. It was as if once he put quill to vellum, his soul would be given to the Christian deity once and for all, and his beliefs would be no more.

He was neither Pict nor Christian. He belonged nowhere!

So he walked away, turning only once to look back at the monastic enclosure which, like Iona's settlement, was composed of church, domestic buildings and guest-house. Once a fortress founded deep in Pictish territory by Columba, the abbey was now a place where Pictish children went to school. He had been one of those children. He himself had gone uncomplainingly but his brother had rebelled, disappearing into the forests to join a sect of Picts who repudiated the new God Columba had forced upon them.

Adomnán, a later abbot of Iona, had even written a *Life of St Columba*, full of propaganda such as Columba's last words, supposedly about foreign nations revering Iona. There was a copy at Deer but the monk had refused to read it. There was still a small settlement on Iona itself, although most of the monks had fled to a new monastery in Erin after Norsemen had pillaged the island, killing seventy members of the community and martyring their leader. They had split his sternum, pulled his lungs from his ribcage and draped them over his shoulders. The Norsemen called this method of slaughter the blood-eagle and, after it was done, they suspended the mutilated body from a stone cross.

The monk got into his stride, and despite his age the miles seemed to flow by. It was an easy route to the sea, through rolling hills and past small settlements. *Christian* settlements, though, he thought sourly. Once he saw a small wooden church. He turned away and spat.

He had thought of his brother often, but had not seen him for many years until a great battle in Fortriu, five years before.

How the high shields had clashed that day, as Scot fought Pict for the final time! Until then, the monk had not left the abbey in many years. He had not really wished to, for he'd been fascinated by the ancient books in the scriptorium. The Cathachs. They had rested there for many years, carrying the words and waiting to take the fight to the barbarians, and chief among them had been a copy of the Gospel of St Martin.

It was said that Columba himself had carried the copy to Deer, and although the monk sometimes felt he should have hated the man and his works, he could not hate the book. It was beautiful, and early in the evenings it almost seemed to glow.

Then the call from the king had come, and once again a Cathach was needed. But to care for the Cathach a dewar was also required. Dewars were a sect responsible for the care of sacred relics like the Cathach. The monk was the nearest thing to a dewar the abbey could find, so they'd given him the job of carrying it in its reliquary on the long road to Fortriu.

The army had camped on the banks of the Tay, wondering when battle would commence. They knew that Picts would be lying in wait in the forest. They did not know that Kenneth had asked to confer with the last of the Pictish nobility.

Kenneth Mac Alpin of the House of Dalriada. Successor to Áedán Mac Gabran who had warred against the Picts for thirteen years. After Áedán had come Eochaid Bude. Then Domnall Brecc. Aed Find. Fergus. Constantine ...

A line of Scots kings whose power-base had shifted inland as the Norsemen had laid waste to the Western Isles and pillaged the west coast of northern Alba. For the same reason, Craig Phádraig had been abandoned as the Pictish High Kings had moved south to Fortriu, settling between the rivers Tay and Earn.

The Scottish House of Dalriada and the Pictish House of Fortriu had mixed, but until the day of Kenneth Mac Alpin, no single king had ruled both Houses.

No one knew where Kenneth had been born, although

it was said he was from Lorne and claimed descent from Domnall Brecc. It was also said that Kenneth had married a Norse chieftain's daughter.

A Scot allied to the Norsemen who could also dominate the Picts would have tremendous power, but the Picts would not just *let* themselves be dominated...

Hence the conference with the Pictish nobility. Politics.

The monk had presumed that the Cathach had been called for as a symbol of past glories and a demonstration of traditional power. Other Cathachs had been there, one in the hands of a monk from Lindisfarne, but still he'd felt uneasy. Kenneth was known for savage violence, not gentle diplomacy.

Kenneth had arrived later that day. The king had ridden along the riverbank with his retinue and waited. As dusk approached, the shadows of the forest coalesced into Picts who'd left the places of their oaks. And as the monk looked at the line of proud, painted men, his eye had been drawn to one in particular. Although he himself wore a corded habit and his hair was properly tonsured while the other was bare-chested and bearded, blood had called to blood. He realised he was staring at his brother.

His brother had turned – the monk noting absently that their profiles were identical – and broken into a smile. The monk found himself smiling back, and for a moment time had seemed to pause.

But then there'd been the sound of swords being loosed from scabbards. The conference was a sham, the slaughter had begun and the monk was an accessory to it.

The Picts fought hopelessly as Kenneth's men made short work of them. Stark images would stay forever in the monk's mind. A severed hand in the shallows of the river. An elderly Pict clutching his own blue-white intestines as if he might replace them in his gut, ripped open by a sword. A figure with an axe embedded deep in his chest staggering about for several moments before the great arteries of the heart gave way, the wretch going down in a frothing torrent of blood. Blood on the water.

And his brother, fighting his way towards Kenneth in a berserk rage. Kenneth coolly drawing him in, smoothly gutting him like a fish.

The monk seemed to see it happen in slow motion. Cathach forgotten, he found himself running to his brother, holding him as he cursed and railed against Christianity and the Scots. Watching him as he died, thick venous blood soaking through the monk's habit.

The water ran red for a time, and twilight fell in a mist of blood through which Kenneth could be seen in outline. The king was squat and broad-shouldered. A small dark man not unlike Brude Mac Maelchon, his long face outlined by a coal-black beard framing blue eyes which burned with frightening intensity.

All of this had happened within sight of Scone.

Kenneth's consecration upon a Stone of black basalt took place two days later. The bodies of the slaughtered Picts had been left crucified outside the gates of the Palace. It was a brutal, obvious warning. No one wished to join the crucified, so no one had disputed Kenneth's kingship of both Picts and Scots. It was a consecration bathed in blood, the antithesis of Columba's consecration of Áedán and confrontation of Brude.

The blood-spattered copy of St Martin's Gospel had added lustre to the ceremony. The monk held on to it throughout the proceedings. First there'd been the oath of accession, then the laying-on of hands (ordination), next the recitation of the ancient line of kings by an elder. Finally, bishops had given fealty and laymen had paid homage. The land of the Scots had been united at last, but only by means of a massacre. Flecks of dried blood were still lodged in the new king's beard.

When, finally, it was over, the monk had fled the palace, found his brother's crucified body and wept bitter tears beneath it.

The book was still beautiful, but terrible things had been done in its name. And he had been party to it.

He'd eventually been allowed to take his brother's body down. He buried it in a place of oaks and offered up his brother's spirit to Cernunnos and Donn.

The monk had thought of vanishing into the forests like his brother had, but there was no sect left to join and his woodcraft had long deserted him. He had thought of killing himself, but he had wanted too much to live.

He was a coward, a wretched coward. He was tied to the Scots, tied to their abbeys, and tied, by the book in his hand, to their God. He hated himself.

The monk reluctantly returned to the abbey with his brothers, but he said not a word on the long march from Fortriu to Deer and once back, had little time for the rules.

He had grumbled constantly, neglected the Divine Offices, left and been received back three times, been rebuked, felt the stroke of the rod and been forced to prostrate himself at the entrance to the oratory time and again.

The only thing he'd still been any good for was taking care of the Cathachs. That was the only duty he did not neglect, and he did not know why.

After five miserable years, his loathing for the abbey and for himself became so great he just walked away. This was the fourth time he'd left and he knew he could not expect to be received back.

He went right on walking.

Late that afternoon, the monk reached the headlands and walked to the edge. He stood there, frozen by wind and soaked by spray. If he'd come here to punish himself, he reflected, he'd certainly picked the best possible location. If he stayed much longer the soaking misery would become unbearable.

He looked out to sea, and it seemed he'd come to a place where Nature held absolute sway: earth, air and water pounding each other in endless trinity. Against that, all the hopes and fears of his life and of those who'd lived before faded away. He was alone with a history that was dust and a future he did not want. He was fated to kneel to a deity he did not trust in an abbey that would never be his home. The monk began bitterly to curse. He cursed Kenneth Mac Alpin for slaughtering his brother. Then, as spray blinded him and his anger built, he cursed his abbot and the other monks. Finally, recklessly, he cursed the Lord.

The wind dropped for a moment, like a sharply indrawn breath. Then the monk saw or felt a whiteness come upon him, lifting him from the rocks upon which he stood and flinging him headlong into a dark well of despair. His breath froze in his throat as it seemed his soul was plucked from his chest in the manner of a spiritual blood-eagle and he realised that, although his carcass might be found on the rocks in the matin, all that he truly was would remain in this well forever, without hope of pardon.

That was worse than sacrifice. Blood sacrifice was *quick*. This Christian Lord would leave you to contemplate your sins for all eternity.

Then it got even worse. Approaching him through the murk, he saw three apparitions shaped like old women. Cold, smoky figures who wafted around him, chanting gutturally.

Witches.

The monk struck out blindly and began to quote St Martin's Gospel.

At first his panicky words had some effect. The apparitions recoiled and seemed poised to slink away, but then they re-formed close by and a cauldron materialised with them. A terrible gurgling came from it and the monk saw what awaited him. Surrounded by demons, he was to be boiled alive for all eternity. The stench of cooked human flesh filled his nostrils and he felt the fraying strands of his sanity begin to snap, one by one.

Inch by unwilling inch, icy fingers dragged him to the cauldron. He looked down, he beheld the cauldron's awful contents, and he screamed. He screamed as he'd never screamed before. Not even as a child, when his father had told him tales of the ancient druids; nor when he'd seen his brother gutted by Kenneth Mac Alpin.

For before him *was* his brother. His brother whom he'd seen dying in agony. His brother who had spat upon the Christian God and died an unrepentant pagan, railing against Kenneth and the Scots. His brother who now rose up from the cauldron, his fishbelly skin seared burgundy by the sour waters, the gaping hole in his stomach plugged by a writhing mass of bloated maggots, black blood bubbling in one empty eye socket, the other eye fixed firmly on the monk.

With a terrible clack, his jaw opened. A maggot or two fell from his lips in a stream of goo and faint words issued from the remains of his mouth.

"Say a blessing for my soul..."

Hearing this, the monk staggered in shock. His brother's rotting hand reached out to him, but the monk realised that if he entered into that embrace, the witches would have him and he would pass into their domain. He would become an unquiet spirit lost in the cauldron's putrid depths, forever without rest or peace. A shadow without substance in a dark pagan world.

"I cannot join you, brother," he said simply. If the witches were going to take him, let them take him, but he would not go *willingly*.

The witches ceased swirling around him, tangling their fingers in his hair, and his brother sank back into the hissing cauldron, his face a mask of pain and sadness. Sadness and pain at returning to those depths but also, half-seen in his one eye, a glimmer of hope.

The monk felt whiteness encroaching upon the corners of his eyes, and welcomed it.

"Say a blessing for my soul..."

The shocking words hung in his memory. Blessing was *Christian*.

Why would his brother ask for this? What had he seen in the afterlife?

The next thing the monk felt was a sensation of peace and warmth, and as he floated up through layers of compressed consciousness the next thing he saw was a shining light.

He opened his eyes. He was back in his bed at the Abbey of Deer. The abbot was at his side. Despite himself, the monk felt grateful.

"Well, you caused us all some concern," the abbot was saying. "Out three days in that awful weather! We'd quite given up hope when one of the brethren found you by the headlands, half-starved and half-dead. It's a miracle you survived the cart ride back to Deer."

Three days? That had to be wrong. He couldn't have lasted three days and nights outdoors without a lot more protection than he he'd taken with him. Surely not.

Late that night, the abbot found the monk in the oratory. They stared at each other in the light of the candles for some minutes. Pict and Scot. Pagan and Christian.

"My brother asked me to pray for him," the monk said finally.

"Your brother died five years ago at the hands of our king."

"He died five years ago. I should have died five days ago. Instead, I see my brother and he asks me to pray for him. To say words from the Cathachs for him. He who died pagan! I do not know why I live. I do not know why he would ask this of me. What did he see in the afterlife? What did he see?"

"Perhaps," the abbot ventured, "your brother saw the Word made flesh, and was converted."

The monk shook his head wearily. He had never understood the metaphor.

"What *is* the Word made flesh?" he finally asked.

The abbot paused, wondering how best to reply. The monk had always been a grudging convert, mouthing the words in the Cathachs with no idea of the meaning they carried. For the last five years he'd been downright impossible. Perhaps he was finally changing. But an intricate answer would get them both nowhere.

"Latin words on calfskin flesh," he said simply. Then, more seriously, he went on. "They are a means of moving closer to, of communing with, God. The words of the Gospels cannot themselves suffice. Pictures alone cannot illuminate, but together the words and pictures in the Cathachs may let the penitent catch a glimpse of the kingdom of heaven. Perhaps that is what your brother saw."

The monk nodded. He had always thought the books were beautiful, but never known why he felt that way. Now he was getting an inkling.

"But who am I, that he should do this for me?"

The abbot ran a hand through his red hair and decided honesty was the best policy.

"I don't really know who you are. You're not a pagan, you're not much of a Christian either. You haven't really got the guts to decide *what* you are. All I can say is that, for all your flaws and frailties, you're a monk like many others living in monasteries all over Christendom, secure in His love and close to His word."

"I don't know if that is enough."

For a moment, the abbot's temper flared. What else could he do, for heaven's sake?

"Well, it's a start, you poor wretch!" he snapped.

A start. The abbot's words stayed with the monk through the night as he wandered the grounds of the abbey. He finally found himself back in the scriptorium where he'd previously been so reluctant to put quill to vellum.

Perhaps he'd been given a new start. He had even been received back a fourth time.

The quill, plucked from a goose's tail, still lay at rest in its conical inkwell. The vellum waited. The calfskin pages had been dipped in lime, stretched taut on wooden frames and ruled into patient lines. He had a good supply of iron-gall ink boiled down from oak-apples and iron sulphate. Then there were the pigments. Beautiful colours applied by brushes made from the soft winter coats of pine martens. Deep browns, emerald greens and chalk whites were mixed locally. Others had to be imported. Shades from pink to purple and known as extract of folium came from Mediterranean sunflowers. Bright red kermes was concocted from the ground-up bodies of North African insects and ultramarine created from gemstones of lapis lazuli.

These were the ingredients, this was how it had begun. The way of the Word, first made flesh by ancient scribes. The flesh illuminated by artists who learnt their skills in the East. The Gospels preserved in monasteries, the monasteries surrounded by the people, the people migrating across Christendom...

Constantine had read the Gospels. Then Martin. Ninian and Finnan. Columba. So many others.

A beautiful tapestry.

The monk looked at the vellum for a long time, and came to a decision. He found a gospel to copy, picked up the quill and began to write.

Liber generationis Jesu Christi filii David, filii Abraham.

A quibis majoribus Christus secundum carnem descenderit: angelus instruit Joseph de Mariae sponsae suae conceptione, partuque futureo...

He wrote for over an hour, seeing the words uncoil smoothly before him until the candles burned low. Finally he sat back, satisfied.

He didn't really understand the words of the Book of Matthew, his copy of the Latin was crude, but it was a start.

He stood, then turned to the oratory where he prostrated himself and prayed for the soul of his brother. It was the first time the monk had willingly humbled himself. Perhaps it was in silent acknowledgement of his role. He was unworthy, but he'd been given the skills of a scribe. He should have died at the headlands, but he'd been given his life.

There had to be a reason.

Perhaps if he illuminated a fine manuscript, created a fine Cathach, his brother's soul would find peace.

A worthy goal.

He himself was a wretch, but that would be his work.

Those words found an echo, far in the past, which gave light to a vision. The monk saw a faded image of a man standing on a knoll by a stream. He had the presence of a great abbot, but looked humbled, wretched, and seemed to be asking for his soul to be blessed.

The image died away and the monk was alone again.

Perhaps the work of God was often done by wretches, he mused. Little men who little knew how well their labours would endure. Now he was one of them, but at least he knew it, and when his work was done, why, he could ask for a blessing on behalf of them all.

All eighty-six folios of the Book of Deer, one of the great Celtic illuminated Gospels combining the Western tradition of the Cathach and the art of the East, were written at Deer in the ninth century by a single scribe. The writer's crude knowledge of Irish Vulgate Latin led to arguments over whether the Book was the work of a Pictish or Scottish scribe; but there was no question that as well as its main Latin text with the Gospels of Matthew, Mark, Luke and John it carried a unique Old Irish Gaelic colophon added by the same scribe at the end of his labours:

"For chubus caich duini i mbia arrath in lebrán collí
ara tardda bendacht for anmain intruagáin rodscríbai."

(Let it be on the conscience of everyone who uses this splendid little book, that they say a blessing for the soul of the wretch who wrote it.)

From the Latin Vulgate and Old Irish Gaelic flowed a new language and, over two centuries later, notes in a new form of Gaelic – Scottish Gaelic – were added to the manuscript to tell the story, by then legend, of the founding of the Abbey of Deer.

Those notes were Scotland's first words:

> Colùcille 7 drostan m̄c cosgreg adalta
> tangator ahi marroalseg dia doib go
> nic abbordobor 7bede cruthnec robomor
> mær bucan araginn 7 esse rothidnaig doib
> īgatraig sain īsaere gobraith omormaer
> 7othosec...

> Columba and Drostán son of Coscrach,
> his disciple, came from Iona, as God guided them,
> to Aberdour; and Bede the Pict was mormaer
> of Buchan on their arrival; and it is he who
> bestowed on them that monastery, in freedom
> till Doomsday from mormaer and toísech...

Once the Book of Deer was written, the nameless monk may have made a pilgrimage to Iona where he found the abbot Indrechtach taking Columba's relics to Erin. Perhaps the monk helped the abbot carry the relics across the sea. Amongst them, there was an unfinished manuscript from Iona which he took to the community's new home. There he and other scribes completed it, and it became the chief gospel of their new abbey.

The Abbey of Kells.

9

I haven't planned ahead! thought Sandiman suddenly. *I haven't worked this out. What am I really going to do with the bloody Book when – if – I manage to steal it?* A tidal wave of worry swept through him. He was throwing his life away, deliberately arranging things so he would end up homeless, jobless and with a criminal record and he didn't know what he was actually going to *do* with the sodding manuscript if he even managed to spirit it out of Cambridge University Library.

Shit, shit, shit, shit, shit...

Okay, stop swearing and think. *You're a librarian, for God's sake. You think all the time. Usually about boring stuff, but you can't have completely lost the habit. Somewhere in this strange fretwork pattern you're sawing will be the answer.*

Just think. Find a somewhere to think – there'll be a bed-and-breakfast place in the next village. Get a room. Stare at the ceiling and work out your place in the tangled scheme of things.

In a fury of fear and impatience, Sandiman found a B&B – run by a stern landlady with a large girth – and in a remarkably short time had settled upon a suitable ceiling at which to stare. He thought back to Ellis's book again. According to the text, the Book of Deer had disappeared sometime in the twelfth or thirteenth century and only been rediscovered four centuries later.

Four centuries. Where had it gone, and why?

The Tale of The Book of Deer

Part Four

Picture the scene: Scone, 1296.
You are the Abbot of Scone and have
been warned that Edward, the King of England,
is approaching and he has vowed to take any
and every symbol of Scottish sovereignty. Do you:

a) Do nothing?

b) Defend the Stone to the death,
lose your life and lose the Stone
thus achieving nothing?

c) Hide the real Stone and replace it with
something else completely worthless
and a wee bit embarrassing?

According to some, the Abbot chose option 'c' and
solemnly handed Edward the lid of a cesspit.

(Scotland on Sunday. 1 December 1996)

By the first millennium, Western Europe was moving away from the dark years after the fall of Rome. European kingdoms were becoming nation-states while the Byzantine Empire corrupted, levying too much money from its provinces to pay for too many lavish churches. Monastic and chivalric orders like the Benedictines, Cistercians and Knights Templar were founded, the monks fighting corruption by preserving the way of life advocated by Ninian and Columba, the knights protecting Christian pilgrims from Muslims.

The move into the light was far from smooth and the road had many potholes. Eastern and Western Christendom split during this time but still began retaking their lands from the Muslims. In the eleventh century Christians captured the Byzantine capital Constantinople, pushed south into Spain and mounted the Crusades to regain Jerusalem. They occupied the Holy City in 1099 but Saladin recaptured it in 1187 and Jerusalem was finally surrendered to Islam in 1244.

As the empires fought, their knowledge continued to change hands. Christians entering the Islamic city of Cordoba in Spain congratulated themselves on vanquishing the barbarous pagans who'd built the second largest city in Europe and equipped it with plumbing and public street lamps. They then turned their attention to Cordoba's library, translating thousands of beautifully bound texts from Arabic to Latin and promptly delivering the essence of Persian, Greek and Arab science and culture to the first universities.

North of the new Europe, Kenneth Mac Alpin's kingdom was now long united as the nation of Scotland. Peace had been made with England and the Royal House of Plantaganet. The Abbey of Deer, which David I of the House of Canmore had enjoined no one should harm, crumbled away and in 1219 Cistercian monks founded a monastery not far from its ruins.

Alexander III of the House of Canmore reigned from 1249 to 1286. He championed Scotland's unity and independence, bought the Hebrides (including Iona) from Norway, and attended the Plantagenet king Edward Longshanks' coronation in 1274. But when he died, the House of Canmore fell and Longshanks began trying to conquer Scotland.

To do so, he intended to seize the symbols of Scottish sovereignty and depose their king, John Balliol, last heir to the House of Canmore. This was how he'd subjugated Wales. He would subjugate Scotland the same way.

It is well known that Edward Longshanks looted the Stone of Destiny from Scone in 1296 on his way home. It is less well known that the Book of Deer disappeared from the monastery of Deer at about that time, *when Edward's crusade had reached as far north as Moray.*

Deer: 1296

The abbot knew trouble was coming. First the sack of Berwick. Next the loss of Dunbar. Then the capture of Andrew Murray, heir to the estates of Moray and a patriotic Scot. Now the news that Longshanks was marching further north than he ever had before, making it clear he regarded Scotland as his own and showing his contempt for John Balliol.

How futile it all was, thought the abbot. He looked out at the green fields of Buchan, musing on the progress that had been made since the days of the pagans. Although nothing could truly compensate for the loss of Jerusalem at least there was trade with Norway. Fine monasteries and cathedrals built with methods learnt from England and France graced Scotland's hills and glens. Scottish sheriffdoms and royal burghs were growing wealthy on the trade of wool, coal and salt. There was peaceful tenant farming. Above all, the Cistercians and other orders were spreading the Word throughout Christendom.

The first Cistercian monastery had been founded in 1098 at Cîteaux in Burgundy. Now there were over five hundred abbeys scattered across Europe, each living a monastic way of life designed to give order and stability to an uncertain world. The design of the abbeys might vary, but all the monks were robed in white and all carried out God's work in the same way.

At the heart of each abbey were the stone pillars of a square cloister garth. This garth adjoined a church composed of nave, oratory, north and south transepts, and an eastern presbytery. Together the nave, transepts and presbytery created the shape of a cross while the garth embodied the cloistered life of the monks, distanced from the outside world's distractions.

To the north of the garth, sheltered by the nave, was the scriptorium where the Cathachs still waited. East of the garth, reached by a passage called a slype, was the chapter house to which the abbot summoned the monks for counsel or reproof. Next to the chapter house was the parlour, where monks could talk freely. On the floor above the chapter house and parlour was the long dormitory, at the north end of which a stair led down to the south transept of the church.

East of the chapter house and separated from it by a paved forecourt were the abbot's house and the infirmary. South of the garth was the kitchen and refectory, and to the west were the workshops where lay brethren toiled. Herb and vegetable gardens did have to be tended, after all, and crops had to be farmed.

The monks' ordered lives were ruled by the Divine Offices of the day: Lauds, Prime, Terce, Sext, None, Vespers and Compline, plus the Night Office of Vigils. It was a healthy rhythm of manual labour, prayer spoken in plainsong, reading after Compline, silence for contemplation.

It was also a battle for holy obedience, leavened with an understanding of frailty.

At Deer the battle was going well, the abbot thought. Little grumbling, few excommunications of monks at fault, even fewer departures of brothers touched by evil. He felt a small stirring of pride, and reminded himself of the words in Luke.

"Quia omnis qui se exaltat humiliabitur et qui se humiliate exaltabitur"

(Whoever exalts himself shall be humbled, and he who humbles himself will be exalted).

Wise words, but the corruption which had made a sixth century scholar called Benedict of Nursia create the rules by which the orders lived still festered. Benedict had retreated to a cave near Rome to write the rules. Some said he'd seen visions of Rome, St Sophia and cities of bronzed temples and marbled halls between the Tigris and Euphrates. There was an old tale that Columba's master, Finnan, had seen something similar before he sent Columba to Iona, but such stories were only legend.

Meanwhile, despite the schism between the Eastern church and the Roman papacy, lavish churches were still being built and the levy imposed by Pope Gregory X on ecclesiastical income to build such churches and finance another Crusade was particularly harsh. The papacy was also allowing Longshanks to collect the levy, but taking money from Scotland would not appease the Plantaganet king. Only complete sovereignty over England and Scotland would satisfy him, and Longshanks preferred rule by force to the diplomatic pursuit of peaceful union.

Futile.

From the south the abbot began faintly to hear the sound of horses. It sounded like a moving column. There was no specific reason to feel a sense of foreboding, but suddenly he suspected the way of life he'd just been exalting was about to be humbled. He called for the porter, who arrived promptly.

"Get the brothers in from the fields. Immediately. I think there's trouble coming."

"Your Grace... what?"

The porter was old, arthritic and deaf. Nor had he been very bright in the first place. Not surprisingly, the tired old brain cells simply refused to comprehend such a change from the routine. The abbot took one look at the porter's blank and rheumy eyes and took the stairs himself, running across the paved stones of the forecourt in his corded habit and frantically ringing the bell to summon the monks. When they presented themselves in the chapter house, the abbot told them of his fears. The monks, thankfully, were younger and more able than his porter. They acted quickly.

When the English knight swept into the monastery at the head of his Northumbrian militia, some of the most important artefacts had already been safely stored away. In the monks' minds, though, was the knowledge that Longshanks' men were perfectly willing to kill them all. The way they'd murdered the Flemings in Berwick, burning them alive in their own house, the Red Hall.

But at first, all seemed peaceful. The knight wearily doffed his helm, asked for food and provisions for his men and horses, and confined his questions only to the whereabouts of the scriptorium. But the question, so casually asked by the Norman, alerted the abbot immediately.

They know of the Book, he thought. *They know of the Book and they want it. More than likely that is the only reason they are here. But even if we hand it over without a struggle, they will likely sack the monastery anyway. If only the Book could be hidden as easily as the Stone of Destiny had been.*

But while a rock could easily be camouflaged, a Celtic work of art was another matter entirely. It was unique.

The night passed slowly as the abbot and the monks waited in an agony of anticipation. It was almost a relief when the door to the abbot's house crashed open and the knight strode in after Lauds the following day.

The abbot forced himself slowly to turn and look at the knight with an expression of mild surprise and kindly interest. He tried not to think about the fate of the Flemings.

"Can I help you, Sir Godfrey? Do your men have any further needs?"

"No... no thank you, abbot. They have been well-fed and watered, and we will be taking our leave of you soon."

"I wish you a peaceful journey."

The abbot saw a cloud cross the knight's eyes. *He doesn't like this any more than I do,* he realised.

"I have been to your scriptorium, but I cannot see which manuscript is the one King Edward commanded me to deliver to him."

The knight was trying to give him a way out, the abbot thought. The options were clear: hand it over and I will leave in peace. Fail to do so and I will carry out my king's orders, no matter how I feel about it.

The abbot knew then that he had reached a turning-point in his life. He could save himself, his monks and his monastery from harm by acquiescing without protest, by deserting his beliefs in the face of danger. Or he could put his faith to the test.

He remembered one of the rules of Saint Benedict, so clearly it hurt.

The abbot himself must fear God and keep the rule in everything he does; he can be sure beyond any doubt that he will have to give an account of all his judgments to God, the most just of judges.

There really was no choice. He *had* to keep the rule.

"I fear I cannot help you," he said slowly, knowing he was signing his own death warrant. "You see, King David once decreed that no one should dare harm either ourselves or our property, or improperly exact from us that which we did not wish to give. Would you spit on the words of a consecrated king?"

The knight looked at the abbot for a long and terrible moment. He was no longer young and the enticements Longshanks had originally placed before him to become a knight – influence at court and a high station in society – had palled. He would never forget the Welsh campaign of 1282 or the slaughter at Berwick. He was here now for no other reason than to avoid the relief he would otherwise have to pay to take over the family estates.

Longshanks would do here what he had already done in Wales. Invade, give no quarter, mercilessly destroy the sacred symbols of another culture. Sir Godfrey was a Christian and in his heart of hearts had long ago admitted to himself that he hated his king's politics of terror. But for all that, he had kissed the ring finger of his liege's hand at the Abbey of West Minster and ridden up from the South with Longshanks. And, above all, he was a dutiful subject of the King of England.

"You damn us both, sir," he grated, locking eyes with the abbot.

Sick at heart, he strode from the abbot's house and told his men to begin the sack of the monastery. The first monk to die was the old porter, his head literally lopped from his shoulders as the soldiers went about their work with rather too much enthusiasm. A fountain of blood erupted from the scrawny neck as the figure in the habit went down, legs kicking frantically. For a moment Sir Godfrey thought the headless man might even run round the forecourt, but the wizened old frame quickly gave up the ghost.

Lighted torches were thrown into the infirmary and soon it was aflame. The monks scattered into the fields as the militia began to run them through for sport, and Sir Godfrey closed his eyes as an auburn-haired girl who'd come from the nearby village of Aberdour to pick herbs was pinned to the ground and raped. It didn't help. He could still see the abbot's eyes burning into him.

If he took the Book now, they could leave this place. He strode back to the scriptorium and broke down the door. Facing him was the Keeper of the scriptorium, an aged cleric with yellowed teeth and weary eyes. The Keeper stood before the manuscripts which, bound in gold, lay chained to long shelves of dark wood. The knight faced him, his hand on the pommel of his sword.

"Where is the book of the abbey, Keeper?"

"I cannot tell you," the old man replied calmly, and Sir Godfrey realised he had no fear of death. The manuscripts surrounding them really had become more valuable to the Keeper than life itself; defending them was his destiny. For a moment Sir Godfrey wondered if he was facing a *librarius* – a magician, prophet and keeper of books – who would leave him languishing in pain and crying for mercy as the flames of Hell consumed him. But the moment passed and the weary old man gave himself away. He involuntarily glanced to his right, at a well-bound but innocuous volume. The gesture spoke volumes to a soldier used to dealing with foes in battle. The knight tried to avoid the inevitable one last time.

"By order of your king, move aside!"

The Keeper merely shook his head, his lips moving in prayer.

Hating himself, the knight raised his sword and ran the Keeper through. He smelt the stench of blood and wondered if that stench would still permeate the books hundreds of years in the future.

And the Book of Deer itself? Now that he knew which manuscript it was, the knight was struck by a profound sense of awe. For this, the monks had been willing to defy a king and lay down their lives. He admired their stand, useless as it had been. He unchained it and leafed through the pages, recognising the Latin words of the New Testament on pages bordered by flowing Celtic knotwork and occasionally obscured by crude renderings of crows, ravens and deer. Then he turned to the colophon at the end of the book and looked at the Gaelic entreaty.

For chubus caich duini i mbia arrath in lebrán collí
ara tardda bendacht for anmain intruagáin rodscríbai.

He couldn't work out what it meant, could not share in the sacrament of the words. Once, as a boy in a country church, he'd seen another illuminated manuscript, had been told it was a gateway to heaven, and had stared at the colours and pictures in wonder.

He didn't have that sense of wonder any more. No man could bathe himself in blood and then look upon God's kingdom. No king should force his will upon a people by stealing their icons, their *identities*.

It was unchristian, but it was the king's will. King first, God after, or so it seemed.

He picked up the Book and wearily walked down to the forecourt with it. Two of his militiamen were waiting for him; the abbot was sprawled on the smooth stones between them. Both of the soldiers were wearing wolfish grins. In memory of the maiden they'd raped, no doubt. They'd beaten the abbot without mercy but left him alive so their commanding officer could apply the *coup de grâce*.

Yet another example of good military discipline.

The abbot looked up at him and waited, unafraid. And suddenly Sir Godfrey rebelled. He'd been ordered to sack the monastery and the burgh if necessary, but he didn't recall Longshanks telling him to kill the monks to the last man. So he wasn't going to do it.

"Stand up, abbot," he said harshly. "There has been enough killing today."

The abbot looked around slowly. Then his eyes fixed upon the girl, used and discarded by the soldiers.

"It will be a long time before you're forgiven," he said simply, but with a depth of feeling that made the knight feel even more wretched. Apart from earning the undying hatred of a kingdom, what had they really achieved?

"It will be a long time before I forgive myself," he replied. Then he turned and walked away, carrying the Book of Deer with him.

The soldiers followed him reluctantly and soon the remnants of the order were alone in the forecourt. The abbey and its burgh was still around them, but its peace and prosperity had been shattered. The work of God and His Divine Offices, the rhythm of plainsong and the glimpses of heaven afforded by the icons had been ruined and replaced with raw hatred for England and the English king. The abbot could smell blood, its odour mingling with acrid wood smoke from the burning infirmary, baking hard into the earth. He walked over to the raped girl, cradling her head in his hands as her green eyes gazed emptily skywards. He tried to think of some words of comfort for her, but then he realised that the Book which held those words was gone. There was nothing more to say, and no more chance of peace.

Perhaps that was what Longshanks had wanted all along.

Edward Longshanks returned to West Minster, collecting the Stone of Destiny en route and confident that Scotland, like Wales, had been beaten into acceptance of sovereignty.

He was wrong. The sack of cities and plunder of precious artefacts like the Book of Deer provoked a rebellion. In the Highlands it was led by Andrew Murray, in the Lowlands by the son of a Renfrewshire knight called William Wallace.

Murray and Wallace met at Perth and jointly led an outnumbered army of Scots to victory over a divided English force at the Battle of Stirling Bridge on 11 September 1297.

Gospel books were doubtless carried to war as Cathachs, but to take the sceptre of their kingdom back into Scottish hands Murray and Wallace knew they would have to pay a high price.

Andrew Murray was mortally wounded. Dictating a letter for his wife to a captured English priest shortly after the battle, he considered the cost of their victory:

But what forces, I cannot but wonder, have we now unleashed by this victory over Edward's army? Scotland, it is true, now has a hero in William Wallace, my colleague today and, I am proud to say, friend. He is a man of ability and no mean spirit but without high rank, surely, an obstacle? His path will not be easy. Edward will seek revenge. Pray to God we are prepared. What has happened here is a cause for celebration but a prelude to agony for us all ...

As he dictated, Murray's gaze fell upon the reliquary at his bedside. It was a small wooden casket overlaid with thin bronze sheets which their own priest had carried in his satchel. Before the battle the priest had opened it, held the Cathach above his head and recited the Word of God to the hardened men standing in ranks before him. Absolute silence had fallen and Murray could have sworn that, as the soldiers listened to the Latin words, a nameless strength had possessed the army.

They had won the battle but their priest had been killed. Not surprising, really. The man had considered himself very much a soldier of Christ, had insisted on staying in the front line and had promptly been chopped in two by an axe. Fortunately the Cathach had been saved by a dewar. Dewars took care of sacred relics but they were not holy men. The only available priest had turned out to be this captured Englishman!

A high price to pay, indeed. It did seem a bit ridiculous for him to go to war against the English king and end up being tended by an English priest...

He almost laughed, but the effort sent a bolt of pain shooting across his chest and he found himself spitting blood.

He had also paid the price, he reflected soberly. But at least he could enjoy the joke.

His mind began to wander. He remembered boyhood tales of King Arthur and Merlin the magician. According to Geoffrey of Monmouth's *History of the Kings of Britain*, Arthur had defeated the Picts and the Saxons centuries before. A prophet from the Borders called Thomas the Rhymer had recently claimed that Arthur was not dead after all. That he was merely sleeping with his knights under Eildon Hill in the Borders and would one day return to unite Britain.

Other legends said Merlin was buried in the Borders, too. But it was also said he would reappear every seven centuries, and that his reappearance would herald a spiritual renaissance. Merlin and Arthur had lived in the sixth century so if the legend was true, Murray mused, Merlin would have returned in the thirteenth century. In the present day. Perhaps, somehow and somewhere, he *had* returned. Scotland had been at peace for much of the thirteenth century, especially during the reign of Alexander III. The young Alexander had had a tutor, a man from the Borders called Gamelin, later Bishop of St Andrews, supposedly a suicide.

A man from the *Borders*. Where Merlin was said to be buried. It made some sense, because whoever Gamelin really had been, he had indeed helped bring about a spiritual renaissance.

Unfortunately the days of Alexander and Gamelin were long past, the Wars of Independence were at hand, and Scotland (like Pictland and Dalriada) was fighting for its way of life.

Murray felt tears streaming from his eyes. He realised he was crying tears of rage and sorrow. Tears for the futility of it all. Tears for those who'd died, and tears for himself, for he would be one of them.

Two painful months later, Andrew Murray passed away. No one knows where his body was buried.

William Wallace sealed his fate with a message to the English commander at Stirling which read:

Tell your commander that we are not here to make peace but to do battle and liberate our kingdom. Let them come on, and we shall prove this in their very beards.

Wallace, defeated at Falkirk, was hanged, drawn and quartered in London in 1305.

The Stone of Destiny (or its duplicate), symbol of sovereignty, was taken to the Benedictine Abbey of West Minster.

The Book of Deer, a small cornerstone of Christendom, vanished from the pages of history.

Over the next four hundred years, although a cultural Renaissance triggered by translated eastern texts spread its light across Europe, the road back to civilisation remained far from smooth. Royal Houses fought like savages for the sceptres of kingdoms while Church and Empire broke apart. Cathachs and calls to arms were used to turn Catholic Christian against Protestant Christian, and a combination of wilful misunderstanding and failed Crusades divided a xenophobic Christendom from a disdainful Islam.

It was futile, it was ridiculous, and it divided the peoples of the Book while bibliophiles bartered for Christian gospel manuscripts illuminated by illustrators from the East at the great book markets of Toledo and Cordoba.

By the late seventeenth century neither the House of Plantaganet nor the House of Tudor held the sceptre. The British Isles had been united under one crown in 1603 by James VI and I of the Catholic House of Stuart. Ninety-two years later, Anne, by now head of the House of Stuart (although she herself was Church of England), was waiting to become Queen of a Protestant (and protesting!) Scotland.

Eleven hundred years after Finnan's acceptance of the challenge at a place of oaks on the borders of Dalriada, it must have looked less – rather than more – likely that Word and sceptre would unite a world. Too few priests and kings had time for the simple sacrament of the gospel books. Too many preferred the fight, the hate and the power.

Perhaps weary worshippers in battered churches were also praying privately for an end to the tortuous theological disputes which had led to violent Reformation and Counter-Reformation. Maybe some longed to go back to the original sacraments, to bathe in the love of Christ and bring the confusion to a close with the clear light of liturgy.

If so, they got their wish, because amid this tangled and intolerant tapestry the Book of Deer was about to return.

It had come back on the scene in 1695 and fallen straight into the hands of Princess Diana's ancestor, Robert Spencer. A statesman – a *politician* – who certainly would have realised the importance of the prize he held...

10

It was a pleasant enough ceiling, as ceilings went. Decorated with Artex, home to a single sixty-watt bulb sheltered by a peach lampshade and distinguished by a little crack at the very edge of his vision. A ceiling beneath a roof sheltering a house in the hills of Moidart, where very little usually happened except, at that moment, for the torrent of thought travelling through Sandiman's mind.

All my life, I felt unable to do anything. I was bored by my job but too apathetic to do anything about it. I drink too much and I'm in real danger of turning into the kind of couch potato I despise. I've come to hate my fellow countrymen. With the exception of Natalie, of course.

Now I'm having a very imaginative midlife crisis, in which I'm switching identities in order to steal an old book nobody remembers for a purpose of which I am unsure.

In other words, I'm cracking up, in the very year that people are saying might go down in history.

Do I care about devolution? Not really. Do I think a new Scottish Parliament is the answer to our prayers? Definitely not. But so what? If we can't even decide to vote *for it, that really would be the end and I don't want that to happen.*

So maybe, just maybe, I'm in the right place at the right time.

Where does the Book of Deer fit into all this? A relic from a time when people died for their kings; when a book like this could, and did, lead armies into battle. But a relic that is still powerful, surely? Could it lead a new army? Could it help me be the guy I should have been?

Sandiman's brain was bursting. He closed his eyes, and dreamed of the Book again.

The Tale of The Book of Deer

Part Five

"The Gaelic poet Sorley MacLean died in 1996.
He once told a startling tale of his brother,
the folklorist Calum Iain MacLean,
who as a very young man had met
in Duirinish, by Kyle, a very old man,
who had as a child known a very
old lady, who in her own childhood
had watched fearfully as homes burned on Raasay ..."

(John MacLeod. *The Herald*. 24 November 1997)

London: 1695

10th. I dined at the Earl of Sunderland's with Lord Spencer. My Lord showed me his library, now again improved by many books bought at the sale of Sir Charles Scarborough, an eminent physician, which was the very best collection, especially of mathematical books, that was I believe in Europe, once designed for the King's Library at St. James's; but the Queen's dying, who was the great patroness of that design, it was let fall, and the books were miserably dissipated.

The new edition of Camden's Britannia was now published (by Bishop Gibson), with great additions; those to Surrey were mine, so that I had one presented to me. Dr. Gale showed me a MS. of some parts of the New Testament in vulgar Latin, which he esteemed to be about eight hundred

148

years old; there were some considerable various readings observable, as in John i., and genealogy of St. Luke.

(extract from the *Diary and Correspondence of John Evelyn*, 10 March 1695)

*I*n *the beginning was the Word, and the Word was with God, and the Word was God...* John Evelyn, European traveller, ardent Royalist and habitual diarist, smiled as he translated the vulgar Latin text of Saint John. Thank God he'd lived to see the restoration of the monarchy! Born in Surrey seventy-five years earlier, Evelyn had lived in Deptford for decades but only the year before had returned to his native shire with his wife, and only the month before had seen her namesake, Queen Mary, lying in state. He shook his head sadly. James VII and II's daughter Anne could now claim the throne, but he doubted the nation would like a Queen with blood ties to a Catholic Royal House in exile.

He wished for a simpler time. A time when only books like this manuscript held the Word and only one church in Christendom gave sovereigns the divine right to rule. But it was no use wishing. The Act of Supremacy and the Reformation had changed all that forever. Still, the words from another age had endured and a manuscript some eight hundred years old would certainly interest his friend and fellow member of the Royal Society, Richard Bentley. Bentley, a theologian who'd just been made Keeper of the dissipated Royal Library at St James' Palace, would certainly be interested in a gospel as old as the Book of Kells! Unfortunately the Earl of Sunderland would much rather improve his own collection and personal standing than donate books to the King's library for the glory of the nation.

Descendant of a family of sheep farmers from the Midlands, the second Earl of Sunderland, Robert Spencer, was a shameless hypocrite who had allied himself to both Catholic and Protestant faiths solely to increase the power and influence of the House of Spencer. At least Sunderland's son, Charles, seemed to be cut from different cloth. Evelyn had met the child at Althorp in 1688 and been hugely impressed by the precocious maturity of a child who could talk assuredly on adult matters but also play happily on the small island in the estate's Oval Lake. A youth of extraordinary hopes, indeed!

He put the manuscript down and glanced at Thomas Gale, canon of St Paul's School and honorary secretary of the Royal Society.

"Sunderland House has an incomparable library and this would be a priceless addition to it. Do you know the provenance of the manuscript?"

"I believe it was brought south sometime, perhaps in the fourteenth century, but as to its more recent whereabouts I am at a loss. The bishop of Norwich would like to have it for his own collection, though. There will probably be a bidding war between the bishop and Sunderland for this book."

Evelyn frowned. He knew that John Moore, bishop of Norwich, was an avid collector of rare books, but it would not do for a bishop of the Church of England to get involved with the likes of Sunderland. In creating the finest private library collection in the country, though, Moore had become more bibliomaniac than bibliophile. Evelyn was a devoted Anglican and would not publicly criticise the conduct of a bishop, but privately he realised Moore wouldn't hesitate to deal with Sunderland in order to own such a book.

Sunderland came over and picked up the manuscript. Evelyn and Gale traded wary glances. Sunderland looked effeminate and had an affected, drawling mode of speech. Perhaps his enemies had been deceived by this. He had been a Privy Councillor and ambassador extraordinary to Madrid and Paris. He had advised the Catholic kings Charles II and James VII and II. He'd even brokered a deal between Charles II and England's greatest enemy, Louis XIV. This was treason, and when the Protestant king William and his consort Mary had come to power Sunderland should have been executed.

But somehow the great charlatan had not only survived, but ended up as William's confidant! It could only happen in an age which had seen the overthrow and restoration of the monarchy, Cromwell's republic and now two Royal Houses vying for one throne. It was an age which invited deceit, and Sunderland had deceit in spades.

Still, the charlatan could be charming, and he seemed genuinely entranced by the Latin words and Celtic knotwork. Evelyn remembered that Sunderland had gone on a Grand Tour of Europe in his youth and, instead of spending most of his time in brothels, had actually become interested in art and culture.

He would surely recognise the importance of the manuscript he held.

Evelyn felt a sense of foreboding. A sacred book in the hands of a man who'd pay any price to be king. Or whose House would.

Then Sunderland spoke. He was not known as a great speaker in Parliament, but he had advised William to form a government with a Whig majority. The Spencers were Whigs, so this development would place Sunderland's House within a hair's breadth of the sceptre of the kingdom. To achieve this had taken Machiavelllian diplomacy, so when Sunderland spoke, men of influence listened.

"This is a book which both King William and Queen Anne could read," he said.

"What do you mean, milord?" said Gale, perplexed. William and Anne disliked each other, and neither of them trusted Sunderland.

Sunderland looked thoughtful for a moment.

"It is a book," he said, "they could read together."

Then Evelyn saw it. If Sunderland could dissolve the tension between the two Houses, the country would be more united, and if it was united against France, the war would probably end victoriously. Then it would only be a matter of consolidating the kingdoms of Britain and a peaceful future would surely come to pass.

With the House of Spencer at the centre of power, naturally. Brilliant.

Sunderland's next words confirmed Evelyn's insight.

"We have all seen great changes and turbulent days, but I believe there will be a Union in my lifetime. We can hardly go on fighting France, Scotland and the House of Stuart as well."

Evelyn nodded and turned to look across Pall Mall to the trees of St James's Park, now shrugging off a severe winter and embracing the spring. Down the Thames, he could also see the popish dome of the new St Paul's Cathedral on the city's western hill. The endless squabbles over sovereignty and the Church suddenly seemed pointless. Future historians would doubtless wonder what all the fuss had been about. He was sure of one thing, though. He, John Evelyn, was done and, for better or worse, Sunderland and the House of Spencer held the future in their hands.

Probably for worse.

He needed a drink.

"With your leave, milord, I think I shall join my honourable friends for a glass of port in the smoking room. I am an old man and my strength is failing. It is a fine manuscript. I hope I will leave a legacy half as noble."

"So do I, sir. So do I."

Sunderland died in 1702, the same year that Anne, last sovereign of the House of Stuart, took the sceptre of the kingdom. Two years later his son, Charles Spencer, third Earl of Sunderland, read before the Lords a report on relations between England and Scotland, which recommended preventing a recurrence of the problems caused by legislation passed by a Scottish Parliament independent of Westminster. With Scotland now also destitute due to the failure of the Darien Scheme, the whispers for a union between countries as well as crowns began growing much louder.

John Evelyn died in 1706 and the third earl of Sunderland became a commissioner for such a union, acting as a leading 'manager' of the debates in the Lords. The Union with Scotland Act was passed by England's Parliament in 1706 and the Union with England Act, designed mainly to prevent Scotland choosing a rival Stuart sovereign but also granting nearly £400,000 to offset the Darien debt, was passed in Edinburgh on 16 January 1707. It was formally ratified when the Earl of Seafield touched the Act with the sceptre of the kingdom of Scotland, bringing the line of Scots kings to an end and dissolving the Scottish Parliament.

The Acts of Union became law on 1 May 1707, creating the Parliament of Great Britain. The Scottish nation first united by Kenneth Mac Alpin in 843 was no more and Queen Anne, lacking an heir, would have to leave the united kingdom to be fought over by other Royal Houses.

In 1714 Queen Anne died and George I of the House of Hanover was crowned on the Stone of Destiny in West Minster Abbey. His new Parliament had a large Whig majority, one of whom was the third Earl of Sunderland. Another was Charles, Viscount Townshend, Secretary of State for Scotland and friend of John Moore. Townshend had the King's ear and most influence over the new administration. John Moore, by then bishop of Ely, had died in July 1714 and his remarkable library, *which now included the Book of Deer*, was being fought over by Oxford and Cambridge. The bishop, however, had been educated at Cambridge. Townshend and Sunderland were also Cambridge men. In 1715 George I bought John Moore's library and gave it to the University of Cambridge.

Did Townshend and Sunderland influence the king to choose Cambridge instead of Oxford, and if so, why?

Perhaps Townshend and Sunderland, both players in the creation of the Acts of Union and both learned men who'd realised the value of the Book of Deer, had become enraged by Scottish attempts to wreck the great work which would be their legacy. James VII and II had died in 1701 but his son, James Francis Edward Stuart (later known as the Old Pretender) continued to claim the throne and had tried to invade in 1708. He'd intended to dissolve the Act and restore the Scottish Parliament, but failed even to set foot on British soil. In 1713 a motion to rescind the Act had only very narrowly been defeated in the Lords and only George I's creation of a majority Whig administration in 1714 *over which Townshend held the whip hand* had saved the Union.

When the Old Pretender's ally, the 11th Earl of Mar, began to rally an army in Scotland early in 1715, enough was enough.

If the Scots could not behave themselves, the Stone of Destiny would never be returned, and by God, neither would the Book of Deer!

So the king donated the bishop of Ely's collection to Cambridge. It was the largest single gift ever made to the University. Criticism of the House of Hanover was silenced at a stroke, the collection gave Cambridge a position of national importance, and Townshend and Sutherland's relations with their old university doubtless benefited.

Townshend probably first bent the king's ear about Moore's collection in September 1714. In May and June of 1715 he helped remodel a bill which declared enlisting and recruiting for the Old Pretender to be high treason. Despite this, the 11th Earl of Mar raised the Royal Standard at Braemar on 6 September 1715 and started looking for soldiers. On 20 September, four days after he became Secretary of State for Scotland, Townshend wrote to Thomas Sherlock, Vice-Chancellor of Cambridge:

Reverend Sir

I have received His Majesty's commands to acquaint you that for the incouragement of Learning, and as a mark of His Royall Favour he gives to the University of Cambridge the Library of the late Bishop of Ely. It is with great satisfaction I send you this notice, which I desire you will communicate to the Heads of Houses and Senate.

This was the first formal confirmation of Townshend's plans for the collection. A day later he had the Jacobite sympathiser, Sir William Wyndham, arrested.

In October 1715, some Jacobite army officers were pursued to Oxford and a Professor of Poetry at the university, still smarting over Oxford's failure to claim the collection, wrote these sarcastic lines:

> *The King observing with judicious eyes*
> *The state of both his universities,*
> *To Oxford sent a troop of horse; and why?*
> *That learned body wanted loyalty.*
> *To Cambridge books he sent, as well discerning*
> *How much that loyal body wanted learning!*

The tragedy unfolded. Much as the Old Pretender's heritage was being buried beneath books at Cambridge, so were his officers and men being rounded up by troops of horse. Townshend relentlessly crushed the rebellion and by November 1715 the Jacobite army was no more. Twenty-two common men were hanged at Preston, two nobles went to the block on Tower Hill and hundreds of clansmen were transported to the colonies. James Stuart was forced into exile, setting up tensions which, thirty years later, would break the Highland clans at Culloden.

Glenfinnan: 1745

Despite the passing of twelve centuries, the trinity of calm blue loch, hard-edged mountain and heavens' vault that Finnan had seen from the place of oaks was much the same. Except now the glen had been named after him and the loch was called Shiel.

A romantic might have said that history turned full circle on the shores of Loch Shiel when Bonnie Prince Charlie of the House of Stuart, the Young Pretender, raised the Royal

Standard to regain his kingdom and restore his Royal House. Like Finnan, he was willing to put a lifetime's beliefs to the test, to face death to safeguard his people's future.

A realist would have retorted that although Charlie was in the right place, he was the wrong man at the wrong time.

The Prince was not a soldier of Christ like Columba, he was not a general like Arthur, he did not have a magician like Merlin by his side and he possessed no icon of Christendom with which to inspire his armies.

Worse, the Celtic Isle of Alba was no more than fading myth half-remembered by Gaelic-speaking clansmen part-descended from Picts, and the idea of a united Scotland ruled by the House of Stuart was fast becoming part of that myth.

So when Prince Charles Edward Stuart stepped ashore in August 1745, there was no one to greet him. A little thunder rumbled in the distance, but there was not a breath of wind. The waters of the loch were still as glass. Looking around, the prince could clearly see every last detail of the rocks, shoreline, ridges and gullies. He realised he was holding his breath.

Where were the Macdonalds and Camerons who had promised to be there?

For a brief, terrible moment he wondered if this was really the role he'd been born to play. He had imagined the clans flocking to the Royal Standard. With the support of Louis XV of France, he had imagined the House of Stuart delivering a grateful populace from the tyranny of the House of Hanover. Most of all, he'd imagined gaining his father's approval. The Old Pretender had landed at Peterhead thirty years before, but got no further than the ruins of an old monastery a few miles inland.

When the *Du Teillay* had deposited the prince and his seven men on the Isle of Eriskay, Macdonald of Boisdale, brother of the chief of Clan Macdonald, had told him to return home!

"I *am* come home, sir," he had retorted. He was a Stuart king, returned from exile in Rome after thirty years, by God!

He would entertain no notion of going back to the place from whence he had come. Either his cause would be vindicated, or he would disappear from the pages of history.

Others had also told him to go home. Only the Macdonald chief's son, Ranald, and Cameron of Locheil had pledged themselves to their Prince.

If he raised the Standard, surely his Highlanders would flock to his cause!

So the prince had sent out letters from his camp at Borrodale on the coast:

I intend to set up the Royal Standard at Glenfinnan on Monday ye 19th instant and shou'd be very glad to see you on that occasion.

They had marched to Dalelia on Loch Shiel's north shore. From there, navigating carefully past a small island with a scattering of oak trees, boats had carried them on to Glenaladale and the head of the loch.

There, with his Highlanders by his side, he would take up the challenge to fight for the sceptre of the kingdom. A kingdom which was his by divine right and which he would regain. Either that or perish in the attempt.

Yet now he was here, and still he saw no clansmen.

There was nothing else to do but wait.

It seemed he heard the tolling of a bell, very far away.

At last, early in the afternoon, the prince saw two long columns of Highlanders coming over the hills and descending down to the loch. He could faintly hear the sound of pipes.

"You sons of dogs, of dogs of the breed, O come, come here on flesh to feed!"

That was the pibroch which welcomed Bonnie Prince Charlie back to his native land. It was a joyous, martial gathering. The Camerons of Lochiel were there, and with them stood the Stewarts of Appin, the Macleans of Mull and the Isles, Macgregors from Balquhidder and MacDonalds of Keppoch, Glengarry, Clanranald and Glencoe. United by the Royal Standard of the House of Stuart.

But it was a sham. For in truth, they were the last Scots of Dalriada and they were the dead. Both they and their way of life were already dead. They would see no renaissance, and they had embarked on the long, low road to their destiny at Culloden.

Lacking a Cathach but rallying behind a bonnie prince, they took Perth and Edinburgh. Scotland was in the Young Pretender's hands. If Charlie had stopped there perhaps the House of Stuart could have restored Kenneth Mac Alpin's kingdom, but he was determined to regain the British throne, so he had to occupy London. At first he had some success. The rebels routed Sir John Cope at Prestonpans and captured Carlisle, but the dream began to die at Derby. The retreat began there and though Charlie was still able to thwart the enemy at Falkirk, a largely Protestant island was turning against a Catholic prince.

Pursued north towards Inverness by the Duke of Cumberland at the head of an army which included the Glasgow Regiment and the Argyll Militia, Charlie made his last stand at Culloden in 1746, near the site of the fort of Craig Phádraig where Columba had faced Brude in 580. It was there that the beginning and the end of the road was reached, and it was there that the starving clansmen of the House of Stuart fell before the disciplined army of the House of Hanover.

The men of Clan Chattan had come to stand with their prince. The Grants, the Frasers, the Chisholms and the MacLeods also stood. With them were the men of the small clans and lastly the common men: Carmichaels, McColls, Livingstones and MacLeays. Brave men one and all, but when Cumberland turned his cannon upon them, the Highlanders could only charge into a hell of musketry and grape-shot, the survivors staggering on to skewer themselves on three ranks of bayonets.

Much as Sir Godfrey's militia had looted the monastery of Deer, Cumberland earned the nickname 'Butcher' by destroying the clans, leaving over a thousand dead at Culloden and putting the Highlands to fire and sword. Then came the Clearances, emptying the glens and scattering the Highlanders to the four winds. Some surviving clansmen who knew nothing except the use of a claymore joined the very army that had broken them.

This was the end for the Highland clans. The descendants of the Scots who had fought the Picts, broken the Ridge and lived among the hills and glens of northern Alba saw their beliefs and traditions pass into history. The House of Spencer, aided by Townshend, Whigs and lowland Scots, had helped create the Acts of Union; and at Culloden the House of Stuart's bid for sovereignty and the last resistance to the Acts had been destroyed. The last civil war fought on British soil was over, the kingdom was united and the House of Hanover reigned supreme.

Exiled in Rome, Bonnie Prince Charlie died in 1788. The House of Stuart died with him, but the fight for the sceptre of the kingdom went on and the House of Spencer continued to do battle. George II took the sceptre from his father in 1727. Sarah, Duchess of Marlborough and Charles Spencer's mother-in-law, quickly offered George II's son, the Prince of Wales, a dowry to marry her grand-daughter, Lady Diana Spencer. The offer was blocked by the first Prime Minister, Robert Walpole, who opposed Sarah's ambitions. In 1981, two hundred and fifty-four years later, a second Lady Diana Spencer succeeded in marrying another Prince of Wales, finally placing the House of Spencer within a hair's breadth of the throne.

11

The *past is another country, is it not? They do things differently there, but it's near to us and we're bound to it more closely than we know.*

It was the only pub in the wee Moidart village where Sandiman was staying. It had an open fire in the hearth, a fruit machine in the corner and a jukebox full of Proclaimers hits. A couple of small dark men were nursing drinks by the bar, the publican was saturnine but amiable and there were no women there at all. All in all, it was a standard issue Scottish howff, proof against the weather, warm and drowsy, spare and solid. A good (or should he say *guid*?) place for a man to nurse a bursting brain and ask himself poetically about the past, aided by a glass or three of Glenmorangie.

Steady rain fell on the hills outside, invisible in the velvet dark. A river ran through the village, feeding Loch Shiel. The past did not feel so far away. In fact, it felt rather close.

Perhaps, he thought, *it is time to remember Jessica.*

He'd first met her in 1991. He was just back from backpacking around Europe and had, he thought, been lucky enough to find a job as a library assistant at a further education college in Glasgow. Not his first choice of job but he'd always liked books. It would do for now. The future, of course, would take care of itself.

Sandiman had taken a short holiday, taken the train to Glenfinnan and drunk too much coffee en route. He'd also had too many pints of lager and a shot of Glenmorangie the night before, then a cooked breakfast that morning – and one of the eggs had been off. As the train pulled out of Rannoch station, he stood up to change seats for a better view and his stomach lurched. It was the kind of lurch, he knew from occasional but never less-than-bitter experience, which presaged vomiting of truly heroic proportions.

He barely made it to the loo in time. He'd had diarrhoea in Turkey once or twice, but this was by far the worst attack through which he had ever had to sit. He crouched on the pot, convinced his plumbing was about to drop right out of his slack, spasming anal sphincter along with the putrid remnants of his breakfast; and felt the peristaltic churning of his gut synchronise with the rhythm of the train's diesel engine.

Before Sandiman knew it they were at Corrour and some pernickety part of his brain insisted he was not allowed to barf into the toilet bowl while the train was at a station. He lurched onto boneless legs, punched the UNLOCK & OPEN control and crashed straight into a young girl who'd just got into the carriage. Bone-tired from a twenty-mile walk and little more than half his size, she was thrown onto one of the seats. Her hip hit the plastic armrest with a thud and she slid to the floor.

He leaned over to help, and promptly puked all over her.

The girl lay there for a moment, flat on her back in the centre aisle of a train passing by Loch Treig with a spreading pile of brown vomit discolouring her Berghaus hiking jacket. Everyone else in the carriage looked the other way, and the two of them were left staring at each other like a pair of shell-shocked soldiers in No Man's Land.

She looked straight at Sandiman and said nothing.

"I don't know what to say," he eventually stammered.

"Sorry might be a good start."

"Yeah, right. Sorry. It was lager. Lager, maybe a Chinese takeaway. A cooked breakfast. I think one of the eggs wasn't cooked."

The girl looked at the jacket upon which most of this was now beginning to congeal, then looked at him. She had nice eyes, he thought. Hazel, flecked with gold. Great cheekbones. Beautiful black hair.

Suddenly, miraculously, she smiled. He helped her up and as their hands made contact he felt a tingle of excitement. Their eyes met again, and he smiled as well. She washed off the puke in the lavatory. They got off the train at Fort William, shared a cup of coffee in the station buffet and ended up going on to Glenfinnan together.

Jessica was a year younger than he, from Kyleakin on Skye, the only daughter of a widowed father who was an elder of the Free Church. Sandiman told her about the Church of St Finnan and as they walked down towards it, rain started to fall. They ran the last few hundred yards and he almost fell through the door of the church. She was just behind him, wasn't she?

He looked around. She was just standing there, framed in the doorway.

"What's up?"

"This is a Catholic church."

"It's a *church*. And it's dry. That's the main thing."

"I've never been in one before," she murmured.

"A church?"

"No. A *Catholic* church."

He didn't dwell on her words at the time, but he thought of them later.

It had taken an hour for the rain to stop, and they left the door half open to see Loch Shiel. After a time, they sat beneath St Finnan's stained-glass window, hands clasped. It was a quiet sacrament, and by the hour's end they were in each other's arms.

Later, they'd waited for the last train to Morar, begged entrance to the Garramore youth hostel after lights-out and walked along the silver sands of the beach the next day, looking in silence at Eigg, Rum and the southern tip of Skye.

Scotland can be cold, damp and full of midges; but when Sandiman looked back on those times with his mind's eye he saw only soft light and sea air. Perhaps he deceived himself, for he felt no awkwardness between them. No uncertainty in her smile, no hesitation when he moved to kiss her.

But he'd gone with her to Kyleakin, and the magic interlude of soft light and silver sand was wiped away in an instant. The wind was chill, the youth hostel was full and a pall of cloud hung stubbornly over the village. Jessica didn't seem to know what to do with the incomer, with *him*, and he realised she'd hardly ever been away from Skye in her life. They spent an evening with a clique of her friends in the local pub, where he felt left out of craic called clishmaclaver conducted mostly in Gaelic. He met her father just the once, a man older than his years, content with a glass of whisky and his dignity as an Elder. Sandiman was careful not to mention he was Catholic, for the Elder was welcoming but his faith was unshakeable. It was a long evening, with gaps in conversation and heavy silences, as if all the awkwardness banished from his relationship with Jessica had found a home with her father.

Late that night, they took a walk along the pier. Sandiman sensed her uncertainty, felt no anger, still believed love would work things out. Love – how natural a word when he looked at her, impossible to believe a feeling so warm and simple could be balked by circumstance and tradition.

As he sensed her confusion, so she felt his worry. She talked vaguely of leaving the island, but had no clear plan. She had a pal in the police who might help her get a job. It was either that or work in the tourist information centre across the Sound in Kyle of Lochalsh. It was dark by then, so he held her close. For once there was no rain, so instead she cried.

"West End or West Highlands?" he said gently. "It shouldn't be such a hard choice to make."

"For you or for me?"

He'd hated leaving but he was due at work. Even so, he could scarcely concentrate on anything that first week and on the Sunday morning ended up sitting with a friend called Andy in a café called Insomnia. Andy was a mournful ex-student with a drug habit who shared a squalid flat in Ibrox

163

with his thin-faced girlfriend Sharon. He would die of an overdose early in 1994.

Sandiman had talked on and on about Jessica as coffee and cheesecake came and went until Andy, sick of all the boring details, had finally asked the question uppermost in his mind.

"So, did you shag her then?"

"No."

"Can't be it, then. You've got to shag her."

"That's it? Love equals Shagging. Shagging equals Love?"

"Yeah, and I can prove it."

"How?"

"Okay, here's the choice. Suppose you could shag this girl of yours for a week, but after that you don't ever see her again. Or you swear off sex for life. Go down the vet's and have the op, but after that she's there to talk to an hour a night for the rest of your life. What do you do?"

Sandiman had taken one look at his friend, across whose forehead the word SHAG might as well have been printed, and found himself breaking into a smile. As decisions went, it was actually one of the easiest he'd ever made.

"Is the vet open tomorrow, then?"

Andy's face had sagged in sheer disbelief. For a split-second Sandiman thought his jaw might literally hit the floor.

"But you've *got* to want to shag her."

"Of course I want to shag her. That's just not all of it."

Andy slowly worked his jaw back into place and went right on staring at him.

"You've just *got* to."

"Sorry, no. At least not like you mean."

Andy just shook his head and left shortly afterwards. Sandiman had stayed a little longer before walking home, light of heart and fleet of foot. It would be the last time he saw Andy alive.

Love did try to conquer all and at first it seemed it would. What started as a holiday romance, that most ill-starred of relationships, developed despite the odds. After a few weeks of mutual pining and misery the phone at the issue desk had rung and Sandiman found himself talking to a weeping, excited Jessica. She missed him, she wanted to come to Glasgow and see him. Would he meet the train at Queen Street? Was Queen Street far from his flat? Did he mind if she visited? A frantic torrent of words, delivered from the red phone box out on the pier at Kyleakin, answered by a fusillade of yeses.

She only mentioned at the end of the call that she wouldn't tell her father what she was doing, would let him think she was staying with a cousin in Dowanhill while she looked at college courses.

Tell him, tell him, he thought to himself late that night. *If it's right there's no need to lie.* But the realist and coward in him talked of compromise and wheedled him round.

They did no sightseeing after he met her off the train. She smelt fresh, sweet and *sans* city pallor, as if she'd really bottled a little of the tangle of the Isles on the platform at Mallaig and kept the bouquet fresh all the way down to Glasgow. No, they saw no sights. Instead, carried away by the heady scent of reunion and a large dollop of lust, he and Jessica made love as soon as they reached his flat.

Her eyes gleamed but she hesitated, and he knew he was her first. Knew it was a great gift she was offering to him.

Afterwards, as they lay in each other's arms in front of the fireplace, he'd said something he would never say to any other woman.

"I want to marry you."

The words had simply floated through his mind. As if they'd been planted while he was still in the womb solely in order to be triggered by the correct hormonal stimulus. Without thinking, Sandiman spoke them aloud.

"I want to marry you."

With no sense of shock, he realised he meant what he said.

She had been playing with the hairs on the nape of his neck. When she heard him, her hands froze. Then she walked over to the window. A light rain was falling. In later days that was how he always remembered her: a dark figure in silhouette, looking out at the rain.

"Let's not talk about it now," she said after a long silence.

The flat was warm but he felt a chill, and the weekend went downhill after that.

He felt a deeper chill when he put her on the train at Queen Street. She'd waved goodbye nervously, and from nowhere other words floated through Sandiman's mind.

I won't see you again. He thrust the thought away, burying it deep in a dungeon inside his head, but it kept forcing itself free as he called her and called her, leaving messages and hearing the empty ringing tones of the unanswered phone. She never did talk about marriage to him, or about anything else, putting off his increasingly frustrated attempts to contact her until he finally went to the house in Kyleakin that October, only to be told by her father that she was visiting another Elder of the Free Church and did not want to see him.

An Elder. He knew some in the Free Church didn't like Catholics, but it couldn't really be that important. She couldn't be so hidebound...

Then he realised she was. He should have realised the moment she hesitated at the door of Finnan's church.

For a moment he had hated her, hated her father, hated his church, hated the sectarian clerics spreading intolerance and insularity. Then that emotion had left him, replaced by an awful hollow emptiness. He would not come to this house again, would not see her again. The rest of his life would pass by without her. One day after another, each as empty as the next. He saw that so clearly it hurt. It hurt about as much, he thought later, as having a knife slipped between his fourth and fifth ribs one inch at a time, and twisted.

He'd walked back to the ferry, oblivious to his surroundings. Remembered nothing of his journey back to Glasgow, awareness only returning as the train drew into Queen Street Station.

Now here I am in a howff in Moidart, he thought. *Six years later, and that knife is still between my ribs.*

He took another sip of Glenmorangie, loosening up his emotions, working around the knife. Feeling pictures rise like bubbles to the surface of his mind. The stained-glass window in the Church of St Finnan. The dome of St Sophia rising above Istanbul and the Bosphorus. The sacrament he and Jessica had shared. All ruined, all desecrated.

He was getting really maudlin now. The knife was working its way on in.

Wait. The colours and light in the stained glass window of Finnan's church. Like the spectrum of shades in an illuminated manuscript.

He could feel the answer. So obvious and so close.

To the illiterate, gospel illuminated manuscripts were windows for looking at God. To priests, they were a means of consecrating kings.

A Book like Deer couldn't conjure Jessica up for him, but why couldn't it reconsecrate a damaged church?

This felt right, but he strained for more answers. A tapestry seemed to be forming.

"You have lost touch with your history but we carry ours with us ... We are people of the Book. To be a custodian of the Book – to be a librarius *– is to be held in high esteem."*

The words of the Muslim scholar in Glasgow, clear in his head. The Book couldn't talk but John Macnab could.

And on the eve of the referendum, there were things he'd waited a lifetime to say. Words he needed to illuminate.

He had to get the Book of Deer out of Cambridge University Library, and he'd need Gavin Beatty's help.

Thank you, Henry Bradshaw. Thank you for finding the Book at Cambridge all those years ago!

It must have been wonderful to come across the Book the way Bradshaw had in 1857. And as Sandiman hurried back to his lodgings to phone Gavin, he found himself wishing he'd been in that other librarian's shoes that far-off day.

The past felt close, like a well-kent friend.

The Tale of The Book of Deer

Part Six

1856. The golden age of the British Empire. Bonnie Prince Charlie had died a melancholy drunk in Rome in 1788 and many Highlanders had reluctantly taken the King's shilling to serve in regiments mustered by clan chiefs like Simon Fraser of Lovat.

They became the footsoldiers of an Imperial Britain united by unchallenged Acts of Union, and Scotland entered upon an Age of Enlightenment centred on an Edinburgh down whose streets walked renaissance men like David Hume, Adam Smith, Robert Burns and Sir Walter Scott. Commerce and the creative arts flowered, and the agricultural and industrial revolutions took hold. The linen trade brought prosperity to the north east of Scotland. The cotton trade advanced by harnessing the power of Scottish rivers. Ironworks and coal-pits opened and roads, railways and waterways bound the nation together. Glasgow, second city of the United Kingdom, became a wealthy seaport and third city of the British Empire.

The Church was still the keystone of this Empire, and the Word still at the centre of the Church. Queen Victoria of the House of Windsor took the sceptre of the kingdom in 1837. By 1856 Lord Palmerston was Prime Minister, Britain was an industrial Master of the World and India the jewel in the imperial crown.

Such material success did generate arrogance, but it also bred a society liberal enough to bear criticism provided by the likes of Matthew Arnold and Charles Dickens, to accept the evolutionary theories of Charles Darwin and tolerate the theological scandals caused by Cardinal Newman and the Oxford Movement.

Acording to Kipling, this was the British Empire upon which the sun would never set. Perhaps the Picts had believed their kingdoms would endure, perhaps the Scots had thought they would remain a nation ruled by descendants of Kenneth Mac Alpin. This time, the British Empire, with its enlightened attitudes and military strength, would be secure for all time.

Wouldn't it?

But on 10 May 1857, the Empire was forced to realise that it too was mortal. Muhammad's people had marched eastwards as well as westwards in the seventh century and the Mughal Empire of Islam had co-existed uneasily with the British in India for many years. Both cultures continued to misunderstand each other and the Indian Mutiny arose from a refusal to use the grease needed to fit a cartridge into the new Enfield rifle. The grease, it was said, had been made from beef and pork fat, and neither Hindu nor Muslim would bite off the paper sheath from a cartridge *"covered with the fat of pigs and cows."*

Eighty-five sepoys of the 3rd Light Cavalry at Meerut were court-martialled and sentenced for their refusal. This was the flashpoint. Hindus and Muslims united against the British Empire. Bloody rebellion boiled out of the native cantonments and spread across India, leading to the slaughter of many British soldiers and the capture of Delhi. The rebellion only petered out with the second relief of Lucknow that November.

Britain had assumed it had sovereignty over India but now that assumption had been shattered. The jewel had been tarnished, and every citizen began to realise that he or she could never again feel quite so complacent or secure.

Now was the time for a jewel in the crown of *past* empires to reappear.

Cambridge: 1857

There was no question about it. Oscar Heun was insane. Deciding he was going to be married, the Principal Library Assistant had bought several white waistcoats and a gun. He later complained the police were not protecting him from people looking at his heart through his green eye-shade. The members of The Museums and Lecture Rooms Syndicate (Syndic) were relieved Heun had resigned before being carried out screaming in a straitjacket, but they'd have to replace him fast. Find someone who could meet Cambridge University Library's urgent need for a new catalogue and also sort out all those books and manuscripts – some of them part of George I's gift in 1715 and *still* not properly catalogued – lying around in the disused Divinity School on the ground floor.

The Syndic didn't have to look very far. A young graduate and Fellow of King's College applied for the job and was appointed in November 1856. His name was Henry Bradshaw and around him history's tapestry would once again weave its threads.

For although Bradshaw was from Lancashire, his father had left him a large collection of rare Irish books and the younger Bradshaw's first teaching post had been at St Columba's College outside Dublin. He would definitely have no trouble identifying ancient illuminated manuscripts.

At first, though, it seemed Bradshaw had been misplaced. He carried out his everyday duties competently but they made him miserable. In truth he was more bibliomaniac than librarian, and compared to the feverish fascination he always felt when he found old books, shelving stock and checking bills bored him to bloody tears.

He spent more and more time poking around the old monographs piled in the Divinity School, putting off the moment he'd have to do the administrative work he hated. The Syndics wanted the space the Divinity School could provide for periodicals and Parliamentary papers. Bradshaw just liked searching through the dust of ages.

It was hard to explain why, even to himself. The room really was thick with dust, but that was not a burden. It felt more like layers of compressed wisdom waiting patiently to be rediscovered. The broken cabinets, dirty slop-pails and ladders lying around did not deter him, although a rusty scythe had nearly sliced one of his fingers off once.

Perhaps it was because he could feel history all around him. A living thing not confined to the guided tour or the lecture hall. So close he could almost touch it. Theology had been taught here. Had John Henry Newman lectured here? The Oxford Movement was still frowned upon by many Dons. Bishop Moore of Ely must surely have passed by at some point. Before him Burnet, Thomas Aquinas, Thomas Stapleton, John Fisher...

And before them?

He had a sudden feeling that there was a presence in the room with him. Someone benign but with a touch of fiery temper. Just around an unseen corner.

Columba? No, that was reaching too far. Columba had died in 597. He could never have imagined his legacy would have lasted so long. Or could he? His friend J H Todd had let Bradshaw see the Book of Kells at Trinity College in Dublin. He knew about icons and Cathachs, and he hoped to hold the Lindisfarne gospels. They had endured, and Columba had had vision.

Bradshaw was still young, but he'd already realised just how hard a road Columba and others like him had walked. His fellow Masters at St Columba's had told him stories of Columba and his mentor Finnan of Moville, and an odd tale about a deer. Before that he'd had some interest in his father's books, but in Ireland it became his passion. As an undergraduate, Bradshaw had badgered Oscar Heun about Irish works and corresponded with him from Ireland. He'd been particularly interested in Adomnán's *Life of St Columba*. So it seemed the Syndic considered him an authority, which was why they'd put him in Heun's old post. Doing bloody paperwork.

Well, the bloody paperwork could wait. He would stay down here in the Divinity School for a while and do some musing instead.

From Finnan to Columba to Newman and on. How proudly Britain's civilisation had climbed to its present pinnacle! A pinnacle represented by these buildings on the banks of the Cam where the sons of the privileged were educated to take their places in Parliament or the East India Company. Or elsewhere in an Empire composed of India, Canada's North-West Territories, the dark continent of Africa and the new democracies of Australia and New Zealand.

Surely Columba's beliefs had reached their fullest expression with the British Empire? British missionaries had brought the Word of God to the heathen, and perhaps one day there'd be another crusade to win back Jerusalem from the Muslims.

One day.

For a moment Bradshaw felt uncertain. The feeling he was not alone nagged at him again but he shrugged it off. There was no reason to feel insecure. Christianity was as much a part of the British Empire as India was and it always would be. Church and State working together for the betterment of all, much as the Holy Roman Empire had done in Constantine's day. There had to be *some* certainties in life!

Enslaved by the bibliophile's obsessive curiosity, Bradshaw began picking his way through the old manuscripts again. He'd already discovered part of Bishop Bedell's Irish Bible, lost for many years. His fingers were literally itching at the prospect of finding another piece of history.

He picked up a small manuscript and opened it.

It *gleamed*. Very faintly.

Bradshaw looked at it intently. There was something familiar about it. Something very familiar. An echo of designs he'd seen elsewhere.

He froze, trying to trap the elusive memory. Then it hit him, like a beam of solid white light.

He'd seen pages like these in Dublin.

My God.

It was another illuminated Gospel! Celtic. It could only be Celtic. But where had it come from?

He made out the flowing Celtic knotwork and key patterns bordering the folios, the bold one-dimensional image of a saint (Saint Matthew?) in an early folio. Another saint holding (of all things!) a book, the painter truly within the portrait. The ornamented initial letters of the Latin Gospels were like shadowy reflections of the calligraphy in the Book of Kells and Book of Durrow. A touch cruder, a little older, but definitely similar.

He was touching history.

Henry Bradshaw sat back for a long moment, gently put the Celtic manuscript down, and stared at the ceiling.

His Latin tutor had once said that Bradshaw would only be able to learn Latin properly by talking to a Roman on the other side of the classroom door. It was a dead language with no chance of resurrection, but just for a moment Bradshaw felt like he'd opened the door and spoken to the Roman on the other side.

Moments before, he'd thought glibly of Newman and arrogantly of the British Empire. But the Word of God had preceded both the Empire and the Oxford Movement. Not only that, the Words had been illuminated by arts learnt from those so-called heathens in the East.

The script seemed to glow in the half-light, and Bradshaw remembered the story of Columba secretly copying a gospel owned by Finnan of Moville, working at night to avoid detection. Light had supposedly spilled from the saint's fingertips in order to do so, but the dull glow coming from the manuscript itself was probably nearer the truth.

As he thought of Finnan and Columba, the presence seemed to solidify, as if a door *was* slowly being pushed open.

But then it drifted away like small clouds on a summer day.

Bradshaw picked up the manuscript again and turned to the last page. He noticed the colophon and saw an odd little phrase.

At first he could make no sense of it. It was not Latin. But all the great Gospel manuscripts were in Latin. Was it Anglo-Saxon or something? Then it hit him. It was *Gaelic*. Early Gaelic! What did it say? Screwing up his eyes, he tried to translate it.

Let it be... That wasn't too difficult. Couldn't make the next bit out. *Book. Blessing?* That had to be blessing... *Blessing the soul...* Blaggard? Wretch? *Wretch! Wretch who wrote it.*

He'd have to find someone with better knowledge of Gaelic than he possessed – Whitley Stokes would do – but what a find! A book to rival the manuscript at Kells, by God.

Tucking the Book of Deer under his arm, Bradshaw walked up the spiral staircase to the main library and headed straight for his office. He reverently locked the Book of Deer in his desk, told the porter he was taking an early lunch and headed down Regent Walk to the Blue Boar where he ordered a rather large glass of stout.

As he sipped his stout and pondered his find, he reminded himself what day it was. He wasn't quite sure. Oh, yes. How could he be so absent-minded? 10 May 1857.

Now there was a date he wouldn't forget in a hurry.

As a result of Bradshaw's finds he was charged with editing the listings of the four thousand western manuscripts finally being catalogued after one hundred and forty-odd years. He did so meticulously, ensuring that the manifest importance of the Scottish Gaelic notations in the Book of Deer was made absolutely clear.

The fifth and final volume of the manuscript catalogue was published in 1867. A few days after its publication Bradshaw became University Librarian, a post he held until he died in 1886. The catalogue he helped create was the best in the Britain of its day, and after being lost for nearly six centuries the Book of Deer had literally re-entered the pages of history, becoming MS Ii.6.32 in one of the greatest libraries of an enlightened state.

But a state upon which the sun, slowly and surely, was setting.

12

He'd taken the salmon, he'd taken the grouse, now all he had to do was take the deer and the wager would be won. Stalking the deer, though, would be the hardest task of all. Especially with every ghillie on Lord Abinger's estate at Inverlochy searching for him. His brother officer in the Queen's Own Cameron Highlanders, Abinger's son, would also be trying to catch him to avoid the forfeit, but dusk was falling and all would be won or lost in the next few minutes.

Those thoughts flicked through Captain Dunbar's mind in a second, but the experienced soldier's expression never altered. It was as if he was in a meditative state. As if he'd became part of Inverlochy's forest, attuned to every rustle, aware of every noise. Waiting for the correct sound as he covered the nearby clearing with his hunting rifle.

At least it made for a more interesting summer than stilted conversations over brandy and cigars at regimental gatherings in Inverness. Which was why he'd announced at a dinner held by the Militia Battalion earlier that summer that, as he'd received no invitation to hunt anywhere that season, he was reduced to poaching. Impulsively, he'd wagered his brother officers twenty pounds that he could kill a deer in any forest in Scotland without being caught, and Abinger of Inverlochy had accepted the challenge.

Dunbar had prepared carefully, hiding out at a fellow officer's house on the edge of Abinger's estate before slipping into the forest in search of game. This was how deer had been stalked in the past. First by Picts, then by Scots, now by poachers and gamekeepers.

His mind had wandered for a few seconds. Annoyed, he returned to his vigil and only then did he see the deer, standing motionless at the edge of the clearing.

It stared unblinkingly at him and he felt a moment's uncertainty. The creature, as finely sculpted as an oak tree, was beautiful. His hand hesitated on the trigger, but only for a moment.

It would be a fine kill.

The bullet took the deer through the eye. It collapsed without a sound.

He thought he heard a brief rumble of thunder, but it passed. He walked over to the fallen animal. He'd never felt regret before, would never tell anyone he felt regret now, but he found himself wishing he hadn't killed so fine a specimen just to relieve his own boredom.

Still, he had won his wager, and telling the tale would enliven many a future regimental dinner. Unless they saw action again soon, of course. The regiment had been at Lucknow in 1858, had taken part in the 1885 Egyptian Campaign and ended up in the Sudan, but for the last decade or so they'd been stuck in Britain.

Despite endless square-bashing, officers and men were stale. War was a grim business, but it was their trade and they were out of practice. There were a lot of barrack-room rumours going around that General Kitchener intended to reconquer the Sudan. Dunbar wondered why Kitchener wanted to bother. The Sudan was the hind end of Africa. Hot, full of flies, malaria and little else. The old sweats had hated it, but since the regiment had been there before it would probably have to go there again.

He didn't want to have to sharpen his skills in the Sudan, but he knew he was rusty and he hated being like that. Perhaps that was why he was really out here...

He heard a sound. Turned sharply.

Deep in the shadow of oaks, a figure was standing at the edge of the clearing.

13

*M*ay gave way to June and July as the pivotal events of 1997 continued to unfold. Diana, Princess of Wales and descendent of Robert Spencer, second Earl of Sunderland, had begun a liaison with Emad 'Dodi' Fayed, son of Mohamed Al-Fayed, owner of Harrods.

Aware of her family's parliamentary past and well-informed about present-day politics but a little wilful nonetheless, Diana caused some controversy by holidaying with Al-Fayed and Dodi in St Tropez. Her sons, William and Harry, had also been invited. The Press sniped about the wisdom or otherwise of allowing a future sovereign to become entangled, however innocently, in the Machiavellian dealings of a wealthy Muslim desperate to become part of the British Establishment.

Cabinet Ministers decided to publish the white paper on Scottish devolution on 24 July. After the Cabinet meeting at 10 Downing Street, a smaller meeting of the Constitutional Reform Policy Committee was held to work out how best to achieve a Yes-Yes vote in the referendum. Previously, ministers had squabbled because they knew the general election had partly been fought on the promise of devolution for Scotland.

And devolution might not work.

A Yes-No or No-No vote could leave Britain with a useless second parliament and all the old prejudices unresolved. New Labour could lose most of the Scottish vote, the British government could destabilise and (as the president of the Adam Smith Institute had suggested) the United Kingdom might even begin to break up. And if the UK degenerated into parochial warring provinces the Proclaimers might have to change their lyrics a little:

Methil no more!
Scotland no more!
Britain no more!

The stakes were high, uncertainty was rife and it was easy to imagine kings like Arthur, Kenneth and Alexander spinning in their graves as their country stood poised to fracture in a flood of legislation.

Less pivotally, or so it seemed, John Sandiman returned to Glasgow and asked Gavin Beatty to write to Cambridge University Library on his behalf. Gavin seemed more than a little surprised when Sandiman asked for that particular favour, but after a few seconds of stunned silence a broad grin crossed his face and he agreed to help.

"If you're to be a rogue, then I'll be a rogue with you," Gavin had said. "And if it's a parcel of rogues we become, why, it'll be something to tell the grandchildren."

Shortly afterwards, Dr David Giles, Keeper of Manuscripts & University Archives at Cambridge, received a letter of introduction on behalf of a librarian who'd recently been made redundant and was now studying the Book of Deer.

There'd been quite a bit of media interest in the Book the year before, when the Stone of Destiny had gone home, but like any nine-days-wonder it had quickly faded away, and the introduction *was* from a Librarian involved with Special Collections.

This letter (read Giles) is to introduce John Macnab as a person in whom trust can be placed. I acted as John's advisor during the preparation of his Professional Development Report for the Library Association. At that time, five years ago, I was Librarian in charge of Reference Services at the Mitchell Library. My current activities as Deputy Keeper of Special Collections at Glasgow City University give me an understanding of your need for some assurance that it is safe to allow

John to consult material in your department.

John is a trustworthy and conscientious person who will treat rare books and manuscripts with care and reverence, as he always does. If you have any queries, please ring me at work or at home.

Yours faithfully,

Gavin Beatty

Giles thought for a moment. He'd never heard of a John Macnab in rare book circles, but he knew Gavin Beatty slightly by reputation. He would give Beatty a call, but it would probably be all right.

Giles called Beatty, minutes later Beatty called Sandiman and a little while later Sandiman put the phone down, his hand literally trembling with excitement. Giles had taken the bait. Thank God for Gavin.

A few days later, at 3.30pm on Thursday 24 July, the Secretary of State for Scotland rose nervously to his feet in the House of Commons, adjusted his round glasses and fiddled with his tie. Slowly at first and then more confidently, Donald Dewar added the white paper on Scottish devolution to the pages of history.

As he was about to sum up, Dewar found himself wishing John Smith could have been there. *The best Prime Minister we never had*, thought Dewar. Smith had been an Argyll man and when he died in 1994, he had been buried on Iona. Achievement always required sacrifice. Dewar had carried on his political soulmate's work and it was now within an ace of fruition. What else would be required of him? He thought about his own surname. Historically, dewars had been those responsible for the safety of sacred relics. A nation was more than its government, and a nation's icons and symbols would outlive many an administration. Above all, Dewar thought, it would be the Scottish Parliament's responsibility to cherish a culture for which so many had fought and died.

He realised he'd paused a beat too long. There were rustles of disquiet on the backbenches. The Tories would fill the vacuum with jeers if he didn't get on with it.

"I am," he said, "a little nervous about my place in history. Like many others in this House and beyond, I have campaigned long and hard for a Scottish Parliament over the years. Few occasions in my long parliamentary career have given me as much pleasure as coming here today to present our firm proposals for that Parliament. In my time I have seen many devolution schemes. I genuinely believe this is the best; and right for Scotland. We have renewed, modernised and improved on the plans agreed within the broad coalition of Scottish interests in the Scottish Constitutional Convention. It will provide a new, stable settlement which will serve Scotland and the United Kingdom well in the years to come."

He was getting a bit wordy, he thought. Cut it down and sum it up!

"I know – none better – the strength of feeling and the intensity of argument that there has been on this subject over the years. Constitutional change requires good will. I believe there will be a broad welcome for our proposals which will reach out across party lines and across the range of communities. It is my belief that it will be so."

That would have to do. Sober and pretty much straight to the point. Just get through the interviews and catch the charter flight to Edinburgh. Suddenly he very much wanted to be back in Scotland.

The interviews went easily and the limousine to London City Airport went swiftly, as if buoyed up by the day's elation. As it headed down Whitehall, Dewar didn't notice (and nor did he have any reason to notice) a man called Mike who'd once worked as a library assistant in Glasgow and was now out on a pub crawl with his brother, owner of a second-hand bookshop in Camden.

Mike gave the finger to the limo, dropped his pants, mooned, and farted.

The departure from London City was uneventful and it was only in mid-flight that the mood changed. Dewar felt the fuselage tremble as the plane skirted the fringes of a thunderstorm. His back twinged and he mulled over his thoughts in the House of Commons. A few inches from the cabin in which he sat, the forces of nature were hard at work. For all the scientific advances of the modern day, the storm could still swat them from the sky with one careless cuff. *To deliver devolution and die for the privilege*, he thought. *What a black joke that would be. The media would have a field day.*

But the thunder died down slowly, allowing the plane safe passage. Dewar's attention turned to the rugby scrum of reporters who would be waiting for him at the airport, and then to the reception in Edinburgh Castle's Great Hall. He hoped they wouldn't overdo it. This was not a day for flag-waving jingoism. George Galloway, MP for Hillhead (reputedly a priapic goat and, thought Dewar, someone with no nous for politics at all) had already called for Dewar's name to be added to *"the whole host of heroes who have stood and fought for home rule for Scotland."*

John Smith's widow, Baroness Smith, was at Dewar's side when he entered the Great Hall. The Stone of Destiny had been returned to the same hall less than a year earlier, but it had been a bit of an anticlimax. After all, a stone could not speak! Dewar could, though, and the white paper could be read.

The evening passed in a haze of laughter and ended with a polite queue of the great and the good standing in front of him to get his autograph on their copies of Scotland's Parliament, as the white paper was called. He noticed the Earl of Mar, descendant of the 11th Earl and as much an opponent of the Union as his ancestor had been its ally. Mind you, he thought, the 11th Earl had changed his mind and damn nearly started the Jacobite Rising of 1715 on his own.

All the while Baroness Smith stood at his side, smiling serenely.

It was almost as if John were there with him.

It was all a bit unreal. He felt a little dizzy and excused himself to walk over to one of the stained glass windows. The storm had passed, but he could still hear a faint whisper of thunder, like gods conferring.

Dewar raised his glass, thinking of the unfinished business which had driven his old friend so far. In the end, perhaps too far. For a moment he thought of John's grave on Iona, and the image of a stag standing silently at bay came to mind.

Again he heard the whisper of thunder and again his mood darkened.

They had begun the break-up of a kingdom united since 1603. Their actions would have consequences, and historical consequences were usually bloody.

He put the glass down suddenly. He had always known he lived in an uncertain world, but up until that moment he had never realised just how uncertain it really could be.

He would never admit it to anyone else, but he was absolutely terrified. He had no idea what would happen next.

What if the new, stable settlement devolution promised *wasn't* stable?

What if it just didn't work? What if it all fell apart?

In the sixth century, Arthur and Merlin had united the border kingdoms of Strathclyde, Rheged and Gododdin against the Picts and Angles.

In the thirteenth century, Alexander and Gamelin had championed Scotland's unity and independence, and made peace with Norway.

But in the twentieth century the break-up of the United Kingdom was at hand, and it seemed no one could stop it. The way ahead was still in shadow, and the Royal Houses would go on fighting like savages to claim the throne. But at what price?

14

It was August, and it surely seemed the United Kingdom would shake itself apart. The referendum regarding the 1997 Scotland Bill would take place on 11 September and journalists were gamely trying to predict the consequences. Between the lines of their copy ran the icy fear that apathy would rule and the Scots, in McIlvanney's words, would stop chapping and back off. In the meantime, the House of Spencer's most famous daughter was in the midst of a love affair with Dodi Fayed. The day after Donald Dewar unveiled the white paper on Scottish devolution, Diana and Dodi flew to Paris where they were booked into the Imperial Suite at the Ritz.

A little less glamorously, John Sandiman locked up his flat and set off for Glasgow Central to take the night sleeper to Cambridge. As he walked onto platform one, he hesitated.

This was it.

Once he stepped on that train, he would be setting in motion the events he'd planned, changing history. Well, it was either that or stay behind and do nothing, an impartial observer relegated to the backwaters of time.

Had Finnan or Columba had moments of self-doubt like this? Of course, but the idea of impartial observation wouldn't have cut much ice with them. Better by far to fuck up doing something you believed in than sleepwalk through a life of parochial mediocrity.

And once it was in his hands, he knew what he wanted to do with the Book of Deer.

He checked his ticket and got on the train.

Looking back in later days, he remembered little of the journey south. There was probably a psychological reason for it. As if after the loss of his job, the decision on the Quirang, the months of planning, the gnawing doubts and growing confidence, all the theory was about to become reality. As the train pulled away from the station, Sandiman fell into a deep sleep. And if a stag was part of his dream, it had no place in his memory.

He hadn't been to Cambridge before, and when he woke and left the train he found a city lodged awkwardly between past and present. Part shopping mall, part cloistered grove of academe with Sainsburys only a stone's throw from Sidney Sussex College.

He was due at the university library at one. Well, he'd have a pie and a pint first. He looked around and a nearby pub caught his eye. The Blue Boar. Yes, that looked as good a place as any.

An hour later, 'John Macnab' was being ushered into the Manuscripts Reading Room. He had had a cordial meeting with David Giles, but despite his best intentions hadn't been able to help bristling a bit at the Keeper's last words.

"The MP Alex Salmond is taking up the cudgels on behalf of the Central Buchan Tourism Group. They want to digitise the Book of Deer and set up a visitor centre at Old Deer. They'd rather have the book itself instead of its image, but I'm afraid it's our policy never to relinquish manuscripts. Once something comes into the library, it stays in the library."

Then Giles had turned to his next appointment, leaving John Sandiman free to look at the Book of Deer.

Now he was standing in the Reading Room, reader's ticket at the ready; and there, on a small table surrounded by ranks of books stacked behind wire mesh, was a blue archival storage box. The bookwatcher on duty, a languid young lady who introduced herself as Leila, gestured towards it.

"Manuscript Ii.6.32?" she said.

Sandiman simply nodded. On the outside he looked cool as a cucumber. On the inside he felt a profound sense of awe, and he was sweating like a horse.

Once again, much as he had at the bookbinders, he

realised he'd paused a moment too long. The girl was looking enquiringly at him.

"Yes, that's the one," he said quietly. "The Book of Deer."

"Please handle the manuscript with care," said Leila. "It must be returned to the archive box ten minutes before closing time. And you'll have to sign the register while it's in your hands."

She handed a pad to him and he quickly did so, hoping the girl was not a fan of John Buchan. He had a feeling Baudelaire or *The Diving Bell and the Butterfly* might be more to her liking.

She eased open the box and stood back, respectful as an acolyte. Now the object inside could be seen she was no longer quite so languid. She knew what was in there.

Sandiman sat down and looked into the box. The old manuscript lay there and for a moment he just looked at it, feeling it might float away like thistledown if he touched it.

"Do you have a pair of white gloves?" he asked.

"I do."

He pulled on the gloves. No fingerprints or acidic traces from his hands could damage the old vellum now. Then, very gently, he eased the ancient manuscript out of its box and onto the book support.

Leila was still standing behind him. He looked round.

"I don't often see the manuscripts," she said. "Sometimes you forget what it's all about."

He smiled.

"Sometimes you do."

Padding light as a library cat, Leila left him and he turned the page; looked at the Vulgate Latin verse. The words of Matthew, Mark, Luke and John. The first letter of each Gospel enlarged and ornamented. The words framed by Celtic key and knotwork patterns, illustrated by surprisingly crude depictions of the Saints. He remembered reading that the Book might be the oldest surviving native Pictish manuscript and not the work of Irish scribes from Dalriada. It was hard to tell. Paganism had not just stopped dead in its tracks and been replaced lock, stock and barrel by Christianity. The faiths had merged, sharing rituals for over a century and only gradually coming under the influence of Rome.

Perhaps that was why there were animals woven into the Book's many folios: the heads of dogs, hares, ravens and deer. The Picts had believed their gods appeared to them in the form of beasts. Beasts common to the Scotland of their day were the wolf, the raven and the deer.

Sandiman knew his Celtic history better now. Cernunnos was Father of the Gods. He was always depicted as part human, part stag. Then there was the God of Death, Donn. The animal drawn in the Book was female, but Donn was a shapeshifter, could become a hind...

To modern tourists, the stag was just The Monarch of the Glen, a symbol on a whisky bottle. What kind of symbol it really was, no one had thought about for years.

It was easy to be an atheist in the nineteen-nineties. Less easy when you were in the presence of a manuscript named after the deer and doires of times past. A world where the Christian God stood side by side with Cernunnos and Donn. Where unfortunates were burned alive in wicker men at Beltane and druids inspected the entrails of human sacrifices to divine the future.

He went on browsing, losing himself in the Latin verse he'd come to learn and love after cordially detesting it at grammar school, that old dump of a building with its broken windows and busted teachers. He grew calmer. An eyeblink and it seemed an hour had gone by.

Sandiman looked up suddenly, his meditations disturbed by a stiff back. Several hours had passed. Where had the time gone?

He looked round. Leila the languid librarian was still there. A vision in a blue print dress.

Ever so calmly, Sandiman closed the book and replaced it in its box. Then he took it over to her, nodded and left.

She'd have no doubt he was exactly what he pretended to be: a librarian researching an ancient manuscript. Indeed, that was exactly what he'd been. He had not been acting. Come to think of it, that was the best way to play a part. John Buchan had written something about that in *The Thirty-Nine Steps*:

> *I remember an old scout in Rhodesia* (Richard Hannay had thought), *who had done many queer things in his day, once telling me that the secret of playing a part was to think yourself into it. You could never keep it up, he said, unless you could manage to convince yourself that you were it.*

Good advice from a good writer. He hoped Buchan would approve of his actions.

Sandiman was careful to create a pattern the following day. Wear the same patched and tweedy clothes. Sit in the same seat. Most importantly, wear the same solid, stolid jacket with the concealed inside pocket, stiffened with cardboard and cut to fit the manuscript.

There was no problem. Sandiman mentally marked off the number of paces it would take to reach the exit from the Manuscripts Reading Room and summed up the security guards stationed at the entrance. They were on the high side of fifty, supplied by a private firm and paid peanuts. Not the sharpest of guys.

The simplest plans always reigned supreme. Walk in with the fake in its concealed pocket, swap it for the manuscript and walk out. The electronic gates which monitored the exits would react only to specially-tagged items. Because of their fragility, rare books and manuscripts were never tagged. Sandiman had checked the manuscript, and as long as he could swap it unnoticed he doubted he'd be caught.

After that, just take the high road and hope for the best.

He'd have to leave by four o'clock. That would give him enough time to take the train from Cambridge to Stansted

Airport and check in. Very simple, but he'd have to keep his cool, because this was for real.

Today was Friday 15 August. His flight would leave on the Monday evening. It was going to be one hell of a long weekend. Sandiman glanced at Leila and for a sexy second he thought about sharing it with her. If nothing else, some release would be of help.

No. Forget it. The last thing he could afford now was any sort of entanglement.

As it was, he was able to pass the time quite easily. After all, his path was set. All he had to do now was walk down it carrying a book.

Sandiman slept in on the Saturday morning, then read the papers for a couple of hours. The news was dominated by Princess Diana and Dodi Fayed. There was little about the Scottish referendum.

Early on the Monday morning, as government information leaflets on home rule began to fall through Scottish letterboxes, Sandiman woke and savoured the view of the ceiling, the light streaming through the faded curtains of the cheap B&B in which he was staying. If he pulled this off, he thought, people would write about the events of this day. Maybe dramatise them. He might even be interviewed by Kirsty Wark.

He dressed in patch and tweed, broke his fast and left for the library. He usually timed himself to arrive there at about 10am so he walked slowly, a slug in a stolid jacket amid a fast-flowing river of people.

He wafted into the Manuscripts Reading Room like an absent-minded professor, took his usual place at the table and nodded to Leila.

Then he signed the register and she passed him the manuscript.

Sandiman felt the adrenalin begin to gather in his belly. This was the moment. He had the Book in his hand, and in a few short hours he would steal it. Win or lose, wheels were now in motion. He pretended to faff around like a fussy academic getting his mind in gear, rubbing his nose, snuffling into a handkerchief, fiddling with a notepad and yawning a few times. It worked a treat. After a few moments, everyone else in the room – Leila, some old fart of a Don and a couple of students – noticed him, registered his presence (bland, boring, fidget) and forgot about him again. And just after he slid beneath their notice, he took the fake manuscript from the concealed pocket and laid it on the table, right next to the real one and half-obscured by papers. It all looked perfectly normal: a librarian sitting in a library, surrounded by books.

He left it that way for the whole day, letting anyone who might notice get used to the sight of two manuscripts lying next to each other. When the moment actually came to make the switch it was a complete anticlimax. It was about three o'clock, Leila was distracted by a kindly old man with a prominent moustache who couldn't find the toilet and Sandiman simply swapped the manuscripts round. It only took a moment.

He noticed he was sweating. He looked at Leila and saw her smile at him. She hadn't noticed anything. But now two books had changed places.

Don't disturb anything. Let things settle. Then put the Book of Deer in your pocket like it was the most natural thing in the world.

Half past three. Sandiman took his glasses off, rubbed his eyes and nodded to Leila. The same gesture he'd used twice before, meaning 'I'm tired and I'm going home soon.'

She hardly noticed, so he quietly put the Book of Deer in his pocket, feeling it slip easily between walls of card, and placed the fake in the archive box.

He wondered if Bradshaw's ghost was watching him.

Quarter to four. Sandiman had spent a few minutes ostensibly writing notes, but it was time to stop shuffling paper and walk out of there. He stood up decisively and handed Leila the archive box.

And this time she opened it.

Sandiman's heart stopped dead in his chest. If she opened the book itself, he was done for.

He cleared his throat. He had absolutely no idea what to say.

"Where did you say the toilet was, my dear? I'm afraid my memory just isn't what it used to be."

No, that wasn't it, Sandiman thought. *I wasn't going to ask that.*

The kindly old man with the prominent moustache and defective bladder had reappeared, as if from nowhere.

Just at the right time, too.

Her attention slightly diverted, Leila turned to the old man, gave him the directions and automatically closed the archive box. The fake lay inside, unopened.

Sandiman's blood started circulating again. He said goodbye to Leila and, like a prisoner scenting freedom, walked out of the Manuscripts Reading Room, keeping up the slow, steady pace typical of the slow, steady academic. The security guard never even looked up as he passed through the electronic gates.

Bless me, he thought. *I'm out!*

He faded into the crowds, heading for the railway station.

Cambridge University Library closed at 9pm and all manuscripts consulted in the Reading Room that day were checked by the Deputy Keeper before going back into storage.

Odd, the Deputy thought, as he opened the box containing manuscript Ii.6.32. The binding didn't look quite right. Suspicious, he opened the manuscript itself. Instead of pages of illuminated Gospels and Celtic art he found himself staring at blank parchment. Something fluttered out of the book as he held it up to the light. He bent down and snatched it up. Found himself holding a short little note:

TO WHOM IT MAY CONCERN

Thank you for giving me the opportunity to return the Book of Deer to the Scottish Nation.

Sincerely,

J. Macnab

John Macnab

15

"If I was able to write my own script
I'd say that I would hope
that my husband would go off,
go away with his lady and sort
that out and leave me and the children to carry the Wales
name through to the time William ascends the throne."

(Diana, Princess of Wales)

If they had discovered the deception by now, it must have been embarrassing for the staff to admit they'd been hoodwinked, but Cambridge University Library wasn't Fort Knox. No one had noticed him swap it for a duplicate, hand the duplicate in its box to the bookwatcher and calmly walk out with the original.

Sandiman's plan was working. He had the Book. He also had a seat on the KLM UK flight to Inverness from Stansted Airport at ten past seven that evening; and he'd be back in the Highlands in a few hours.

For a moment, exhilaration gripped him. John Sandiman *was* John Macnab and, one way or the other, he'd just joined the ranks of popular Scottish heroes. He wondered what Ian Hamilton, who'd stolen the Stone of Destiny, would think of it all and decided he didn't really care. He was becoming the man he really should have been, and it felt damned good.

No one could ever take this moment away from him. *John Macnab was alive.* And there was more to be done.

The feeling of exhilaration rose up again when he landed in Inverness. For the first time in seven hundred years, the Book of Deer was back in Scotland. As Sandiman slid by knots of people clogging up the concourse the temptation to shout out loud what he'd done was nigh on uncontrollable. He looked at the lights of Inverness for a while instead, remembering his next move.

His destination wasn't exactly recommended by the Scottish Tourist Board, but whatever happened the Book would be safe. He'd made sure the case in which it now lay would act as a modern-day reliquary, keeping the manuscript clean and free from humidity, however gruelling the outside conditions.

Speed was essential. Discarding his tweeds, Sandiman changed into standard hiker's garb in the toilets, made for Farraline Park Bus Station and took the next bus to Invergarry. Waiting for him at an Invergarry hotel was a room he'd booked and a package he'd left a week before. Except for water, it contained all he needed to survive outdoors for several days. He checked in, collapsed into bed, wolfed down a full Scottish breakfast the next morning and set off for the cave he'd found a few months earlier.

It was the morning of Tuesday 19 August 1997. The events due to occur over the next twenty-seven days would touch lives from the Shetlands to the Scillies, but in the meantime John Sandiman, sitting comfortably in a cave just above the treeline of South Laggan Forest with a good view of Loch Lochy, enjoyed a pleasant interlude. A nearby burn provided drinkable water and several paperback novels kept tedium at bay. Sometimes he wondered when his theft would be discovered or if a walker would come across him over the next fortnight. But he only left the cave when necessary and all another hiker would see would be a fellow wanderer complete with the usual accoutrements. The Book of Deer rested invisible in its reliquary.

Sandiman had decided that going to ground for a couple of weeks would be the best idea. He was not good enough to create a false identity or a plan Machiavellian enough to ensure he got away scot-free. That wasn't the idea anyway. All he wanted to do was stay at liberty for long enough.

So don't run around thinking you're a revolutionary, he mused, *don't try to be too clever. Just sit tight and sweat it out. They don't know who I really am, they don't know where I really am, and it's not as if they give much of a shit anyway. I'm not some fiendish criminal mastermind secreting a nuclear bomb in a suitcase, merely a loony librarian who nicked an old book. Scotland can be a* very *big country in which to look for a nutso needle in a haystack not even intent on doing harm, so why bother?*

Meanwhile, news of the theft had become public knowledge and as the referendum drew nearer, the newspapers were having a field day. It was mid-morning in Glasgow's West End and Natalie, staying in her uncle's flat on Hyndland Road and temping after resigning from the college, was enjoying herself reading headlines with John Macnab's name all over them when the policeman came to call. **'Theft Costs Library Deer'** made her smile, but the wondering awe in the words **'Who Is John Macnab?'** and **'Has Fictional Hero Come To Life?'** sent hot sensual thrills shooting up her spine.

It was so damn sexy knowing her man had really *done* something. She'd never forget the way some of the students had cheered when the news broke that their librarian had stolen the Book of Deer. There was a highly believable rumour going round that that old prune, Miss Partridge, had a cousin who dealt in drugs and kept a stash in her spinstery flat for safety. When the news broke about Macnab's theft, she'd tried a little sample before phoning the bemused police and insisting 1) that John Macnab was actually John Sandiman and 2) that they come round and arrest the white spiders climbing up her walls. There'd been a general upsurge in interest in Scots history as well. Numbers paying to see the Stone of Destiny had trebled. Ian Hamilton had been interviewed and said it'd been about time some other daft young patriot had stolen something important; and while

Donald Dewar publicly condemned the theft she'd heard other highly believable rumours that he'd been privately asking whether the Book of Deer could be acquired by a Scottish university...

But that was all she knew and all she could tell the police officer, a small man with a big broad Lanarkshire accent and a bent nose.

They shared a pot of tea by the bay windows while he took notes.

"And you've known Mr Sandiman since...?"

"A couple of years now. We always got on well."

"Has he tried to contact you?"

"Not since he left the college."

Well, that wasn't entirely true. There was the night they'd made love, but she wasn't going to tell the police that, and anyway she hadn't seen him since. She wanted to, though. Bloody men. They could just do it and walk away. Women were left missing the bastards.

Hell, she *did* miss him. Why couldn't he just have stayed with her instead of trying to be the new John Macnab? Damn. She could bloody murder him. Though she was proud of him in a funny way, too.

All these thoughts flickered across Natalie's face in a fraction of a second, and the policeman saw them.

"And you've also left the college?"

"Yes. I hadn't liked it there for some time. Shortly after I went, the principal was charged with viewing porn over the Internet."

She smiled at the memory of the red-faced principal being interviewed by the police and released on bail. He'd apparently gone home and his wife, who'd spent the day drinking Martinis and staring white-faced at the wall, calmly smashed an Etruscan vase over his head. The principal wobbled like a drunk as she then picked up several exquisite willow-pattern plates and flung them at him. Off-balance and concussed, he spiralled daintily through a set of French windows and crashed onto the patio. The paramedics arrived to see her calmly standing over him and rhythmically kicking him in the groin. He lost a testicle. She spent a night in the cells. They were now separated. The newspapers had had a field day with that, too. Natalie suspected Mike had had a hand in it. He'd probably even tipped them off.

Just another example of how modern technology could bring people closer together.

"Is there anything else you can tell us?"

"Not really," she said truthfully. "He's a natural loner. He can do without company longer than most so I'm sure he won't contact me, and I know he won't harm the Book. The last time I saw him he said he was going to do something. He certainly has done something, but you already know that. I just don't know what he'll do *next*. He can't sell the thing. It's too easily identifiable. He'll probably just give it back sometime, but I don't know when."

The officer shrugged his shoulders. He'd known the likely answers before the start of the interview, but he'd had to ask the questions.

"Well, if you hear anything else, please get in touch."

He got up to go.

"Officer?"

"Yes?"

"Maybe he didn't steal it. Maybe he just took it out on loan and now it's overdue."

To his credit, the policeman smiled.

The Macnab enquiry continued and so did the countdown to the referendum. If the House of Windsor had any misgivings about the greatest political shake-up of Great Britain since the Acts of Union had been ratified, they did not say so. The Royal Family spent time at Balmoral and, as Natalie was being interviewed on 21 August, Diana flew to Nice with Dodi Fayed for a cruise on his father's yacht, the *Jonikal*.

The last days slid by, calm and unhurried.

Dawn on the slopes of Lochnagar, and a single deer stood silently, looking over hill and glen. Its gaze rested briefly on the estate of Balmoral where a boy born to be king slept; and in a cave in Lochaber John Macnab woke for a moment from a dreamless sleep.

It was the early hours of Saturday 30 August.

On that day Diana and Dodi left the *Jonikal* off the coast of Sardinia, took a private jet from Olbia airport and touched down at Le Bourget, ten miles outside Paris. From there they were chauffeured to the Ritz in a black Mercedes followed by a Range Rover driven by the Ritz's acting chief of security, Henri Paul. And like ravens circling their prey, the paparazzi pursued the princess and her lover.

At the Ritz the couple checked in to the Imperial Suite and Diana had her hair done at the hotel's salon de coiffure. At 7pm they left the Ritz in the Mercedes for Dodi's apartment near the Arc de Triomphe. Once again, they were escorted by the Range Rover, now being driven by Jean-François Musa. Earlier, believing he had finished work for the day, Henri Paul had handed the keys to Musa and gone home, stopping off at a bar en route.

At 9.30pm Diana and Dodi left his apartment, driving down the Champs-Élysées to a dinner date at the restaurant Chez Benoît. But the paparazzi were clustering ever more thickly around them. Dodi angrily cancelled their reservation and decided to dine at the Ritz instead.

On such small decisions are the fates of Royal Houses decided.

As the couple entered the hotel's restaurant, L'Espadon, paparazzi gathered at the hotel's main entrance on the place Vendôme. The night security officer called Henri Paul who decided to come back and take care of the situation. Arriving at the Ritz shortly after 10pm, the chief of security drank a few liqueurs at the hotel's Vendôme bar and awaited orders.

Enraged by the paparazzi swarming at the main entrance, Dodi Fayed concocted a plan to leave the Ritz via the service exit at the rear, using a different Mercedes and chauffeur. Protective of his fiancée's security, he wanted Henri Paul to be the chauffeur. He got his wish.

The only car available, a smaller Mercedes, was driven up to the service exit at 12.19am and left a minute later with Henri Paul at the wheel. Diana's bodyguard, Trevor Rees-Jones, was in the front passenger seat. Diana and Dodi sat in the rear.

Instead of taking the most direct route back to Dodi's apartment via the Champs-Élysées, the car turned on to the cours la Reine, the westbound dual carriageway on the right bank of the Seine. Pursued by paparazzi on motorcycles it accelerated rapidly, its driver drunk and overconfident. Less than a mile ahead lay the Alma tunnel, an underpass beneath the Pont de l'Alma. The Mercedes entered the tunnel at over 60 mph. It scraped the rear wing of a white Fiat Uno, swerved as Henri Paul over-reacted to the glancing blow, brushed the kerb of the central walkway and crashed into the corner of a support pillar. From there it spun round in a half-circle and smashed into the north wall of the tunnel.

Henri Paul and Dodi Fayed were killed outright, Trevor Rees-Jones was badly injured, and Diana began to haemorrhage.

For many years afterwards, anyone around at the time could always remember what they'd been doing on 22 November 1963 – the day President Kennedy was assassinated in Dallas. For a new generation, many of whom had not even been born when Kennedy and his Camelot passed away, 31 August 1997 would have the same significance.

To anyone with TV, radio, mobile phone, personal computer or fax, that is.

Early on the morning of 31st, at about the same time as the Queen's Private Secretary was telephoning the Pitié-Salpêtrière hospital to be told that Diana, Princess of Wales had been declared dead, John Macnab awoke. He felt refreshed, relaxed and fit. He automatically checked that the

Book of Deer was by his side, safe in its case, then stretched. There was something beautiful about waking up to complete silence, and this morning it seemed as if he really was the only creature alive. He couldn't even hear birdsong. There'd been birdsong every other morning. Every one of the thirteen mornings he'd woken up in the cave. Sometimes he had spent an hour lying in his sleeping bag, just listening.

But this morning, nothing.

He shrugged and went outside to make his toilet. Even the birds had to take a day off sometime. Tomorrow would be his last day here anyway. Tomorrow, he'd walk down to the village – just another hiker with a rucksack – and see what was happening in the world.

What *would* the papers be saying about him?

He looked about. Such a quiet morning. And no mist at all. He gazed at the waters of Loch Lochy and across to the ridges of the Monadhliath Mountains, remembering that Columba had believed sea and sky to be elements of the House of God, a natural temple in which to worship. He felt like whispering something, but did not know the words.

And at the same time but in another place, someone who did know the words sat by the bed upon which the body of Diana lay, and prayed for her soul.

As John Macnab rested, the Prince of Wales broke the news to his sons that their mother was dead. The Prince then drove to Aberdeen airport and flew to Paris. Diana's body was returned to British soil later that day and arrangements for the funeral began. Bouquets of flowers appeared at the place de l'Alma and outside the gates of Kensington Palace, left there by a quiet sea of people which just grew and grew. A sea which filled the streets of the cities and spilled out into the shires, so few able to understand what had come to pass.

As the sea of flowers grew, night fell. In the morning, as the body lay in the Chapel Royal of St James's Palace and the Prince of Wales took a long lone walk on the moors around Balmoral, John Macnab came down from the mountain. It was an easy stretch of the legs to Laggan Locks, across the Caledonian Canal and onto the A82. Once on the main road he could catch the bus to Fort William or change at Spean Bridge and take the West Highland Railway. It wouldn't be a problem. He looked so much like any other hillwalker – lean, tanned and outfitted by Berghaus – that it would take an abnormally sharp eye to detect anything out of the ordinary. In truth he *was* a hillwalker now, and the face he saw in his shaving mirror every morning had little in common with the discontented fizzog he'd had to acknowledge ownership of a few months earlier.

As he reached Laggan, he was itching to know what had been happening over the past two weeks. There'd be lots of wrangling about the forthcoming referendum, of course, but would his theft have been discovered?

The bus would be along in an hour or so. Macnab looked up and down the road and stepped into the general store. Under the benign gaze of the square-jawed proprietor he looked at the papers, scanning the headlines intently.

He didn't get it at first. The papers were nearly sold out. Not a normal occurrence for nine o'clock in the morning, to be sure. There was not an *Inverness Courier*, *Press and Journal* or *Herald* to be seen, but there was a *Times* and a *Daily Mail*. The *Mail* didn't seem to have a headline. All he could see was a picture of Princess Diana.

He felt a moment's irritation. The union was likely about to break up and all the papers could do was go on about some spoilt princess...

Then he looked more closely, and he froze.

Below and to the right of the picture were three simple lines:

Diana, Princess of Wales
Born: July 1 1961
Died: August 31 1997

"Died?" he said.

"Aye, in Paris yesterday. She was in a car crash with her boyfriend. Terrible, it was. The newspapers and TV have been talking about nothing else."

"I... hadn't heard. I've been walking. Out of touch."

Macnab's head was whirling. He quickly bought the two papers and left the shop, found a seat by the bus stop and started reading.

He acquainted himself with the facts in moments. The Mercedes. The tunnel. The crash. Something occurred to him.

The histories of the Royal Houses were intertwined with the gospel of the Church. Kings consecrated with icons, Cathachs carried by them into battle.

The Book of Deer had been in the hands of Robert Spencer in 1695. A man willing to pay any price to be king, or for one of his descendants to be king.

Diana, his descendant, had desperately wanted her son to be king, but with the help of the Scottish referendum his kingdom, the *United* Kingdom, was coming apart at the seams.

No Royal House would want that.

Then, just before all this is due to happen, just before history is due to take a different path, John Macnab steals a symbol of ancient power, venerated by Church and State.

And what of Diana?

It was weird. As if there were subtle connections he couldn't quite see. An X-file worthy of Mulder and Scully.

He turned to the paper, finally found an article about his exploits on the inside pages. All it said was that the thief had been identified as John Sandiman and enquiries were continuing.

He was far from the centre of attention. But at what a cost.

More than a little shaken, Macnab took the bus to Spean Bridge and walked down to the station with its green-trimmed Victorian canopy, unchanged for decades. The train was not due until twenty to twelve, so he had a while to wait. The station was unmanned, adding to the stillness of a warm September day. Flowers in little rockeries on the platform were still in bloom. He sat and waited, and despite everything his mind drifted.

Imagine weaving a tapestry. You, the weaver, can see only a small part of the design until, once the tapestry is complete, you stand back and look upon the whole picture.

What if you are not even a weaver but merely a thread, part of an inconceivably complex pattern you cannot even begin to comprehend?

Macnab felt a trickle of real, cold fear. He was out of his depth, but he couldn't stop now. Maybe he'd never even had the choice.

The train was coming. He got to his feet.

It was a short trip round the Ben to the Fort. Head still whirling from the day's revelations, Macnab sat down on a bench in Fort William's High Street and tried to decide when to make his next move. He was being careless, but Diana's death had thrown his timetable out of kilter and he needed time to think. He'd have to work out when the best time would be to carry out his plan. He certainly couldn't do anything for the next few days. Churches all over the country would be flooded with mourners and flowers.

Preoccupied, Macnab didn't notice a nearby figure glance at him, stop dead in its tracks and then walk nervously up to him. Nor did he notice it stop behind him, only reacting when a hand came down on his shoulder.

Macnab nearly pissed in his pants, expecting to see the stern face of a policeman telling him the jig was up and would he mind coming quietly. But then he heard a familiar voice say his name.

He looked up, realisation slowly dawning.

"God," he said slowly, "Jessica?"

16

It was the best of times, he thought, remembering his Dickens with an eerie clarity, *it was the worst of times.* He hadn't seen Jessica in nearly seven years, not since a cold October day in Kyle. To do so now was wonderful, but this was the worst possible moment.

Not only that, the last he'd heard she'd been planning to join the police. Oh shit, the *police.* If she had, she'd probably been taking a particular interest in his case for the past week or two. Even if she hadn't, his identity had already been revealed in the papers. He had a sudden vision of a carefully woven tapestry being ripped to shreds.

"John?"

"Jessica?"

He relaxed. If this was how the game was to end, so be it. He stood up and looked at her. Despite everything, he couldn't resist glancing at her ring finger. No evidence of matrimony there, anyway.

She was wearing a short brown raincoat. Her black hair was just as thick and smooth, her hairstyle had hardly altered and her face was much the same. But perhaps no longer quite so sweet.

"I thought it was you," she said softly. "You look just like you used to."

That was true, he thought. He'd felt a lot more like his old self in the last few months. He met her eyes and thought he saw something calculating in her gaze. That, and a certain sadness.

Whether or not she's with the police now, if she's been reading the papers then she knows what I've done. But there's just a tiny chance she hasn't. So all I can do now is act naturally and keep my cool.

"Yeah," he said. "I've taken up walking again. Been up around Sligachan the last few days. So, er, how are you?"

"Fine, er, fine."

He suddenly found it all rather funny. She was the only woman he'd ever wanted to marry. He'd thought of her every day for nigh on a decade. Now she was standing right in front of him, probably well able to put an end to his criminal jaunt on the spot, and what were they doing? Acting like a couple of tongue-tied teenagers.

"Want to get a cup of coffee?" he said. If he was going to be arrested he might as well have some caffeine first. Colombian Supremo would do. She looked at him nervously, then nodded.

Fort William was well stocked with tearooms. They soon found a window seat in a nearby establishment with tartan décor and plastic tables. He glanced over at the shops, noticed Peter MacLennan & Co, outfitters and grocers to the Lochaber gentry since the days of Captain Dunbar.

Then he looked at the crowds flowing past, a colourful stream propping up Fort William's fragile economy. Youths wearing orange cagouls and baseball caps, backpackers from Europe in red raincoats by Berghaus and Karrimor; elderly ladies with plastic rain hats, the occasional local in fisherman's jersey and wellingtons, all window-shopping and washing up outside the Tourist Information Centre in Cameron Square like flotsam and jetsam propelled by the ebb and flow of the tide. It passed him by without rhyme or reason as he sat there, looking across a plastic tabletop at a woman who'd been the love of his life.

"I never thought I'd see you again," he said.

"You shouldn't talk like that. You knew where I lived. I only moved here a couple of years ago. I've got a flat here now, off Lundavra Road."

He thought of the last few times he'd gone to Glenfinnan, stopped off in Fort William, probably been no more than half a mile away from her. So many opportunities lost, so much time wasted.

"I thought you made it pretty clear you didn't want to see me any more."

He saw a sudden spark of something in her eyes. Anger? Fear?

"I had a long time to think about it," she muttered, looking down for a moment. "It all smoothes out after a while, you know."

"*Smoothes out?* Like what? Like cottage cheese or something?"

God, it had hurt. He'd forgotten how much it had hurt. But now he was being reminded. Slow anger welled up inside him. Not the little fighting flame of the Celt this time. Something a lot stronger and deeper.

"I wanted to marry you," he said slowly, realising he'd been waiting to say those words for years.

She was silent. Feeling like a weight was lifting, he went on.

"I wanted to marry you. I never wanted to marry anyone else. I came to your house and you wouldn't even see me, wouldn't answer my letters. Nothing. No reason. Ever."

"It wasn't like that."

"Actually I think it was. You see, I was there. I remember it very well."

"I didn't mean..."

"I don't care what you meant. It was what you *did* I wasn't too keen on."

"This isn't the place..."

"Yes, it is," he said wearily. "These things are never easy." He took her hand, felt that hand tremble. "Why did you do it?"

He'd wanted to ask that question for so long, and as he waited for the answer he felt that familiar old knife twisting between his ribs again, still working its way on in.

"If I'd gone off with you, my father would never have been able to hold his head up in the street again."

The sentence hung in the air. As an answer, it wasn't up to much.

"Yes he would have. This isn't the nineteenth century."

He saw a shadow pass over her face.

"Isn't it?"

For a moment, he saw it from her point of view. To live all her life in Kyleakin, her world bounded by the Free Church and the townspeople. And then to fall for a Catholic. But this was the nineteen-nineties, for God's sake! Girls had done things their fathers disapproved of before.

Not in Kyleakin, apparently.

"All this," he said, "all the chances you have. All the world around you, everything. And you let yourself be ruled by the opinions of a bunch of old farts in Kyle. It's gutless. Dress it up any way you like, but that's all it really was. All it really is. Gutless."

The words came out tiredly, all passion spent. He felt numb, detached from it all. Not even caring what her answer might be.

She looked out at the High Street for a moment, her face expressionless.

"Perhaps it is."

For six years, nearly seven, Jessica had haunted him. Now she was facing him, and he didn't know whether to rip her head off or make love to her. That awful conflict had been conceived on a cold October day in Kyleakin, the day Jessica's father had told him she didn't want to see him. A slow-burning hatred of mindless social mores and parochial tradition had begun to form. A flaming Celtic anger filling the emptiness within him, looking for targets to lash out at.

He'd lashed out at Natalie. He'd lashed out at that bloody student. He had *really* lashed out at Guy Mannering. Now he was lashing out at the neds who'd vandalised the church and most of all, at the cringers who had let them do it.

Six, seven miserable years like this. Seven years of trial. For what?

All this shot through his mind in a second. Then he came back to the present. Her hand was still trembling.

Then her eyes turned away from the street, focused on him.

"I'm in the police now. I know who you are."

17

*"As far as I'm concerned,
Scotland will be reborn when
the last minister is strangled with
the last copy of the Sunday Post."*

(Thomas Nairn)

"You're John Macnab."

"Yes."

"I couldn't believe it when I saw it on the news. Then your picture was faxed to the station. I just couldn't believe it."

"You going to turn me in, then?"

"That's my job."

"If you're going to turn me in, why haven't you done it already?"

She shrugged, as if the question needed no answer.

"Yes," he said. "If you were going to do it, you'd have already done it. But that's the way with you, isn't it? Go right up to the edge but no further, because you're scared the light might scald you. Scared you might actually have to *do* something."

"I'm not scared. I just want to know why."

"No, you don't. You just want to put off doing something."

"So why did you steal the book?"

And that, he thought, was the question. The question he'd tried to avoid asking himself in case he came across the truth under all those layers of symbolism, of history, and of bullshit.

"I was – I've been – I am... I'm so sick of being a cringer. I just wanted to do something. Prove that the Scots weren't just a bunch of cringers. Prove it to myself, at least."

"How did you get like this?"

"*You're* asking *me*? You were the biggest cringer of them all. If you'd actually stood up to your father, actually *told* him you wanted to be with me, he might just have said okay. But you never did."

She was silent.

"I'm going to take that book back to Finnan's glen. To the church we went to, the church a bunch of Scots kids vandalised because they didn't know or care about their own culture. I'm going to take that book back and tell them all who wrote it, why it was written, and what it stands for. That's what I'll do. I don't care what happens afterwards."

He stood up slowly, no fear left in him.

"That's all there is to it. You can stop me if you want."

He paused.

"Or you can make a decision for yourself."

She looked at him, and he saw something in her eyes. A fire in shadow perhaps, or a flame. They faced each other for a long moment, then she deliberately turned her attention to her empty coffee cup, not watching as John Macnab took the satchel holding the Book of Deer and walked away into the crowds.

She sat there for a long time, watching people passing by. After a while, she noticed her reflection in the glass and saw that she was smiling. Then, shaking her head in bemusement, she made her way home.

18

*"When Tweed and Pausyl meet at Merlin's grave
Scotland and England shall one monarch have."*

(Thomas the Rhymer)

In Lochaber, John Macnab made his final preparations to return the Book of Deer. In London, final preparations were made for the state funeral of the Princess of Wales at Westminster Abbey on 6 September.

The Stone of Destiny was gone from the Abbey now. In a few short days, power would devolve from Westminster. It may have seemed that the death of Diana signalled the end of the House of Spencer's bid to take the sceptre of the kingdom, for the kingdom was itself eroding as the Acts of Union, created in part by the ignoble machinations of Diana's ancestors, began to splinter.

But if the union fell apart, what would replace it? Who would seize power?

Well, some did remark, as Prince William walked behind the gun carriage that carried his mother's body, that he was half-a-head taller than his father and in look and gesture every inch a Spencer.

As the union stood poised to fall, a deeper unity was forged in the terrible silence surrounding the gun carriage as it bore its burden through the streets of London. A silence which spoke of sympathy for the boy who would be king standing in the shadow of his mother's coffin.

Diana's brother, Charles Spencer, gave the eulogy and during it he said:

It is a point to remember that of all the ironies about Diana, perhaps the greatest was this – a girl given the name of the ancient goddess of hunting was, in the end, the most hunted person of the modern age.

For three centuries the House of Spencer had stalked the throne. Now their quest was coming to an end.

Three days later the 'up' train to Mallaig came smoothly to a halt at Glenfinnan station. This was a modern train. Not one of the 'Glens' built at Cowlairs and once synonymous with the West Highland Railway. Fate had chosen a blue ScotRail SuperSprinter to deposit John Macnab at the stop for the Church of St Finnan.

Not that anyone would have recognised him as the man who'd stolen the Book of Deer. This man, clean-shaven, seemed to be in his mid-twenties and a bit of a scruff – baggy trousers, slightly oversized sunglasses and a baseball cap inviting onlookers to 'Feel the Force', all courtesy of Oxfam. However, unless there was someone very imaginative in the Northern Constabulary on his trail there was no way to link Glenfinnan with the Book of Deer. Of course, Jessica could have had police staking out the whole village but he didn't think that was going to happen.

All the same, remember what that old scout from Rhodesia said. Walk casually, blend in, don't draw attention to yourself. Out there, there just might be someone better than you. So don't take anything for granted and perhaps, just perhaps, you'll manage to make a little bit of history.

The stranger with the worn satchel drifted past the villagers collecting the morning papers and mail, walked down past the red telephone box on the A830 and made his way to the church.

The deputy manager of the Glenfinnan House Hotel usually opened the doors of the House of God to all and sundry at 10am. So Macnab waited, clutching his satchel and looking out at Loch Shiel. He considered the events swirling around him. Princess Diana's funeral had taken place three days earlier. Since her death every place of worship in Britain had become a place of mourning, but he still had to deliver the Book of Deer to the Church of St Finnan before the referendum. It was going to be a tight squeeze. Sunday the seventh had obviously been out, Monday had been too close to the funeral, and Wednesday the tenth too near the referendum for his message to reach the public. It had to be Tuesday, so he had to take the risk and be done with it. The hysteria should have died down enough for him to make the drop.

Tuesday might well be the perfect time. Labour, the SNP and the Liberal Democrats had united in order to argue for a Yes-Yes vote in the referendum. Polls were also showing a lot of support for devolution, but a 60% turnout was needed for the vote. Too many people might not bother.

If enough did, like a beam of light entering a refracting prism, the whole melting pot of the United Kingdom – Church, Sovereign and State – might be transformed, painfully and bloodily, into something new.

Or it could all go to pieces.

A symbol of unity was needed. A Cathach in the hands of a king, perhaps. Then he heard a key turning in an old lock and all other thoughts fled from his mind. Macnab froze as the deputy manager walked into the church, glanced at the stained glass window depicting St Finnan's Bell, then went about his business.

Five long minutes later Macnab strolled into the church and up to the altar, trying to give an outward impression of casual ease. There were flowers to Diana there, the odd wreath, a few notes, but no mourners.

He ducked under the ropes, stood before the altar and opened his satchel. He looked at the stained glass window, thinking of the vandalism of the building he loved, of the neglect of the past by the ignorant.

He had the Book, and he had the penultimate message from

John Macnab. It had been almost impossible to try and say so much in so few words and he'd spent weeks rewriting it, but now it was ready. The words carefully honed, illuminated in a few brief *suras*. More of his father's words had come back to him, and he'd lashed out at a few sacred cows, too.

He brought out the Book of Deer and, together with the message, laid it gently upon the altar.

The tableau was complete. Bathed in sunlight filtered by stained glass the ancient manuscript seemed to glow, as if satisfied it had been returned to its proper place. It was like a quiet consecration. Or *re*consecration. A house of God, once defiled, now restored.

The gilded designs were faded now, the vellum brittle and old, but still the union of words and colours was a sacrament. The clear light of liturgy opening a doorway to elsewhere.

Macnab felt warm radiance fill the church with light. A nameless strength washing down the pews and soaking into the walls, cleansing God's House of sacrilege. He felt no more hatred for the vandals. Mean little men who could see no further than the end of their small grey streets would always exist, but others would walk the long drove roads in search of their Edens or Meccas.

Columba had sailed for Iona, Muhammad had walked to Jerusalem and before them there had been the Word, given by God to the peoples of the Book, copied by calligraphers from Baghdad, illuminated by holy men from Deer and Kells. The wisdom of East and West combined, without which the sacred manuscripts could not have been created.

From the spires of Christendom and the minarets of Islam, both peoples had spread the light of liturgy, but too often their wisdom had been wasted. Too often they had clashed over Jerusalem and belief in Jesus. Too often Church and State had fought for power rather than spread the gospel.

The words of the Muslim scholar from the Southside came back to him, as clearly as if the man was standing at his side:

"You and I, we fought over Jerusalem and we fight still, though the illuminated gospels prove that your culture is part of ours and our culture is part of yours!"

The church was still, quiet as St Sophia.

He looked at the loch through the half-open door to calm himself and suddenly, clearly, he remembered Jessica. The quiet sacrament of rain as they sat together in a pew. It had been the most beautiful moment but the promise of a life together had been false, founded on a girl too scared and hesitant, fading away over too many nights of old whisky and self-pity. Too many maudlin, silly, selfish thoughts. All because he hadn't been able to face the fact she wasn't the one for him.

At least he hadn't fallen completely into a fog of despond. Instead he'd flared up like a flame, blown away his professional ethics, torn up his pathetic little career plans and destroyed his future. Hell of a way to get closure.

Funnily enough, though, he'd never felt more like a real librarian in his life. The classic keeper, classic *dewar*, willing to make any sacrifice to restore an icon to its people.

He looked at Loch Shiel through the half-open door. For a long time that door had only opened onto memories of the past. Perhaps now it would open onto a future, if not Paradise.

John Macnab walked through the door and into the sunlight.

An old gentleman in tweed jacket and flannel trousers was there, sitting on the bench and looking at the trinity of land, sea and sky. Macnab thought he could just about make out a small island away in the west. It looked like a tiny keystone, balancing the trinity. Perhaps it was Finnan's Isle, and if so, it certainly *was* a keystone. A fulcrum upon which history had pivoted.

"Yes. It is Finnan's Isle."

The words were spoken in an accent he'd never heard before, answering a question he hadn't asked aloud. Old and deep, but not unkind. The way an ancient Celt might have sounded. Macnab looked at the old man more intently. He had a long, lush moustache and a shock of thick white hair. It was an odd style, just a little out of place.

Macnab looked more closely. He *knew* the man from somewhere.

"Haven't I seen you before?" he said.

The old man turned and their eyes met. The pupils, Macnab noticed, were a strange dark brown.

Like the eyes of a stag.

"I have been here before," the old man said. "When the deer roamed the Caledonian forest, when the longboats wandered the seas from Byzantium and the horse warriors crossed the plains of Europe, I was here."

Macnab's first reaction was to laugh, and had it been any other day he would have. But not on this day. Not after what he'd seen and felt.

After all, a doorway to elsewhere could work both ways.

Macnab felt like he was teetering on the edge of the impossible. There were no such things as magicians!

Then a memory just had to go and fall into place.

"The library – Cambridge University Library – you were *there*. You distracted the librarian. You helped me steal the book."

"Yes."

"Why?"

"With the blessing of the oaks, I have intervened three times. Three times I have persuaded history to take a different path. With Finnan and Arthur, with Alexander, and now with William."

"To what end?"

"To unite the world."

"And the Book of Deer?"

"An icon. A kingdom cannot come together if it does not know its past. The Book is a window to that past and a door to the future. By your actions, the kingdom of the Scots will be reminded of this at a turning point in history and another path will be taken."

"Diana. What of Diana?"

The old man's eyes darkened.

"No fine future was ever forged without sacrifice."

Macnab felt, quite simply, too terrified to ask any further questions. He had come to the edge, the very edge, of something so dangerous it defied the imagination; and if he went one step nearer he knew he would never return.

"You really are a magician."

"I prefer the word *librarius*."

A shaft of sunlight flashed through the fog in Macnab's mind. He found himself looking east through another's eyes. Seeing a far-flung city of cathedrals and olive groves. Another city laced with a filigree of gold and silver spun around the dome of a great church. A third and final city crowned with spires and minarets where scholars read from tablets written in a strange script.

Like morning mist, the visions faded away. Then he saw another sight. A vision of the future, or of one possible future.

William, a prince of the House of Spencer. Consecrated King of England. Separately, King of Scots.

William stood, surrounded by his honours, sceptre in hand.

Amidst the honours, symbols of his sovereignty. The Stone of Destiny, returned to Westminster for his consecration, and books like Deer. Both icons a testament to the ceremony first carried out by Columba.

William stood. The Once and Future King. A monarch of rare majesty.

And by his side, a figure in shadow. A familiar to the future king. As he had once been familiar to the old king.

Then this vision, too, began to fade. Soon he could only remember a single sentence, softly spoken.

"You will not remember me..."

Then everything faded to black.

19

About two hours later, the shit hit the fan. More precisely, a tourist from Stockholm noticed an old book and a strange document on the altar and spent a couple of minutes poring over them.

A little while later, he asked about John Macnab at the Visitor Centre.

Then the shit *really* hit the fan.

Less than an hour after that, the local representative of the Northern Constabulary was on the scene. He was about to photograph the document and bag it as evidence, but then he started reading it and, for a short while, police procedure came to a complete and unscheduled halt:

TO WHOM IT MAY CONCERN

I first came to the North-Western Highlands in 1897 after a sojourn shooting in East Africa with Jim Tarras. At the invitation of Lord Abinger I was to spend the summer on his estate at Inverlochy, but I found it a dull experience so I wagered Abinger that I could bag a salmon, a brace of grouse and a deer from his estate, escaping detection all the while.

Using the pseudonym Captain Dunbar, I succeeded in doing so, expecting only to amuse guests at luncheon with my tale. I did not know that one such guest would be the author, John Buchan, who bestowed upon me a kind of literary immortality.

Buchan resurrected me in 1925 and Andrew Greig did the same in 1996. On both occasions I was pleased to demonstrate the art of shikar taught me by Jim Tarras, and on both occasions we had sport with the establishment.

But this time, I have returned to the church bordering the estate where I first hunted for a greater reason.

Once I lived only to chase the deer over hill and glen, but shortly after the events chronicled in Greig's work I came upon this Church and saw it had been vandalised. This touched me as no wager ever could. This was Finnan's Church, built in memory of one of the first missionaries to bring the Word of God to Scotland. Such men were soldiers of Christ and, many died for their beliefs.

Yet it seemed they'd been forgotten. So I made a wager with myself to restore part of your heritage to you. To remind you all of whom you really are, to make you hear the echo of your fathers' voices, which still whisper in the cloisters of the church.

This is why the Book of the Abbey of Deer has been brought to Finnan's Church. To prove to you that your history is still with you.

What of the men who were part of that history?

What of Columba, founder of Deer, and his teacher, Finnan of Moville?

They were your fathers and this is the work they wrought. Do not forget what they did.

The Declaration of Arbroath said that, "the which Scottish nation, journeying from Greater Scythia by the Tyrrhene Sea and the Pillars of Hercules, could not in any place or time or manner be overcome by the barbarians ... they won that habitation in the West, which though the Britons have been driven out, the Picts effaced, and the Norwegians, Danes and English have often assailed it, they hold now

... In this kingdom have reigned 113 kings of their own Blood Royal, and no man foreign has been among them".

One nation, united by Robert Mac Alpin, fought down through the centuries for their freedom. One nation, led by a line of consecrated kings, rallied to icons like the Book of Deer whose illuminated gospel led them to stand before God. Gospel books carried by clansmen into battle and known as Cathachs.

One nation, devout in its beliefs.

But what are you now, that you would allow the desecration of Finnan's church? A nation which has forgotten the meaning of its own name, forgotten the words which forged it, and forgotten the men who died for it.

Look well upon yourselves.

Look upon the Book and remember who you are.

Let all the battles and honours vanish, let all the good and evil be forgotten, let it be as if the long brawl of your history never happened. Let all this come to pass unless you look upon the Book and remember who you are.

Make your decision and act upon your beliefs, or say no more forever!

I myself have done what I had to do, and now I am finished. But if my words make even one amongst you think again then my actions will not have been in vain.

Sincerely,

John Macnab

The policeman finished reading the words. He stood there for a moment, musing, then turned and looked out at the loch.

When he handed Macnab's message in at Fort William that afternoon, the *Oban Times* was on the case. A copy of the message was in their hands half an hour later. Fifteen minutes after that, courtesy of an ambitious reporter loyal only to himself, it had been faxed to the editorial department of the *Herald*.

Threads began to come together. The political truce called between the parties for Diana's funeral had ended on Sunday 7 September and all over Scotland ballot papers were being prepared at council offices, but England's post-funeral depression and Scotland's apathy might have led to a rerun of the 1979 devolution débâcle. Now, just in time, John Macnab and the Book of Deer had prodded the electorate awake.

Some of the doubters just rolled over and went to sleep again. Others laughed at the naïve speech from the man out of time, buttered their toast with a silver knife and turned to the financial pages. A few wrote pompous letters to *The Times*. Most did nothing but some – perhaps romantics, perhaps artists or historians, or perhaps just professional cynics desiring redemption – woke up to the importance of the vote.

The papers called it 'The Macnab Factor', and it shifted Britain's mood just enough for it to face the future on 11 September 1997 and decide what kind of nation it would become.

20

*"If the vote is lost today devolution is dead.
If the vote is lost today, moreover, there will
be only one alternative remaining. If the vote is
lost there can be no more excuses,
no more complaints, none of the old,
sour grievances. Should Scotland vote No
the status quo will be vindicated
beyond doubt and independence will
become the last counsel of despair."*

(*The Scotsman*. 11 September 1997)

If it had begun quietly, with the settled will of an ancient sitting alone on an island near the dawn of history's long brawl, then it was fitting that it began quietly to come to an end with the settled will of a people near the dawn of a new millenium.

At first it seemed as if the cringers would, after all, have their day. Few voters appeared when the polling stations opened their doors at 7am and the hope of a sixty percent turnout seemed like wild optimism.

Once again there was stillness, a quietness broken only by occasional soundbites from politicians with an eye on careers in a Scottish Parliament. A bunch of activists who'd been sitting in a Portakabin in the shadow of Edinburgh's Calton Hill since 1992, vowing to go on with their vigil until such a Parliament was elected, began to wonder how long they might actually have to hang around. They huddled by their brazier, waiting.

Donald Dewar cast his vote in Glasgow early on. He hesitated for a moment outside his polling station in

Anniesland, thinking of John Smith and unfinished business, then walked through the doors. Alex Salmond continued to campaign in Banff and Buchan, at one point passing the ruins of the monastery of Deer on his way to Peterhead, but the stillness persisted and the turnout stayed low. Offshore, hundreds of potential voters had been stranded on oil rigs when bad weather grounded their helicopters. In the Borders, low-paid workers were wavering over the question of tax-varying powers. Orkney, given to Scotland by Denmark in 1468 and ill-treated by the Stuarts until 1707, was reluctant to be part of any new handover.

Then the trickle of steps crossing the threshold began to turn into a flow, and from a flow into a flood. As the media watched the giant video screen at the Edinburgh International Conference Centre, results started to come in. At 12.45am on 12 September Clackmannanshire, home to the Earls of Mar, became the first county to declare a vote of Yes-Yes.

Then, also voting Yes-Yes, came the rest of the counties. It was a quiet landslide. 74 percent of the nation voted Yes for a Scottish Parliament and 63 percent for tax-varying powers.

At 1.45am Donald Dewar walked up to the podium, adjusted his glasses, and said:

"This is a great day for Scotland, one of the most important days in our country's long history. The people have seized the moment and we have done the business and given an emphatic thumbs-up to a Scottish Parliament with real powers."

As dawn broke, Dewar headed for Calton Hill. Before facing the media circus awaiting him there, he paused and looked out at the city. He could hear the sound of street parties going on. They would probably go on all day.

He found himself unable to be angry with that obscure librarian who'd become John Buchan's John Macnab, and even a little envious. His gesture might well have made a greater difference than anyone knew. There had been real fear amongst the party faithful that the electorate might have voted No to tax-varying powers. If that had happened, a

Scottish Parliament with no real power would have been the result.

But that was *not* what had happened, and hopefully it would not happen in the future. Like the party faithful, he didn't feel so afraid of the future now. Certainly not as scared as he'd been that night in Edinburgh Castle's Great Hall. For a while he really had been worried by the prospect of a United Kingdom not devolved, but fundamentally disunited.

Of course, the people partying wouldn't be thinking about the consequences of a Scottish Parliament. Power always caused corruption, then there was the Barnett formula and the West Lothian question. The devil might very well lie in details like those. But come what may the United Kingdom had been transformed. First politically, then emotionally with the death of Diana, Princess of Wales, and now constitutionally, British history had been radically reshaped.

With an equally radical clarity, these thoughts came to him:

The long brawl is over.
The unfinished business is finished.
If there is a price to be paid, I'll pay it.

He was a dewar, after all.

He turned to the reporters.

A day later, not far from where Dewar had stood, the activists doused the brazier that had burned for five years and started to pack up their Portakabin. There were some tears from otherwise hardened, streetwise men, and when the rhetoric was over and done a brief ceremony took place. Glasses were raised and a toast drunk to John Macnab – wherever he was.

Macnab himself had been at a party which had gone on for a long time. Highlanders truly loved a 'wee dram' and a party could easily last until dawn, ending only when the revellers rolled out of the pub and down to the beach, peed on the rocks and blinked at the sun rising over one of the Hebrides. In this case, at the very moment Donald Dewar was turning to the reporters on Calton Hill, John Macnab was unzipping his flies by the seawall in Mallaig. He could see Eigg, Rum and the southern tip of Skye and they had seldom looked better. A new day had dawned. Damned if he could think of a better way of welcoming it.

Three days before, he'd got off the steam train in Mallaig and before his feet hit the platform all his ideas about muddling the trail had evaporated like so much morning mist. Why bother being an outlaw any longer? He'd done what he wanted to do, the matter was settled and he was going to give himself up shortly anyway. Jessica knew who he was and more or less where he was. He was low on money, high on overdraft and just didn't give a damn any more. He would simply book into the local backpackers hostel and wait for the result of the referendum.

The only thing niggling at him was his inability to remember anything between leaving Finnan's church and getting on the train. Well, best put it down to stress and forget about it. After all, he'd resurrected John Macnab, poached a Cathach from Cambridge, seen the Royal Houses humbled by the death of a princess and the United Kingdom redefined.

Quite enough, one at a time, but all at once...? That would surely jumble the thoughts in many a head better than his.

He took a good long piss, emptying his bladder slowly and satisfyingly into the sea. He noticed a sodden copy of the *Sunday Post* stuck flapping to a rock and took particular care to urinate on it, too. He had no love for that coven of tight-fisted old men in Dundee: a non-union dictatorship living in the past. Scotland would indeed be reborn when they were gone, and he would gladly strangle the managing editor of the *Sunday Post* with the last copy of their stinking paper himself. He smiled at the thought and walked back to the hostel.

Later that day, a letter addressed to the Chief Constable of the Northern Constabulary was delivered to Fort William police station. Macnab, still full of a sense of freedom, had dropped it in himself. He judged the chance of bumping into Jessica to be pretty low and anyway, he didn't care.

It was quickly opened and read. Although always officially denied, a tale was told in Lochaber for many years afterwards that a group of senior police officers had gathered in the Chief Constable's office and drunk a toast to John Macnab. The letter itself was quite straightforward:

TO WHOM IT MAY CONCERN:

Now that I have wagered my liberty and lost, I am bound by my word to hand myself over to the authorities.

If an officer of the Northern Constabulary would consent to make himself available on the platform of Corrour station at 1pm (or thereabouts) on Saturday 13 September 1997, I give my word as an Edwardian gentleman that I shall place myself voluntarily in his custody.

Sincerely,

John Macnab

On the thirteenth, Macnab found himself standing in the doorway of the youth hostel on the shore of Loch Ossian, a mile or so from the halt at Corrour. Definitely a good location to pick for a dramatic final gesture, he thought. He could have just turned up at the nearest police station, but he'd first met (okay, puked all over) Jessica at Corrour. That was where the chain of events had begun which had led him to John Macnab, the Book of Deer and the Church of St Finnan, so it seemed fitting to bring things to an end back where it had all started. Not only that, it was a beautiful place. Ben Alder lay in the distance and beyond it the Grampians. Thousands of square miles of territory lay before him. Thousands of years of history lay behind him. At least he had played his part in the long brawl. A brawl begun with Calgacus and still ongoing.

Renton, he thought, remembering the scene from *Trainspotting* shot at Corrour, *you were wrong. It's not shite being Scottish.*

Another thought came to mind, and it had no intention of vanishing.

Will she be there?

Jessica would certainly have heard about the note and he found himself hoping she might turn up to take him into custody.

He shook his head ruefully. All those long centuries of brawling, and all it ever seemed to come down to was politics and women.

What *had* it all been for?

So he could say he'd been part of history? Or at least that John Macnab had been. That was part of the answer. But of course, he wasn't John Macnab. Not any more anyway. That honour belonged to the man who'd stalked his prey on Abinger's estate a century before. It was too heavy a mantle for John Sandiman to wear for long.

A long time ago, he'd taken his copy of *John Macnab* to the library. It had stayed in his satchel ever since. Now his fingers flipped listlessly through the pages. If Dunbar had had any idea what his story would lead to, would he have told it in the first place? Probably. Stories were there to be told. That was what made them last.

He walked outside, looked at the hard-edged mountains. Listened to the quiet lapping of the loch's waters, watched for the morning train from Glasgow.

A Celtic priest would have considered the land his church. The dawn a sacrament.

Land, sea, and sky. All part of a country on the way back to being a nation again. There were worse things I could have fought for.

A strange tapestry indeed.

I guess it's nearly complete.

But when did it begin, and who was the weaver?

He didn't know he already had the answer.

He heard movement to his left. He looked round and saw a stag grazing near the youth hostel. He hadn't noticed it the night before. Half-tame, no doubt. Used to getting scraps.

He thought of the stag he had seen at Glenfinnan and found himself smiling. Stags had been chewing the cud for a long time, from Columba's day to his.

He thought of Natalie. He'd missed Natalie. She had guts. Not like Jessica.

Had it been worth it?

Yes, by God!

Time to go.

He put Buchan's novel back in his satchel and walked up to the station, enjoying the feeling of the sun on his back. He saw the weather-vane first, then began to hear the din of a diesel generator. There was still no mains electricity at Corrour, the railway still the only means of access for those who didn't fancy a twenty-five mile walk from Tulloch. The train should have pulled in by now. He expected they'd be there to greet him.

He wondered if he'd end up like Rab C. Nesbit, down in the police cells getting a right good kicking...

He contented himself with the thought that his plan had somehow all gone like clockwork. He'd taken the Book of Deer back to Finnan's glen and told everyone what it stood for. Not only that, he was a far cry from the miserable wretch who'd trudged up the Quirang a year earlier.

He crossed the rails, saw the dark blue of the police uniforms and strolled onto the platform without a care in the world. Then he saw who else was waiting for him and realised it hadn't gone quite like clockwork after all. There was a walker there as well, someone who *had* walked twenty-five miles from Tulloch to be there, and he recognised her face.

21

*"I saw a future for myself, at best,
as an assistant librarian in a mouldy
town somewhere, occasionally getting a
blowjob in a public bog."*

(Stephen Fry)

"I guess I'm just not your average librarian."

It was his last comment of the day. He'd been helping the police with their enquiries for most of the afternoon and he was damned tired. His whole body felt as deflated as his bladder had been the other morning. There really was little else left to say.

He wondered where Jessica was. Perhaps she was somewhere else in the building. Perhaps putting the finishing touches to the John Macnab file with a certain tender loving care. He hoped so.

It didn't really matter, though. It had not been Jessica who'd walked from Tulloch to meet him. It had been Natalie. Natalie, who didn't even much like walking. There'd been the momentary shock of (all right, admit it) disappointment, before he realised how stupid he'd been and how lucky he was. Six years of yearning, all wasted on the wrong woman while the right woman had been standing in front of him all the time.

She had looked so beautiful, too. She'd been tired, strained and limping, but Sandiman had seen only a proud Celtic princess, like Eithne of myth.

"How did you know where I'd be?" he had asked.

"You remember my uncle with the flat in Hyndland Road? My uncle the *policeman*? My uncle for whom the flat was a secondary pension plan? The same uncle whose flat was going to burn down if he didn't tell me everything he knew?"

"You wouldn't really have done it, would you?"

"Put it this way, I had the matches and I was in the mood."

"All this for me?"

"I just wanted to see the return of the masked avenger."

"How are your feet?"

"They hurt, you idiot."

"You know, you could have taken the Rannoch station road. It's shorter."

Her eyes had flashed dangerously, the police had chosen that moment to arrest him, and she'd waited with them all for the train back to Fort William, stroking Sandiman's hand and telling him what an idiot he was.

It had taken a lot of guts to bluff her uncle like that. If only he had met Natalie, not Jessica, at Corrour in 1991.

The inspector dealing with him had been courteous but dispassionate. Sandiman was being freed on licence while Cambridge University Library mulled over whether or not to press charges. Considering the time it took academia to decide anything, he'd probably be formally arraigned in May or June of 2021. He could not have cared less. The splendid little book was back in Cambridge but moves were afoot to transfer it to Aberdeen University Library.

"So I can go now?"

"Yes. You have to report to a local police station once a week until the matter is resolved, but apart from that you're free to go about your business."

"That's it then?"

The inspector nodded. "Yes, that's it. We don't like to make too big a fuss about these things. Of course, Mr Macnab, if you'd like to spend a night or two in the cells we could probably arrange it."

"My name isn't Macnab."

"Oh? I thought it was."

Sandiman thought he saw a glint of humour in the inspector's eyes, but it was gone before he could be sure. He found himself smiling. Then a thought struck him.

"By the way..."

"Yes?"

"Did you catch whoever vandalised the church at Glenfinnan?"

"We did. We made a point of it. I am an Elder of the Kirk myself."

"I'm a Catholic."

The inspector shook his hand and showed him out.

Out in the corridor he took a deep breath, feeling the tensions slowly ease; tensions which had been with him every day for most of the past year. He'd known there would be consequences, but now he'd faced them and he was still on his feet. It could have been worse.

Then he saw Jessica. She came briskly round the corner, heading in his direction. She was a picture of crisp efficiency. At least, she was until she saw him. The timing of her gait went awry and her jaw dropped. He stood there as she walked towards him, unsure what to do next. It was, all told, a very long moment and the silence that drew out between them was something he would remember all his life.

Into that silence, unbidden, came a thought.

I really did do it all for you.

Once again he found himself smiling. A similar smile crossed her lips as if she'd heard the thought. Then the moment came to an end and she was walking past him. She looked back as she turned the corner, and then she was gone.

You always were the kind of girl who'd chap on a door and then run away when someone opened it, weren't you? You've changed a bit, I'll give you that, but you've got a long *way to go.*

He felt laughter welling up from deep inside. Now, now, that wouldn't do at all! There was the outside world waiting for him beyond the doors of the police station. Some media, no doubt. It wouldn't be easy for them to try to interview a John Macnab sitting on the steps of the police station laughing his head off.

He waited for the fit of mirth to subside, wiped a few tears from his eyes, and headed for the exit. What would he do next? This brave new world they'd voted for would still have all the old one's problems. Death and taxes would remain, no doubt. But other things could change.

He would stay at Gavin's for a bit. Then he'd spend some time with Natalie. She had guts, that girl. She really did. She hadn't run away. She was the kind of girl he had always wanted Jessica to be. The kind of girl Jessica would never be.

Why on earth hadn't he realised that sooner?

Perhaps because time really was a circle, he mused, and you had to go back to your past to realise the truth about your present. After all, here he was in Fort William, right next door to the West Highland estates where his ancestors had worked. Perhaps their ghosts had been watching over him all the time.

He pondered this thought, and as he did so an image from an old tale, long forgotten, suddenly came into focus.

A figure standing at the edge of a clearing, deep in the shadow of oaks.

22

A tale may have a beginning, a middle and an end. But a tapestry created by Allah has many tales within it, and even more loose ends.

Hence:

On Sunday 28 September 1997 Frances Shand Kydd, mother of Diana, Princess of Wales, attended a memorial mass for her daughter at St Columba's Cathedral in Oban. She had lived for many years on the nearby Isle of Seil. On a clear day one could see Ben More on Mull from the Isle, and not far beyond the Ben was Iona.

The congregation listened in silence as she talked of Diana. The images it evoked stayed with them for many years.

... A message from a schoolfriend of Diana's reminded me of the sunny days of living when she was a girl. She wrote of her memory of 'Diana's Scottish home on the Isle of Seil' *and of a particular memory she had of myself and Diana together in a boat hauling lobster pots in on a warm and calm Scottish day. She said* 'I remember the softness of the ripples on the water like silk. Wherever Diana is right now, I hope it is how it was then. I can't believe that it will be any different ...'

... Charles asked if I wanted him to row me across to the island where Diana rests, and at that moment I declined. But later that morning, walking in the gardens, I was drawn to the lake. The boat looked overwhelmingly tempting, so I rowed myself across to the island. As I rowed back I noticed a thin covering of weed on the water cut in two by the boat. I looked back and saw it join like

a curtain as a lone swan glided past. At that point I could feel my beloved Diana was at peace. Her earthly life was short but complete. I knew then that all she had to do was completed; that all was well. Very well.

Not long after, Sandiman returned to Glenfinnan. He and Natalie drove up from Glasgow via Inveraray, taking the coast road past Dunadd. They spent some time at Finnan's Church, then took the footpath up to the viewpoint. He sat there, looking out towards Finnan's Isle, while she unpacked the sandwiches. There was a white horse grazing in the field below, he noticed. One of the girls who worked at the Visitor Centre had a horse. Perhaps it was hers.

"They say Columba looked back at Ireland from a hill on Colonsay when he was crossing to Iona," he said presently.

"Columba wasn't his name."

"No. He might have been called Crimmthan or Colum Cille. And before it was Iona they called the island Ioua or Í. Celts weren't even that bothered about churches. They just thought the world around them was the House of God, held services outdoors in places like this. Natural amphitheatres."

They were silent for a time.

Natalie spoke up.

"Was it worth it?"

"For me or for him?"

"For you."

"I don't know yet. If devolution stops the Scottish cringe I'll be quite happy. If it puts an end to us blaming the English for everything I'll be very happy. If it stamps out sectarianism it'll be a bloody miracle.

"But Parliaments aren't sovereign. They're only bureaucracies. A Parliament might run the state machine but only a king can command a nation's soul.

"I maybe made a difference, though. Power devolved, yes, but a kingdom still *united*. Not broken into bitter pieces."

"Well, if the bell tolls for anyone on Judgement Day, it'll surely toll for you."

He looked at her for a moment.

"It already tolled for me. A long time ago."

She frowned. "You talk in riddles, Obi-Wan."

"I don't mean to. I just remembered something the other day. An old story my father must have told me. Something about his grandfather. Like a buried memory someone just dug up for me."

"Any idea who?"

"No. I think I'd know if someone had been messing with my mind."

Even as he said it, Sandiman felt unsure. There were still gaps in his memory from that day at Finnan's church. Thoughts he couldn't bring into focus.

"Anyway," he said more firmly, "my great-grandfather was a ghillie at Inverlochy Estates. When Captain Dunbar was stalking the deer, my great-grandad was stalking him, silent as a ghost. But he didn't deny Dunbar the kill. Buchan certainly based the story of the wager on Dunbar, but he might have based Jim Tarras on my great-grandfather."

Natalie shook her head slowly. Such revelations on such a calm and clear Highland day were surely rattling her brain.

"Then you really *were* John Macnab."

"I suppose I really was. History set me up for the role but I had to act it out. Now I know why it was so easy for me to make the connections."

She went on shaking her head for a long time. He began to think she'd dislodge her brain if she kept it up much longer.

"Brought any coffee?" he asked after a while.

"Yes."

"Colombian Supremo?"

"Of course."

"We're just poor sad people, aren't we?"

He looked at her lovingly. He felt sure there was a proud Celtic princess or two in her ancestry. She and Jessica were like two sides of a coin. One shrinking from the sun, the other embracing it, no matter what the cost.

He knew which side he preferred, and he'd stay on that side, no matter what storms might come.

"I wouldn't say that," he said out loud. "I wouldn't say that at all."

Epilogue

The old man was dying. Once he'd seen angels standing on a rock in the sound between Iona and Mull. Perhaps one had been Gabriel, but they hadn't approached him then. God had seen fit to grant him another four years of life. But when those years were past, they would cleave the soul from his tired flesh very swiftly indeed.

He welcomed the idea. He was old and tired, but his life had been a rich one. The hands which had defeated Broichán at Craig Phádraig were frail and shaking now but the Abbey of Deer, symbol of the breaking of the Ridge, had survived. The last he'd heard, Drostán and Eithne had made it home to many fine manuscripts; and one day the abbey's scribes would no doubt create a new manuscript. A Book of the Abbey of Deer.

Perhaps they would speak of him as they spoke of Arthur but whatever they did, he was satisfied with his lot.

His fingers faltered over the psalter he was translating. He could no longer concentrate. It near his time. He called his servant Diarmait, left his cell and made his way up the hill overlooking the monastery. He stopped to pat the muzzle of the white horse the monks used to carry milk pails to the monastery, then walked on. He always seemed to end up facing his destiny from the tops of hills.

As he climbed he felt a comforting presence. Someone benign but with a touch of fiery temper, helping him onwards.

Finally he reached the top. He could not see the shores of Erin, knew he would never see them again. Knew that was the price he'd had to pay.

He thought of Finnan's tale. The vision of cities between the two rivers crowned with spires and minarets, their temples places where scholars read from tablets in strange script.

But of course his script would seem just as strange to them. Every man made the Word flesh in his own way. There was no need to fight about it. No need at all.

It had taken him so long to understand.

But what to say? What to do? How to put into words the conflicts, the stories and the dreams? How to tell the unborn of the beliefs of those who had gone before?

He was only part of a great tapestry and there were still so many tales to be told. Not all would be illuminated by scribes. Many stories would be distorted, fragmented, lost.

What more could an old man say in the little time left?

He thought again of Finnan's tale. Of the words of the deer beyond the sunset.

Carry the word over the Ridge and beyond. Into the East. Take the sceptre of the kingdom. Let Church and Empire carry that sceptre and, with it, unite a world.

The druids and the ancients had desired unity. People could not be united by force, but tribes could become allies if kings like Arthur led them into battle. If they looked upon the images of icons, rallied around Cathachs...

Yes, it was possible. A chance for real unity. Between East and West, even between Christian and barbarian.

One day, he dreamed, an abbot of Iona would converse with the scholars in the East. Perhaps a longboat would sail from Dalriada to Jerusalem...

A wondrous thought.

How to summon that future? What to say?

Then the words came to him. Subtle, open to interpretation. Certain to be misunderstood, but still words he had to speak.

He raised his arms and let his last words take shape:

"This place, however small and mean, will have bestowed on it no small but great honour by the kings and peoples of Ireland, and also by the rulers of even barbarous and foreign nations with their subject tribes.

And the saints of other churches too will give it great reverence..."

Acknowledgements

Acknowledgement and thanks to Gordon Alexander Jennings for dialogue, chapter four; and to Roy Ellsworth and Peter Berresford Ellis for their very helpful work, *The Book of Deer* (Constable, 1994).

Sources / Further Reading

Scottish History

The Declaration of Arbroath, edited by John S Adam: Herald Press, 1993

Life of St Columba, Adomnán of Iona – [New ed.]: Penguin, 1995

The Stone of Destiny: symbol of nationhood, David Breeze & Graeme Munro: Historic Scotland, 1997

Alexander III: King of Scots, Marion Campbell: House of Lochar, 1999

Surviving in Symbols: a visit to the Pictish Nation, Martin Carver: Canongate, 1999

Scotland and the Union: 1690-1715, Richard Dargie: HarperCollins, 1999

The Book of Deer, Roy Ellsworth & Peter Berresford Ellis: Constable, 1994

Columba, Ian Finlay – [3rd ed.]: Chambers, 1992

Stone of Destiny, Pat Gerber – New ed.: Canongate, 1997

The Heart of Glasgow, Jack House – [New and rev. ed.]: Hutchinson, 1972

The Gaelic Notes in the Book of Deer, Kenneth Hurlstone Jackson: Cambridge, 1972

The Picts and the Scots, Lloyd and Jenny Laing – Paperback ed.: Alan Sutton, 1994

A History of Scotland, J D Mackie: Penguin, 1969

Alba of the Ravens: in search of the Celtic Kingdom of the Scots, John Marsden: Constable, 1997

Bonnie Prince Charlie, Rosalind K Marshall: Her Majesty's Stationery Office, 1988

The Scottish Regiments: 1633-1996, Patrick Mileham – 2nd ed.: Spellmount, 1996

The Lion in the North, John Prebble – [1981 ed.]: Penguin, 1981

History

Library: an unquiet history, Matthew Battles: William Heinemann, 2003

The Indian Mutiny, Richard Collier: Collins, 1966

The Rule of St Benedict in English, edited by Timothy Fry: Liturgical Press, 1982

The Oxford History of Christianity, edited by John McManners – [Paperback ed.]: Oxford, 1993

Arthur and the Lost Kingdoms, Alistair Moffat: Weidenfeld & Nicolson, 1999

The Sea Kingdoms: the history of Celtic Britain & Ireland, Alistair Moffat: HarperCollins, 2002

The Druids, Stuart Piggott – [1st paperback ed.]: Thames and Hudson, 1994

The Druids: Magicians of the West, Ward Rutherford: Aquarian Press, 1983

The Spencer Family, Charles Spencer: Viking, 1999

Airborne Operations: an illustrated encyclopedia of the great battles of airborne forces, edited by Philip de Ste Croix: Salamander, 1979

The Quest for Merlin, Nikolai Tolstoy: Hamish Hamilton, 1985

Biography

Diary and Correspondence of John Evelyn, edited by William Bray: Bohn, 1859

John Buchan: the Presbyterian Cavalier, Andrew Lownie: Constable, 1995

Diana: her true story – in her own words, Andrew Morton –
[Completely rev. ed.]: Michael O'Mara, 1997

Non-fiction

The Autonomy of Modern Scotland, Lindsay Paterson:
Edinburgh, 1994
The Closing Headlines: inside Scottish broadcasting, Kenneth
Roy: Carrick Media, 1993
Death of a Princess: an investigation, Thomas Sancton &
Scott MacLeod: Weidenfeld & Nicholson, 1998

Fiction

John Macnab, John Buchan – [Repr. ed.]: Penguin, 1956
The Thirty-Nine Steps, John Buchan: Penguin, 1991
The Return of John Macnab, Andrew Greig: Headline, 1996
Highlander, Garry Kilworth: HarperCollins, 1998
Sarum, Edward Rutherfurd: Arrow, 1987
The Key Above the Door, Maurice Walsh – [New ed.]:
Balnain, 1992

Reference

Atlas of the British Empire, [New ed.], edited by Christopher
Bayly: Toucan, 1989
Islam for Dummies, Malcolm Clark: Wiley, 2003
Larousse : dictionary of literary characters, edited by
Rosemary Goring: Larousse, 1994
*What People Wore: a visual history of dress from ancient
times to the twentieth-century*, Douglas Gorsline – [New
ed.]: Orbis, 1978
The Dictionary of National Biography edited by Sir Leslie
Stephen and Sir Sidney Lee – [New ed., repr. 1973]:
Oxford, 1973

And, lastly, that splendid little book:

The Book of Deer, edited for the Spalding Club by John Stuart
  – Edinburgh: Printed for the Club by Robert Clark, 1869 –
  (Spalding Club; no. 36)